D1025165

# THE YEOMAN'S TALE

# THE YEOMAN'S TALE

## M.J. Trow

SEVERN
HOUSE

First world edition published in Great Britain and the USA in 2022
by Severn House, an imprint of Canongate Books Ltd,
14 High Street, Edinburgh EH1 1TE.

Trade paperback edition first published in Great Britain and the USA in 2022
by Severn House, an imprint of Canongate Books Ltd.

severnhouse.com

*British Library Cataloguing-in-Publication Data*
A CIP catalogue record for this title is available from the British Library.

ISBN-13: 978-0-7278-5068-3 (cased)
ISBN-13: 978-1-4483-0757-9 (trade paper)
ISBN-13: 978-1-4483-0756-2 (e-book)

*All Severn House titles are printed on acid-free paper.*

MIX
Paper from
responsible sources
FSC   FSC® C013056
www.fsc.org

Typeset by Palimpsest Book Production Ltd.,
Falkirk, Stirlingshire, Scotland.
Printed and bound in Great Britain by
TJ Books, Padstow, Cornwall.

# ONE

F ye Gillis had always loved the river. When she was a
girl, she drove her father's geese to the banks of the
Scheldt, tapping them gently with her stick and hissing
gently if they looked like straying. Some of them were nearly
as tall as she was, haughty and mean with it. They spat at her
if they were in a certain mood, screamed at her with that harsh
cry of theirs, just to let her know who was *really* in charge.
If they let her drive them to the river, it was because that was
where they wanted to go all along. And she watched them
with that love–hate relationship which all little girls had with
the beasts of the field. They pecked in the river slime, their flat,
grey feet squelching in the ooze. The down from their breasts
would make new pillows, beds and coverlets by winter, soft
as a sigh and warm as a hug. The English, she knew, made
flights for their arrows from the wing feathers of these creatures. To her, this showed that she lived in the right country;
one which made soft comfort as opposed to one which wanted
only to kill. Straight willow, a clothyard long, and feathers
that sang through the air to thud into the straw of their targets.

She had never seen an arrow hit a man. She had no idea
the harm it could do. Her father and her uncle told tall tales
around the loom as it thudded and banged, the shuttle flying
backwards and forwards. Tales from before Fye was born,
when the Goddamns came north out of France, looking for
plunder, wine, women; *anything* that didn't belong to them.
The English and the French had been at war for ever, but the
people of the Low Countries, mending their dykes against
the rage of the sea, had not been part of that. Not until the
Goddamns came their way.

Now, it was a different river. Not the Scheldt with its flood
plain, the flat and level land that barely crept above the surface

of the water. Now it was the Thames, rolling and thundering below the bridge, carrying the flotsam of the greatest city in the world. And Fye Gillis had no time now to shepherd her geese. Now, her hands were hard and callused from her years at the loom, her shoulders as broad and muscular as most men's. Her own Magge was nearly full grown now, old enough to drag the heavy wool, expert at teasing out the burrs and the sheep shit. In her quieter moments, Fye wondered how she had got here from her tranquil, sleepy Scheldt to this foaming ferment that buffeted, brown and dirty, the cogs and cats that rode at anchor below the bridge. All right, it had been Arend's idea, to cross the North Sea and set up his weaving trade yards along the Thames. But who had put the idea into his head? This was the land of the Goddamns, the men who killed Flemings as easily as they killed Frenchmen; as easily as they killed geese for their arrow flights.

She hadn't wanted to leave her family, her friends, even the geese. But she was young then, and in love. The world seems very small when you are in love, she remembered, and they had packed their things and set off, into a glorious sunset, as she remembered it. And here she was, however it had happened, in another river, in another world. It was night and she couldn't see very much. The sunset had been unspectacular, as all sunsets had been to her for many a long year. She couldn't see the cranes in the Vintry or the bobbing masts and the anchor chains. She couldn't see the church spires or the stars in God's heaven that sprinkled the sky. She couldn't hear the river's roar either, the thud of boats harried by the tide. And she couldn't feel the cold of the water, for all it was high summer now, lapping around her body. It was gentle enough, in an English sort of way, but it was not the Scheldt.

Fye Gillis could not see anything. She could not hear anything. She could not feel anything. Because, as she slid silently against the black uprights of the Steelyard jetty, Fye Gillis was dead.

'So, what did he mean?' Jack Chub had had enough already. It wasn't mid-morning by the sun and his back was in half. He stretched, felt his spine click and sat on the tree stump.

And because they were sawing together, if he stopped, Will Lorkin had to stop too. It was the way of the world.

'Who?' Lorkin wiped the sweat from his forehead and spat onto the sawblade, wiping away the greasy dust.

'Whatsisface – that knarre you heard preaching.'

'Oh, John Ball.' Lorkin eased himself down onto the log pile. There was no doubt about it, Scots pine bark cut through woollen hose to a man's arse like nothing else, but it was the way of the world and he put up with it.

'Him, yes. Priest, is he?'

'S'pose,' Lorkin shrugged.

'So what did he mean?'

'How do you mean, what did he mean?'

'That rhyme thing. About Adam and Eve.'

'Ah.' Lorkin uncorked his water sack and took a long swig, giving himself time to remember just how it went. '"When Adam delved and Eve span, Who was then the gentleman?"'

'That's it.' Chub wasn't sure that had helped him much but waited a while before adding, 'What did he mean?'

Lorkin looked at the man. He had known Jack Chub since they were knee-high to the nettles. They'd been born in the same village, were christened in the same font. They'd caught rabbits and beaten bushes for His Lordship when they could barely reach his stirrups. And when the time came, they'd both swived the same girl, though not on the same night; friendship only went so far, after all. Be all this as it may, Lorkin realized his old friend, his brother of the saw, was actually a moron.

'Well,' Lorkin passed the water sack to the man beside him. 'In the beginning, what was there? On the sixth day, I mean?'

'Er . . .'

'And God created Adam . . .' Lorkin hinted. It was like pulling teeth.

'In his own image.' It was all coming back to Chub now, the rare occasions when the parish priest actually spoke a language that anyone could understand.

'And then,' Lorkin was in full flow, 'he created Eve, as his companion.'

'Right!' Chub's face, with its dusting of sawdust, positively beamed. It was all falling into place.

'So, we have two of 'em, right? Adam and Eve.'

'And the serpent.' Chub didn't want his friend to think he was a complete idiot.

'Never mind all that.' Lorkin was a master of logic. 'That comes later. Before the tree and the apple and things, there was just the two of 'em, Adam and Eve.'

'This was when the Lord was resting?' Chub checked. 'On the seventh day.'

'Yes, yes, no doubt.' Lorkin didn't remember that coming up in John Ball's harangue. 'So, who was the gentleman?'

Chub looked confused. 'Well, Adam, naturally.'

'Why?'

'Well, 'cos he was made first. And because he's the knarre. He's the man.'

'Yes, all right, I grant you that. But, put it another way. You and Mildred. Who wears the hose in your house?'

'Well, I do.' Jack Chub was starting to have serious doubts about this man and gave the water sack a surreptitious sniff. But apart from the lingering goat, there was nothing amiss.

'Yes, literally, I know. But . . . let me put this yet another way. When your pig died, who buried it?'

'Er . . . Mildred.'

'After she'd cooked the good bits, yes. And when your little Ramekin came along. Who gave him that name?'

'Um . . . Mildred.'

'Do you see a pattern here, Chubby?'

'Are you being offensive about my wife?'

'No, no.' Lorkin patted the man's shoulder. 'I'm just saying. Men and women of our position are equal, aren't they? Well, sort of.'

'Up to a point.' Jack Chub had his pride, after all.

Lorkin looked from left to right under the spread of the chestnut boughs. 'In that paradise, that Garden of Eden, where was Sir Bloody Roger de Bloody Graham?'

Chub blinked. 'Er . . .'

'Exactly!' Lorkin had made his point. '*That's* what John Ball is talking about. When Adam was digging the garden and

Eve was spinning her wool, there *was* no Bloody Roger de Bloody Graham.'

'You're right!' Chub beamed. Then he frowned. 'So . . .?'

'So, John Ball went on to say, who gave these people, the Grahams of this world, the right to lord it over us? Roger de Bloody Graham shits the same colour as the rest of us, don't he?'

'Er . . . I s'pose so.' Chub had never really thought about it.

'So what right has he got to tell *us* what to do?'

'That's right.' Chub tried to sound convinced, but somehow it fell hollow even on his own ears.

A silence fell.

'So what's John Ball doing about it?' Chub wanted to know.

Lorkin looked from side to side again, then leaned in to his man. 'He's plotting.'

'Is he?' Chub was gripped. 'Against who?'

'All of 'em.' Lorkin spat onto the sawblade again. 'All them stuck-up arseholes with their devices and their Latin mottoes and their frilly clothes.'

'What?' Chub looked horrified. 'You mean he wants to kill 'em?'

'Stands to reason,' Lorkin shrugged. 'Change is coming, my lad, and don't you doubt it. Ever since the Pestilence, it's been . . .'

'Hoo, you fellows!'

The voice made both men jump and they were on their feet in seconds, hands to the saw.

A knight cantered up from the river, batting aside the chestnut branches and hauling on his reins. 'I don't pay you to sit around, drinking my water and chewing the fat.'

Lorkin and Chub could barely hear him as they redoubled their efforts with the two-handed saw. The knight wheeled his horse away, cantering across the deer park.

'That's the point, though, isn't it?' Lorkin muttered under his breath. 'Roger de Bloody Graham don't pay us at all.'

'And you know the creepy thing?' Chub's eyes were wide. 'He don't make no sound neither. Riding a bloody great courser like that and I didn't hear a bloody thing.'

'No, you wouldn't. Never mind, Chubby, my boy. It'll all be different soon. John Ball says so. The men of Kent won't take this lying down for ever. You mark my words.'

Geoffrey Chaucer was squeezing the last moments out of the night in his comfortable feather bed. He wasn't, even in his wildest dreams, a man who liked to rough it. His creature comforts had become more important to him as he had got older and, although Harry Baillie charged a king's ransom for his pilgrimages, the beds could never be described as comfortable. He remembered one night, to be fair, when he had had a bed to die for, soft, warm and inhabited by neither flea nor fellow pilgrim. He had had the sleep of his life, hardly spoiled at all by the news the next morning that not only was it a bed to die for but a bed to die in – the landlady's mother had done just that only the afternoon before. But he was younger then, and death's breath on the back of his neck was not as chill. So – and he snuggled down a little deeper – he was going to make the most of his bed in his little room above the Aldgate before he set off on his pilgrimage in this year of his Lord thirteen hundred and eighty-one.

He still hadn't opened his eyes and he was pretending it was not even dawn yet, that he still had hours in this little nest of his. He was looking forward to the pilgrimage; of course he was. Last year's, after all, had been a complete and utter washout, what with one thing and another. But even so . . . his eyes ceased to be screwed up against waking and closed in sleep.

Suddenly, all hell seemed to break loose. One by one, every church for miles around began to ring for Matins, but not all at once, oh, dear me no. There was the tuneless whine of St Katherine Creechwood, the scream of St Olave's by the Tower. He sighed. One day, surely, they could all get together and decide what the time actually was. Once one began, the others all followed, one by one, clanging in their own fashion, the cracked Old Purgatory of Holy Trinity coming in last and flat, as always. It was pointless trying to sleep once they got into their stride. With the bells came the cries of the costers, the shrieks of the fishwives, the bleating of sheep and the occasional goat making their way reluctantly to market.

With a sigh, Geoffrey Chaucer threw back the covers and clambered out of bed, ready to greet the day. He was still standing at the window, scratching a buttock in a desultory way when Alice came in, all but invisible behind a pile of starched and smoothed clothing. Chaucer hastily stowed his buttock and turned to greet her, with his nightshirt decorously lowered. He had never worked out what Alice thought of the male body and how she would react if he proffered part of his, but he always kept it in mind that her husband was not only his source of food and drink and his creditor to quite some account, but he was built like a stone chantry and had an uncertain temper.

'Excited, Master Chaucer?' Alice put down the clothes on the tumbled bed and raked beneath it for Chaucer's bag. 'Going on a pilgrimage and all?'

Alice didn't really see the draw of going all that way to see a musty old tomb. She believed in staying close to home, where you knew everyone and everyone knew you. Foreign parts, even if it was only Kent, were all right for some, but not for Alice. But she liked Master Chaucer and if it made him happy, it made her happy. Not forgetting that she would have ten mornings when she wouldn't have to empty his chamber pot or see him scratching his arse looking out of the window.

Chaucer looked stern. 'I don't go to Canterbury for the excitement, Alice,' he said. 'I go the holy martyr for to seek.' Then his face split in a grin. 'But yes, I am rather excited. Last year wasn't the same, without my usual trip.' His face fell and he gestured at the toppling pile of clothes on the bed. 'Is that . . . is that my green liripipe?' The garment in question was poking out, about halfway down, a virulent shade among the browns and greys.

Alice turned from her packing. 'Yes,' she said. 'It was such a disappointment that you didn't get to wear it last year.' She looked at him closely; he seemed unconvinced. 'It's still all the fashion. Not *quite* as much as last year, but . . . you still see the colour in the streets.'

Chaucer didn't want to hurt her feelings, but neither did he want to go to Canterbury looking more of an ass than some of the transport. 'I think we'll let that become part of a story that was never told, shall we, Alice? It . . .' He waved a hand across his face. 'It makes me look a bit . . . sallow, do you think?'

Alice privately thought it made him look an absolute idiot, but she was too kind to say so, and so she simply removed the offending item from the pile and carried on packing his bag. 'Say no more,' she said. 'It will be donated to the Poor Clares' Clothing for the Indigent before nightfall.'

Chaucer smiled his thanks and waited until she had finished her work. Being caught scratching your arse was one thing; stripping off the nightshirt and dressing in front of a woman was something else entirely. This might be the fourth year of Good King Richard, but there were still standards.

With expert fingers she folded, pressed and cajoled until every item – except the bright green liripipe – was in the bag and the flap was firmly tied down. She doubled the strap and slipped it over her head, lifting it effortlessly. 'I've got a carter downstairs ready to take this to the Tabard for you, Master Chaucer. Your clothes for today are in the press,' she said. 'Your shoes are there,' and she pointed to the end of the bed, where they peeped out from below the tumbled covers, 'freshly mossed and brushed. Doggett has toed and heeled them, so you won't get wet feet, even if the weather turns.' She looked around the room. 'Is there anything else you need?'

Chaucer smiled at her. She was like the mother who, to all intents and purposes, he had never had. 'No, Alice,' he said. 'I think that you have thought of everything. I'll get dressed quickly and be on my way. And, tell me . . .'

She turned in the doorway, head cocked expectantly.

'Are *you* excited about me going on a pilgrimage? Ten whole days without an annoying old man to look after.'

She winked at him. 'Why, Master Chaucer,' she said. 'You're not annoying.' And he could hear her laughing all the way down the stairs.

'Geoffrey Chaucer!' The voice rang around the Tabard's courtyard.

'John Gower!' the Comptroller of Woollens called back.

For a moment, two men the wrong side of forty grinned at each other, arms outstretched. Then they ran to each other, slapping backs and shoulders like wrestlers on Lady Day.

'It's been . . .' Chaucer laughed.

'. . . nearly a fortnight,' Gower finished the sentence for him.

'Yes, I know, but that's business.' Chaucer broke the choke-hold. 'I'm talking about pilgrimage.'

'Two years ago,' Gower said. 'I'd just finished the *Mirrour de l'Omme*, if you remember.'

'I do,' Chaucer said, 'and bloody good it was, too.'

'Oh, now, Geoff,' Gower lowered his eyes modestly. 'We both know I'll never hold a candle to the *Book of the Duchess*.'

Chaucer punched him gently on the shoulder. 'You're too modest, Johnnie – you always have been. What are you working on now?'

The wool-merchant-not quite-brave-enough-yet-to-become-a-poet glanced from side to side. Who knew who was lurking in the Tabard's nooks and crannies, and Harry Baillie himself had never met a secret he hadn't blabbed, to the right person for the right amount of silver. 'It's called *Vox Clamantis*,' he whispered.

'Very scholarly,' Chaucer nodded. 'How's Marian?'

'Unstoppable as ever,' Gower told him, following his fellow poet to his horse hitched by the stables. His sister had been an old friend of Chaucer's wife and he always asked after her, every pilgrimage, like clockwork. 'Grandmother three times over now, of course.'

'Ah, where have the years gone?'

'Where indeed?' Gower pulled up short. 'Good God.' His eyes were fixed on a grey mare standing disconsolately a few places along in the stable yard. 'You're not still riding Bertha?'

'What have you heard?' Chaucer was momentarily startled. 'Oh, I see, the horse. Yes, yes indeed. You forget, Johnnie, that as Comptroller of Woollens, I have to make do with a fixed salary. Not for me the profits of a wool merchant.'

'Profits, my arse. Last year, as you know perfectly well, was a disaster. But that's enough about the state of the economy. How's Philippa? I haven't seen her for years.'

'She's thriving. Thriving.'

'Still at the court of . . .?'

''Fraid so. She comes home for Christmas, that sort of thing. Visiting the children is her priority, as I'm sure you can imagine . . .'

'Oh, yes. Marian's the same. Always seems to be dandling some child or another on her knee. Still, you must miss her.' Gower watched as Chaucer checked the cinch and the stirrup leathers. 'Ride much, these days, do you?'

'There's seldom the need.' Chaucer looked along his horse's body towards her withers. She was getting a bit portly, now he came to look closely. 'She spends most of her time in the stable, eating.' He patted her rump and small puffs of hay dust rose up. He must speak to his liveryman – corners were being cut somewhere, he was certain. 'Tell me, have you met any of our fellow pilgrims yet?'

'Shady crowd,' Gower murmured out of the corner of his mouth. 'As usual, all human life is here. *There*'s one I shan't be turning my back on.'

Chaucer followed Gower's furtively jerked thumb in the direction of a bear of a man with a huge, fuzzy beard. His beaver hat was wide and studded with pearls and his horse a tall bay with silver-shelled harness.

'Gilbert Maghfield,' Gower said. 'Dealer in just about everything. He's got a house in Billingsgate I could put mine down in six times over.'

Chaucer had dined at Gower's house; Maghfield's house was *huge*. 'I've heard of him,' he said. 'Merchant Venturer, isn't he? Links to Middlebergh?'

'That's the one. He'd sell his granny – if he hadn't already done it ten times over. Then there's . . . the old boy over there. The one fiddling about with the harness on the rouncey.'

Chaucer took the man in; a florid gentleman with snowy hair and beard. His houppelande was striped in a most unpleasing design and the cap of estate he wore was more than a little shabby. 'Didn't I give him alms on my way here?' he whispered to Gower.

'Ah, don't let the scruffiness fool you. That's Ralph Ellesmere, a franklin. Owns half of Sussex, by all accounts.

You know, there's nothing like a pilgrimage to bring out the eccentric in a man.'

There was a sudden kerfuffle at the gates and Harry Baillie's minions scurried to their task. As the wood swung inwards, a tall lady, sitting her saddle in the new trend, both legs to the side, trotted in on her chestnut mare. Behind her rode a nun, in the same Benedictine black as the first. But she was shorter, less eye-catching and wearing nothing of the gold paraded by her mistress. Chaucer was reminded of an illustration in a book – the first one limned in gold leaf with costly embellishments, that on the second page essentially the same, but in drab black.

Harry Baillie, who had been lounging on a settle outside the door of his inn, was suddenly on his feet and, nimbly for one of his innkeeper's bulk, was at the woman's side. 'Madame Eglantyne.' His fawning was chaste but effusive, his cap doffed, his bow almost to the ground.

Chaucer and Gower looked at each other and mouthed the name together. 'Is it me, Johnnie,' Chaucer asked, 'or is that a nun?'

'Prioress,' a voice grunted at Chaucer's elbow. 'Runs that convent down in Stratford-atte-Bowe.'

The poets turned to the coarse, squat knarre who was leading his unmade bed of a horse past them. He wore a blue surcoat over his fustian and a heavy sword clanked at his side. Neither poet knew quite what to make of the bagpipes over his shoulder. The man himself looked like a gargoyle.

'I know,' the man checked his nag, 'on account of how I am miller to Her Holiness.' And he walked on.

Baillie was still fussing over the woman, holding the horrible, snappy little lapdog while two flunkies helped her to the ground. Nobody afforded a similar service for the nun, who had to dismount by herself. It was the way of the world.

'Master Baillie,' the poets heard the prioress say. 'Have you any milk for my Woo-Woo? He's come so far.'

Again, the poets turned to each other. 'Woo-Woo?' they mouthed.

'I don't think there's much doubt about it, Geoffrey, my old

Comptroller,' Gower said. 'This is going to be one *very* strange pilgrimage.'

Soon, everyone who was going to be there was there. Some, like Chaucer and Gower, had tended to their own mounts and were standing patiently at their heads, ready for the off. Others had dismissed their grooms. Others still had horses so decrepit that no amount of care in the world could make them look any better than meat for the hounds. But on a pilgrimage, as Harry Baillie was often at pains to remind everyone, all were equal. Except perhaps Madame Eglantyne, who was a touch more equal than others. And Master Maghfield, of course. In truth, Harry Baillie had never met a double leopard he didn't like and, as far as he was concerned, where they came from didn't matter. It was simply a matter of personal preference that made him ensure that he rode alongside Madame Eglantyne, as sweetly smelling as the flower for which she was named, rather than the miller, who had a distressing flatulence problem.

As was the custom, Harry Baillie clambered up, with help from some stable lads, onto a mounting block and clapped his hands for quiet. Eventually, every head turned to him and almost twice as many eyes. He held out his arms as if to embrace his pilgrims. It was an easy gesture to make and meant that he would not have to go any closer to the majority of them as they made their way to Canterbury and back.

He plastered his best ingratiating expression across his face and beamed it at them all. He had a full complement this year. He noticed that even that famous welcher Chaucer had managed to make it as far as saddling up and stowing his bag on the cart. Madame Eglantyne was a bit of a catch; he could do with more of her sort. Soon, and he mentally rubbed his hands, soon he wouldn't need to make up the numbers with millers and yeomen and, yes, civil servants. He would lead a train of nobs so rich that his head would swim. 'Pilgrims all,' he called across the stable yard in his best mine host tones, 'we go to Canterbury, to the tomb of the Blessed Thomas. The sun is shining on us in benediction and the way is set fair. Is everybody ready?' He extended his arms and waited for their response. Only the miller shouted something back and, luckily for everyone, the echo distorted the exact details of his reply. Baillie smiled nonetheless and clapped again. 'To horse, everyone. To horse.' And, to muted applause, he clambered from his mounting block onto his palfrey, which visibly wilted as the weight hit her back. 'Canterbury, ho.'

And so they set out from the Tabard as the sun reached the height of noon. Baillie led the way, as usual, making small talk with Ralph Ellesmere, the franklin who owned half a county. Next, her Woo-Woo duly fed and watered and curled up in her side-turned lap, Madame Eglantyne and her sister-servant who had yet to say a word. Gilbert Maghfield rode behind them, totting up figures with a tally-stick and an abacus fixed to his saddle. He nodded often enough to be polite to the merchant riding by his side, who appeared to Chaucer to be trying to sell him something. Chaucer had not got everyone's name off pat, yet, but he suspected he would not be able to pronounce it if he knew it; the man was speaking Flemish and, as far as Chaucer was concerned, he could have been clearing his throat, the sounds were much the same.

There was a yeoman, tall, strong and clear-eyed. His hair was cropped short like the Goddamns that Chaucer remembered from his youth, the stalwarts of England who stood in French furrows like oxen, sullen and immoveable. Across his shoulders he carried a great bow of finest yew and the quiver at his hip was stuffed with arrows fletched with the rainbow colours of the peacock's tail.

Beyond him was a jostle of heads and hats and the sound of laughter and merry-making in the early afternoon. Chaucer and Gower rode with them, clattering past the high houses out of Southwark onto Great Dover Street to the Old Kent Road. The river looped and sparkled in the sun at Deptford and the Isle of Dogs, and they all halted briefly at the Watering of St Thomas, where the old milestone stood crumbling in the summer heat. Flies flitted around the horses' ears as they drank from the old well.

'Trust the saint to look after us,' a voice at Chaucer's elbow made him turn. 'The holy blissful martyr,' the voice said, pointing to the little statue over the dark water. 'St Thomas himself.'

'Yes, indeed, Father . . .'

'Buckley,' the priest said. 'Cog Buckley, although I don't go by my given name any more. Father Ambrosius.'

'Geoffrey Chaucer.' He shook the man's hand. 'Comptroller of Woollens.'

'Ah, we're all God's sheep,' the priest smiled and urged his horse back from the water.

It was about then that Chaucer realized why the miller had been carrying bagpipes. A wailing sound erupted as the tail of the column swung into view beyond the stand of elms that hugged the road.

'Mother of God!' Maghfield bellowed as his horse jinked sideways.

'Sorry about that, Master Maghfield,' Harry Baillie said. 'I'll have a word.' And with a face like thunder, he cantered over to everybody's least favourite musician.

The Falcon swung in its fetterlock, creaking above the front door. A gentle breeze was drifting from the river that first night, rattling the inn's shutters a little as the day cooled and a warm Kentish glow crept over the solemn tower of Holy Trinity Church.

'Dartford,' Baillie had announced it. 'Gateway to the garden of England.'

There was another party of pilgrims here, from somewhere to the south, and the place was noisy and crowded. Chaucer sat with Gower and Harry Baillie under a leaded window, watching the Kentish world go by.

'Excellent mortrews of flesh, I thought, Master Chaucer.' Harry Baillie was still nibbling his lamb bone.

'Capital, Master Baillie,' the poet said. 'Tell me, are you going all the way with us this year?'

'As far as Rochester this time,' Baillie said, clicking his fingers to a lackey for more ale. 'Mistress Baillie – my beloved Barbara – is with child and I don't want to be away for long.'

'What number is this, Harry?' Gower asked. His Marian looked after their offspring and he'd never understood why men collected children in the way that pilgrims collected holy badges. Mistress Baillie's belly always seemed to be either full or just vacated, as summer came around.

'Six, God willing,' Baillie told him. 'By the way, Master Gower, you're a pilgrim tried and true. You know this road like the back of your hand. Does that parish priest look familiar to you?' The innkeeper angled his head towards Father Ambrosius, sitting in earnest conversation with the prioress and her sister-in-waiting.

'Seen one, seen 'em all,' Gower said. 'Looks a bit threadbare, though.'

'To be able to afford one of Harry Baillie's pilgrimages, you mean?' Chaucer muttered.

'Now, now, Master Chaucer,' Baillie said. 'I know you don't mean that. If it's quality you're after, you must expect to pay for it. For instance, did you see what that other lot,' he tossed his head contemptuously at the other band of pilgrims, all sitting disconsolately along a single trestle across the crowded room, 'did you see what they had for their evening repast?'

Chaucer and Gower shook their heads.

'*Bread*,' Baillie said, in horrified tones. 'Bread and a morsel of cheese. If you could *call* it cheese. Weevils, more like. And no butter. No ale, just water.' He clicked his tongue. 'That's what you get when you don't travel with Harry Baillie.'

Chaucer squinted in the dying light to look more closely at the men across the room. He hadn't really taken that much notice before, what with the crowd and the savoury dish in front of him. But now, everything was clear. 'They're crutched friars, Master Baillie,' he said, somewhat crisply. 'I wouldn't expect them to be paying your prices. Although, when it comes to a vow of poverty, it's easier to achieve after travelling with you.'

Baillie opened his mouth to argue that his pilgrimages offered the best experience at the best prices, a phrase he had dreamed up recently and of which he was rather proud, but before he could speak, a ragged woman was looming over the trio. Her hair hung greasily to her shoulders and one of her breasts had popped out of her gown.

'Lose yourself, harlot,' Baillie snapped. Clearly, this woman

was not of the quality for which he charged and he could see
his justification of his prices going out of the window.

'I ain't no harlot, master,' she said through what teeth she
had left. 'I lost everything I own in a fire not four days since.'

'You poor woman,' Gower frowned. 'Have you no husband?'

'Dead, sir,' she said, 'of the ague this long year. Along with
my babbies.'

'And the Church?' Gower was already reaching for his
purse. 'Can they not help?'

She spat volubly onto the flagstones, her dark eyes darting
from one churchman to the next in that loud, rich room.

'Point taken,' Gower said, and the silver was in his hand.

Baillie covered it immediately, curling the poet's fingers
back into his palm. 'Don't fret yourself, Master Gower,' he
said. 'Nell here has never lost anything in a fire in her life.
And she hasn't lost a husband either – who'd have her? I've
got a memory like a misericorde's tip, Nell Poulter, and
you've been trying this one on every year since I started
running pilgrimages. Take a good look, gentleman. Nell is a
living example of a practitioner in the dark art of begging.
Ever since she was a kinchin mort, not above five years old.
Oh, she looks the part, I'll grant you. If you can bear to get
up close enough to sniff her, she even smells of singeing.
And she can recite the names of all her little babbies from
here to Ospringe and back. But none of it's real. Nell is a
demander for glimmer, a soul lost in an imaginary fire. Don't
fall for it, Master Gower. Put your money away.'

'You bastard, Harry Baillie,' the woman shrieked and, across
the room, the nuns crossed themselves and Madame Eglantyne
covered the tufted ears of her little Woo-Woo. Then, as
suddenly as she had arrived, Nell the glimmerer had gone.

Chaucer and Baillie looked at Gower; neither of them realized he was such a soft touch.

'Crossing the river tomorrow, gentlemen,' Baillie said,
standing up. 'Bright and early start. I'll bid you goodnight.'

The stars were as bright and early as Harry Baillie promised
the next day's start would be. The garden of the Falcon was
violet-scented, with the sweet rocket self-seeded in the nooks

and crannies of the walls; beyond the warm joviality of the inn, the only sound was the occasional click of the moorhens dabbling in the reeds of the Darent.

Geoffrey Chaucer missed gardens. In his little eyrie over the Aldgate, he could see the green fields of Whitechapel and Spital and watch the kites circling high over the grey, misty Essex marshes further east. But *this* county, he knew, was the garden of England, heavy with corn at harvest time and green with hops that criss-crossed the land like a cat's cradle. He was looking forward to the morning, the little cavalcade clattering through Brent. He wondered which way Baillie would take them, to the winding north along the Thames's bank, with Swanscombe along the old legions' road, or south, via Singlewell and St Thomas's. He knew both routes and really had no preference. He chuckled as he thought of dropping his reins in the morning and seeing which way Bertha took; the mare was as much of a pilgrim as he was.

A shiver of leaves made him turn and suddenly he was behind a bush, a poignard in his hand. The Pilgrims' Way was full of footpads, counterfeit cranks and Abram men; any one of them would happily slit the throat of a well-fed Comptroller of Woollens, just for the moss in his shoes.

For all it was a clear night, he couldn't make out, at first, the couple whispering in the orchard. As he focused, he recognized the woman; Nell, the demander of glimmer, in earnest conversation with a man. Chaucer couldn't see his face, but the tonsure and grey hood were unmistakeable.

'The letters?' he heard her say.

'Ready,' he murmured, 'but you'll have to be careful.'

'Who are we talking about?'

'Baillie, certainly. Maghfield. The old franklin. It'll put the fear of God into them.'

They saw him nearly as soon as he saw them and broke apart, Nell dropping to one knee and bowing her head.

'*Pax vobiscum*, my child,' Ambrosius made the sign of the cross over her and she bobbed upright and darted away. 'Good evening, Master Chaucer,' the priest said. 'A fine night.'

'Indeed, Father.' Chaucer's face must have said it all. Something, and he couldn't quite place it, was not right here.

'The poor woman has lost everything,' Ambrosius said by way of explanation, 'in a fire. I gave her what comfort I could. Two groats doesn't go far, these days.'

'Indeed not,' Chaucer said. 'Tell me, Father, your parish. Is it local?'

'Pebmarsh,' Ambrosius told him. 'Essex.'

'Yes, I know of it,' Chaucer smiled. 'I'm a Suffolk man myself, at least by upbringing. You'll know Bishop Aldemar.'

The priest smiled. 'I think you must mean Athelmar, Master Chaucer. Aldemar left us years ago.'

'Ah,' the Comptroller of Woollens said. 'Where do the years go? Are you a regular, to the Holy Blissful Martyr's shrine, I mean?'

'Canterbury, no. St Albans, now, that's different. I am a regular there. And Walsingham. Ely, once or twice.'

Chaucer pointed to the man's chest. 'I see you wear the clamshell,' he said. 'Compostella.'

It was too dark to see the churchman blush, if blush he did. 'I have a little confession to make,' he said. 'This was given to me by a fellow traveller. I have never been to Spain in my life.'

'It's not all it's cracked up to be,' Chaucer said. 'Although, just between you and me, the almond cakes they sell on the way in are to die for.'

'Tricky when you're on your knees, though?' the priest laughed.

'Ah, that's the beauty of it,' Chaucer remembered. 'They catch you along a little lane just before the genuflection begins; sort of sets you up for the pain.'

'It is nothing,' Ambrosius reminded him, 'to the pain Our Lord suffered.'

'Indeed not, Father.' Chaucer felt a little shamefaced, though it was true that his knees did give him gyp in wet weather and that had only happened after the cobbles of Compostella.

'I'll bid you a good night, my son.' Ambrosius made the sign of the cross over the comptroller's head and swung back to the lights of the Falcon, his bald head gleaming gently in the starlight.

'Not wise to be alone out here, sir.'

Chaucer whirled to the voice behind him. His poignard was back in his hand, but there was another, faster, deadlier, its tip glinting at his throat in the starlight.

'Just making a point.' The man slammed the weapon home at his hip.

'Point made.' Chaucer swallowed hard. 'Master . . .?'

'Hardesty,' the yeoman said. 'I didn't mean to startle you, Master Chaucer.'

'Do you know me?'

'Court Poet and Comptroller of Woollens?' Hardesty said. 'Who doesn't?'

'I had no idea my fame had gone before me.'

'It's a small world, Master Chaucer,' Hardesty muttered, 'and getting smaller.'

'We cross the Darent tomorrow,' Chaucer said. 'A quarter of the way there.'

Hardesty smiled. 'Three quarters of the way to go,' he said.

# TWO

Wednesday dawned bright and early and, even though Harry Baillie knew the Falcon's breakfast fare did not compete with the Tabard's, for the sake of the mark-up he got from his pilgrims, he had to pretend that it did.

'Kentish cheese, eh, Master Ellesmere,' he elbowed the franklin at the table next to him. 'Best in the world to break your fast on a summer's morning.'

'I'm something of a traditionalist,' the old man said. 'Breaking your fast before the sun is barely up is un-Christian. Where do we dine mid-morning?'

'Well, that's just it, sir,' his host told him. 'When on the road, we have to adjust a little. I agree with you, of course, mid-morning is the *only* time to eat a proper repast, but by then we'll be in the Kentish levels east of Southfleet. The only hostelry is the Leather Bottle and, trust me, you don't want to eat there. Think of this as an adventure, eh? Something to tell your . . . um . . . great grandchildren.'

Ellesmere looked at the man. 'How old do you think I am?' he asked.

'Well, I . . .'

'Master Baillie, Master Baillie, come quick,' somebody called. 'Master Chaucer's horse . . .'

Baillie sprang back over the bench and hot-footed it into the Falcon's yard. He could see Geoffrey Chaucer, hands on hips, arguing the toss with a rough-clad yokel. The poet's grey looked fine, standing patiently as ever by her master, ready for the off.

'Problem with the horse, Master Chaucer?' The host was at his side.

Chaucer looked at the grey, her bridle bedecked with silver scallop shells, her eyes patient and faithful. 'Not at all,' he said.

'Oh, yes there is,' the yokel grunted in the vowels of a man of Kent. 'She's just pissed all over Wat's wall.'

'Wat's wall?' Baillie and Chaucer chorused. Was this some dialect neither of them had heard before? Some local epithet?

The oaf pointed to a low mound of stones that was indeed splashed with horse urine, still gently steaming. 'That's Wat's wall, that is. And yonder,' he pointed to a near-derelict hovel, 'is Wat's house. You're not showing proper respect.'

'Who the hell is Wat?' Chaucer asked.

The local's head came up, rising from his bull neck like a word unspoken, a promise to be kept. 'You'd better pray,' he said, 'that you never find out. Not where you're going.'

'Now, look . . .' Geoffrey Chaucer, Court Poet and Comptroller of Woollens, had never backed down from a fight in his life – or almost never – and he squared up to the keeper of Wat's wall.

'Come, now.' Harry Baillie could grease the wheels in Hell when push came to shove – which for him, it hardly ever did – and he opened his purse. 'Shall we say, a groat for the wetting of the wall?'

'And the insult to Wat?' The man stood his ground.

'Two, then.' Harry Baillie was a generous man.

'Make it three and I'll forgo the matter,' the wall-keeper grunted, a glint in his eye.

Baillie tutted and cursed the man under his breath. He would be adding the coins to Chaucer's incidentals bill at the end of the pilgrimage, but still. He didn't open his purse unless he really had to – spending money was for other people. He handed over the coins and the man bit each one separately and went on his way. Quite a crowd had gathered outside the Falcon and Baillie was regretting not asking Hardesty to settle matters with his bow instead. The host clapped his hands. 'Nothing to see here, lordings,' he beamed. 'The sun's up and we have miles to go before we sleep.' He scowled at Chaucer and opened his mouth to speak but the comptroller beat him to it.

'On my incidentals, Harry,' he sighed. 'Just don't forget, I saw how many coins you handed over, so don't try and make it four, because I won't pay it.' He looked at the retreating back of the wall-keeper, and shook his head. 'What's the matter with the hoi polloi these days?'

Chaucer remembered the hermit of Holy Trinity from the last time he had taken this road two years before. If anything, the miserable old bugger had got even more miserable *and* his prices had gone up. It was always a wonder to Chaucer that the old man could still summon the strength to haul the chains so that the flat-bottomed barge shuddered and grated its way across the eddying river. He had stopped wondering some years ago how standing out in the open with his hand out for the fare made the man a hermit; some things were just better left unexplored. Madame Eglantyne's horse did not enjoy the crossing at all and the lady had to dismount, holding her Woo-Woo in one hand and her throat with the other, muttering 'By St Loy' throughout the crossing.

'Thank you, Master Hermit,' Chaucer said, having passed the obligatory silver to the man. 'Always a pleasure.'

'Ain't it, though?' the old man grated. 'Hope you make it back.'

'Make it back?' Chaucer repeated. 'Why wouldn't we?'

'Can't say,' the hermit said.

'Let's not be maudlin, Master Chaucer,' Father Ambrosius led his nag off the running board, 'but no man knows his dying day.'

John Gower was angling his stirrup to remount.

'Is it me, John, or is *everybody* a shit-sack this morning?'

'It *is* you, Geoff,' the poet said, swinging into the saddle. 'First one to the Leather Bottle gets 'em in.'

They had taken the southern road out of Dartford, bypassing Gower's Leather Bottle altogether, and had reached Betsham when the miller, riding at the rear, struck up his pipes again with that irritating screech that sounded like a calf being strangled. For a while, no one said anything, but the pleasant murmur of conversation had risen to a cacophony as everybody was forced to shout over him.

'Mother of God!' Gilbert Maghfield suddenly bellowed, clawing free a murderous-looking falchion, its blade gleaming in the sun.

'Hoo!' Harry Baillie, riding alongside him, steadied his arm. 'No violence, Master Maghfield, please. We have ladies present. Nay, nuns.'

'I'm not going to kill the stupid shit,' the merchant growled. 'Just puncture his bloody pipes.'

'No, no,' Baillie begged. 'Leave it with me.' The host had played Solomon to his pilgrims for so long, it came as naturally as breathing. The company watched as the keeper of the Tabard wheeled his bay and cantered back to the miller. They heard raised voices that dropped to a muffled series of oaths. At one point, there was a brief tussle when Baillie tried to wrest the pipes from under the miller's arm, to no avail; the man was built like a wrestler. Eventually, both of them rode to the head of the column and Baillie raised his hand for a halt.

'Lordings,' he said, noting that Maghfield had not sheathed his sword yet and that Hardesty had an arrow nocked in his bow, held low by his side. 'Lordings, Miller Inskip here and I have a novel idea.'

'Joy,' they heard the franklin mutter.

'What if, to entertain us on our merry way, we each tell a tale?'

There was silence.

'A tale?' John Gower found his voice first.

'Anything at all,' Baillie said, staring at the most unforgiving audience he had seen in a long time. 'Master Chaucer, you, I know, have a fund of stories. And you, Master Gower. Master Ellesmere, you can tell us about the good old days, eh? And Master Maghfield, the cut and thrust' – the host immediately regretted his phrase – 'of the European markets. Those burgers in Bruges, eh? What larks! And . . . Madame Eglantyne, I know you could . . . Er, I mean, life in the convent; well, it must be . . . And the best news of all is that Master Inskip here has agreed to tell the first tale. There will be a prize to be awarded by my good self in Canterbury, for the best story. What do you all say?'

The pilgrims looked at each other. Most of them were seasoned travellers, some as far as Rome and Jerusalem; they had never heard of anything so preposterous in their lives.

'Can I just point out,' the yeoman said, 'that there are

twenty-five of us in this party. That's a hundred hoofs clattering on the road at any given point, not to mention the baggage cart. How are we supposed to hear . . .?'

But Robin Inskip, caught up in the chance to hold forth, albeit without his pipes, had nudged his heavy cob alongside the pretty chestnut of Madame Eglantyne and led her forward, yelling at the top of his voice so that all could hear, 'There was once a thick knarre,' he began, 'famed through all the land, for the loudness and the stench of his farts.' He bent over in the saddle, overcome with the hilarity of his story, and it was some time before he could carry on. 'His name was Nicholas,' he managed to gasp out, clinging to his saddle bow to stop himself falling off his horse into the dust.

And the only two people who heard more, becoming ever more horrified, were the prioress and her nun. Everybody else hung back until the three were a suitable distance ahead and, as Tom Hardesty had predicted, the clop of hoofs drowned out the narrative. Although Madame Eglantyne might disagree, Harry Baillie had done it again.

The column halted at St Thomas's Well as the sun was high in the heavens. While the horses were tended by grooms and annoying children tried to sell the travellers little ampoules of Thomas Becket's blood – 'guaranteed two hundred and eleven years old' – John Gower took his turn to tell a tale.

To be fair, the man was cheating. He and Chaucer were, after all, professional storytellers, and the poet gave a beautiful precis of his *Mirrour de l'Omme,* which only Chaucer had read, so it sounded new and fresh. Everybody clapped, although the miller, belching as he finished his bread and ale, knew that it wasn't a patch on his. Madame Eglantyne and her nun had had to find a shady spot in which to lie down and recover from the exploits of the redoubtable Nicholas the farter and missed Gower's poetry altogether.

Apart from the nuns and the two Flemish merchants, who were ensconced under another tree, calculating furiously on their abacuses and tying knots in a piece of string in lieu of a counting table, Gower had a good audience. More people, he later complained to Chaucer, than ever read anything he wrote down. Poet to poet, Chaucer patted his friend's shoulder gently and clambered up from the ground, ready for the off. He never had any trouble getting down, but always wished he were alone when he had to scramble back to his feet; it was not a pretty sight.

Then, they were on the road again, clattering south-east along the Roman road, the great castle of Rochester a vague, grey monolith in the summer heat. It was Tom Hardesty who saw them first, a dark line emerging from the woods of Shorne, the sun glinting on what looked like spear points. The archer's eyes narrowed and he shielded them from the glare. He'd seen this sort of thing before and it had never ended well. He urged his horse forward to the head of the column, where Baillie rode with Chaucer, Gower and the Flemish merchants.

'I'd advise caution here, gentlemen,' he said, standing in his stirrups to get the best view.

The column halted, everybody looking ahead to where the road seemed to vanish into the grey mass.

'What is that?' Maghfield asked.

'Peasants, sir,' Hardesty said, 'to the south-east. Thousands of them.'

Chaucer looked at the others. Their mouths hung slack, their eyes wide. Not many of them had seen that number of people together in any one place in their lives. As the line drew nearer, the glittering spear points sharpened into glaives, billhooks, pitchforks, the implements of the field and furrow. Here and there, makeshift banners floated, the cross of St George high over the multitude.

'That's not peasants,' Maghfield growled. 'That's an army.'

'Is that singing?' Gower asked, straining his ears in the stillness. Without the clop of hoofs and the groan of the cart, the silence was oppressive. Even the birds had fallen silent.

'It's a psalm.' Ellesmere was sitting his gelding alongside them.

'Never in a thousand years,' said Father Ambrosius, shambling up from halfway down the column, where he had been calming Madame Eglantyne and her nun, still a little jumpy and prone to a twitch about the eyes whenever the miller's voice rose above the general hubbub. 'That's a song of the people.'

'The people?' Baillie frowned at him. 'How do you mean?'

The horses were frisking by now, unused to the steady tread of the men and women marching towards them. Only Hardesty's bay remained steady, the yeoman himself upright in the saddle, his bow unhooked and ready in his hand, a more worthwhile target than the miller's pipes in his mind.

'What the hell are you going to do with that?' Maghfield asked. 'Kill them all?'

'No,' Hardesty said, not turning round. 'I've got twenty arrows in my quiver. See that banner? The St George in the centre?'

They all did.

'Whoever their leaders are, they'll be there. People are creatures of habit. They rally to the centre like moths to a flame. I'll just kill the twenty under the cross.' An arrow flipped from the quiver at his hip and was already resting at the nock, the iron tip pointed downwards.

'Well, that only leaves three or four hundred,' Baillie said.

'Make that ten times the number,' Hardesty told him.

'Right, lordings.' The host whirled his horse. 'Time for home, I think. The Holy Blissful Martyr can wait another day.'

'Too late for that, Master Baillie.' Hardesty nodded to left and right. The line of peasants was closing in from both wings, like the claws of a scorpion. Chaucer was glad he had worn his brown hose that day. Even Maghfield, with his great falchion at his hip, felt decidedly exposed and alone.

'Keep still,' Father Ambrosius's voice rose above the deep hum of the singing and the rising hysteria of the pilgrims. 'We have two women and one man of the cloth with us. There is no cause for alarm.'

'No cause, my arse!' Maghfield grumbled and drew his sword.

'Put it away, man,' Chaucer hissed.

'Oh, so you've deigned to speak to me now, have you, Chaucer?'

John Gower caught the moment. 'Er . . . do you two know each other?'

'You might say that,' Maghfield sneered.

Suddenly – and it made them all face front – the chanted singing stopped and the mob stood stock still, in a ring of iron around the little pilgrim band. As Hardesty had predicted, a knot of men was pushing its way through the crowd from under the banner of St George. At their head stood a solid, square-looking man with plate armour across his chest and back.

'Pilgrims, are you?' he asked. It was a Kentish accent.

'We are.' Ellesmere the franklin was the first to answer.

The armoured man whistled and two others jostled their way forward, carrying staffs, shells, gourds and palm leaves in their arms. They dropped them at the hoofs of Baillie's party.

'We met others on the road, east of here,' the armoured man said. 'They were foolish enough to think we didn't mean business.'

'The Medway's red with their blood,' another man grunted, grinning through blackened teeth.

'Who are you?' Maghfield asked. 'What do you want?'

'I am John Nameless, and we'll start with your weapons, purses, anything you're carrying.'

'And if I refuse?' Ellesmere said.

Nameless swept his hand across the spoils of an earlier victory. 'Then something like this pile will be all that's left of you.'

'Tell me,' Hardesty was standing in his stirrups, his arm locked back against the arrow flight at his ear, his eyes narrowed on Nameless, 'would you like my arrows all together or one at a time?'

'Stop!' Father Ambrosius bounced down from the saddle. 'Masters all,' he pleaded, 'there is no need for this.' He was staring at John Nameless. 'We are just going to worship at the shrine of the Holy Blissful Martyr.'

'Becket was a long time ago, priest,' Nameless said. 'John Ball's never mentioned him.'

'Ball?' Gower said. 'Who's that?'

'He's a priest,' Ambrosius told him. 'Something of a prophet, I believe.'

'You will leave your belongings here,' Nameless said, 'and any weapons you carry. Then, you will kneel one by one before the cross of St George and pledge your oath to King Richard and the Commons of England.'

'King Richard?' Ellesmere echoed. 'I have no problem with that. But the Commons of England? You unwashed rabble have lorded it long enough . . .'

But he never finished his sentence. From nowhere an arrow thudded into his forehead and blood spurted over his face, the white of his beard splattered red. Hardesty's arrow was a split second behind, hitting the man with the black teeth between the eyes. There was a roar from the silent crowd as he went down and the pilgrims' horses shied and reared, to a background of screams from the women and snarls from the men.

'In the name of God!' Ambrosius shrieked as his staff with its cross finial pierced the sky. 'Enough!'

Clearly, the man was used to giving orders and, slowly, the tumult subsided. Hardesty was already lining up Nameless in his deadly trajectory and Ellesmere's body had only just hit the ground.

'Lordings,' Ambrosius said to his party. 'For God's dear sake, do as they ask. Swear whatever fealty they demand. Nothing is worth a life.'

There were murmurings and mutterings all round. Geoffrey Chaucer was the first to see sense. He unhooked first his purse, then his poignard, throwing them onto the pilgrim heap on the ground. Ambrosius's cross joined the pile and Madame Eglantyne's gold bracelet.

'And the dog,' Nameless said.

The prioress gasped and tried to hide the little yapping thing at her breast, but the miller grabbed it and threw it into the crowd. 'He'll be all right,' he said, raising his voice to try to drown the frantic yapping. 'These are Englishmen born. They're all dog lovers.'

Madame Eglantyne, with a last frantic cry of 'Woo-Woo!' collapsed in her saddle, supported by her long-suffering nun. 'Canterbury,' they heard the prioress whispering. 'I must get to Canterbury.'

Harry Baillie dismounted carefully, edging his way towards

the cross. Chaucer and Gower were with him, hearing Maghfield's falchion clatter to the ground. Hardesty was the last to dismount. He threw his quiver onto the pile, then snapped his bow in two and threw that down too. One by one, to the jeering of the crowd, each of them swore fealty to their king and the Commons of England, who crowded round them, chanting and laughing.

When it was all over, Nameless raised both hands and the crowd fell silent. 'You can keep your horses,' he said. 'Ride back to London. And as you do, turn back and look behind you. As night falls, I reckon, you'll see the sky red with flame. That'll be Rochester Castle burning. And you're next. Tell them in London. Tell them all. London will burn too. And we're coming. We're *all* coming.'

And Geoffrey Chaucer would hear those words ringing in his head for the rest of his life.

# THREE

From the Old Kent Road, London had never looked so welcoming. The pilgrims, tired and out of sorts, had had time, at least, to wrestle with their individual thoughts and weigh up the pros and cons of what had happened west of Rochester.

And they *had* paused, if only briefly, to see the sky red and glowing over that city along the Medway as it curled and smoked to the sea. Each of them had felt his or her heart sink a little at the sight; had the world gone mad? Then, they had turned their backs on the terror, shut their ears against the low chanting of the mob and the thud of their clogs on the road and they had ridden at a steady Canterbury pace for their homes and safety.

Nothing here had changed. Southwark was still Southwark as night fell and the glow of fires lit the darkening streets. They heard the last comforting bells of St Mary Overie, the barking of dogs in the smock alleys and that strange, haunting howl of the bears in their pits. Men sodden with drink tumbled out of the stews; others scuttled up alleyways with the Winchester geese, the women's breasts bare in the cool June night and their skirts hooked up, ready for business. Steam drifted with smoke from the baths and the cackle of harlots and the grunts of the fornicators welcomed the pilgrims home.

'Lordings,' Harry Baillie could see that Madame Eglantyne, for one, could not take much more. 'Can I suggest we all retire to the Tabard?'

'How much will it cost us, Baillie?' Maghfield wanted to know.

'No, no,' the host did his best to smile. 'On the house, as it were. Everything'll look better in the morning and we can take stock then.' Like the others, he could hardly believe what he had seen that morning and it was beginning to seem like a particularly vivid dream, in amongst the normality of a

Southwark night. 'After a full English' – he caught the merchant venturer's eye – 'and free breakfast, we'll all feel better. It's the least I can do.'

'What are you going to do, John?' Chaucer asked. 'Make for home?'

Gower lived in lodgings along the river, in the precincts of St Mary Overie. It was a stone's throw, but somehow he needed company tonight that didn't involve Marian; he wasn't ready to explain his adventures to her just yet. Sleeping under stone in the general company of lily-livered monks didn't exactly fill him with confidence, either.

'No, I think I'll take up Baillie's offer for the moment. See what the morning brings. Perhaps we'll be able to set off again.' His voice belied the words – at that moment, no one wanted to leave the comfort of London. 'You?'

Chaucer's home over the Aldgate was small, but his own, thanks to the generosity of the Duke of Lancaster and Nicholas Brembre. It was in the wrong direction for the Kentish rabble and Ludlum, the gate-keeper, ate troublemakers for breakfast. But Chaucer was the King's poet. He had news to impart. If only half of what the Kentish rebels threatened became reality, London was in danger – they had all seen that glow in the sky. Nothing would happen tonight, but dawn would tell a different story.

'I'm for the Tabard,' he said.

Tom Hardesty, the toughest man there, even without his bow and dagger, rode past him. 'Where we'll all sleep with one eye open,' he said, 'if we're wise.'

The bells of London were ringing out to herald a new dawn. The city had slept the sleep of the unjust and the people whom Chaucer rode past that morning had no idea that hell was on the way. The bridge was murder as usual on Thursdays, the river roaring under the nineteen arches, splashing the banks north and south as it hurtled to the sea. As it hurtled towards the mob even now on its way. To his right, the Comptroller of Woollens saw the sullen grey walls of the Tower, steady and solid in the morning sun. The gulls wheeled and dipped along the wharves where the cogs and caravels rode at anchor, their sails furled, their flags flapping. To his left, the river narrowed, the banks crowded already with filthy children scratching in the slime for anything a careless traveller might have dropped in the ooze. Ahead of him, flanked by the shops now opening their shutters for the day and the turrets of Baynard's Castle beyond, he saw the drawbridge lower with a grind and a clank and a company of liveried men of the City Watch, with jacks and kettle-hats and halberds, fanning out to begin their watch. Thank God, Chaucer found himself muttering, for men like that.

The bottleneck was always here, no matter what the crisis, what the scare. There were too many people in London, that was the truth of it. And Doomsday itself could come but these people would get into the city, no matter what.

'The queue's down there, mate,' a Cockney voice called as Chaucer's mare threaded her way past a hay cart.

'Queue is a French word,' Chaucer called back, 'and this, when I looked last, is England.'

'Stuck-up ponce!' somebody else called, 'all hose and liri-pipe, some people! That's about to change!'

Chaucer rammed home his spurs. There was no time for politesse this morning. 'Comptroller of Woollens,' he shouted. 'On the King's business.'

At the drawbridge, as lumbering oxen waddled out of his way, he flashed the King's silver hart badge, the one he routinely carried to get himself through crowds, and the guard let him pass. He crossed himself briefly at the chapel of St Thomas, halfway along, and vowed to restart his pilgrimage at some other time. Then he urged the grey through the tangle of streets that lay beyond the north bank. Somehow, now that he was inside the city walls, he felt safe. Then he remembered that those walls had already stood for eleven hundred years; just how many years did they have left in them?

'Geoffrey, Geoffrey. Calm down. It's nothing. Name me one year when the riff-raff didn't go on the rampage.'

Geoffrey Chaucer had had a love–hate relationship with Nicholas Brembre all his adult life. He was the richest man Chaucer knew, and the shiftiest. Yes, he owed his home over the Aldgate to him but he also knew, wearing his comptroller's hat, that Brembre had more fingers in somebody else's pies than anything found in the Shambles. At times like these, however, the comptroller had to speak his mind.

'Don't be ridiculous, Nicholas.' He paused – his poet's soul shuddered at the doggerel.

'I beg your pardon?'

'Oh, come off your high horse, Brembre. One of our party was killed. You might know him – a franklin called Ellesmere.'

'Doesn't ring any bells,' Brembre shrugged.

Chaucer looked the man squarely in the face. 'You've got a nice little thing going here, Nicholas,' he said.

'What do you mean?'

'You know what I mean. I'm not going into all the ins and outs with you today, all the many reasons why the ecclesiastical courts and the King's Bench would be interested in talking to you.'

'How dare you!' the merchant snarled. 'I'll have you remember I was recently Lord Mayor of this fair city.'

'Not above the law, though,' Chaucer reminded him.

Brembre blinked first. 'All right,' he said. 'King's Bench, I'll grant you. But the ecclesiastical courts? It was all entirely consensual, that business with Mistress Griselda, I assure you.'

Chaucer sighed. 'I'm not interested in your peccadilloes, Nicholas, to be honest. Suffice it to say that Mistress Griselda was only one of many. Most of them were Carmelite nuns and at least one was a crutched friar.'

'That's outrageous!' Brembre was beside himself, crimson in the face and letting spittle fly in all directions. 'They were drunk. It was dark . . .'

'That may well be,' Chaucer said, 'but that doesn't change the fact that unknown thousands of knarres are making their way towards your fair city and we've got to do something.'

'Like what?' Brembre asked.

'How about paying a visit to the *current* Lord Mayor of London?'

'Walworth? Walworth, the bloody fishmonger? Don't make me laugh.'

\*    \*    \*

William Walworth the fishmonger sat on his gilded chair in the receiving room of the Guildhall that morning. He was unusually still because he was having his portrait painted, for posterity and a triptych, by a visiting artist from Florence. He didn't appreciate the intrusion from two busybodies who both saw themselves as Walworth's superiors. 'Many, Chaucer?' the mayor repeated. 'What do you mean, many?'

'Several, Master Walworth.' The comptroller was trying to be civil. 'As in plural. More than one.'

Walworth looked at Brembre, whom he hated more than the devil himself. 'Has this man escaped from somewhere?' he asked.

'I'd trust Geoffrey Chaucer with my life,' Brembre said, although no one knew how he'd got that line out without laughing. 'If he says it's a rebellion, it's a rebellion.'

'I'd go further,' Chaucer said. 'I'd venture to suggest that it's a revolution.'

'A rev . . .? Oh, come now, Chaucer. That's preposterous! Didn't you just tell me you were made to swear fealty to the king?'

'I did.'

'Well, that doesn't sound very revolutionary to me.'

'And to the Commons of England.'

'Well, what's wrong with that?' Walworth wanted to know. 'Knights of the shire. Good men and true. Landowners all. Those peasants sound particularly patriotic to me.'

'Not the Commons as in members of Parliament, Master Walworth.' Chaucer was exasperated. 'Commons as in thick knarres. People of the clay. Morons.'

'Oh, now, steady on,' the mayor said. 'I've done a lot of work with these people.'

'At Billingsgate?' Chaucer checked.

'Well, yes, as it happens.' Walworth was not ashamed of his background. Without people like him and those who worked for him, half of England would starve every Friday.

'Ever noticed how slick they are at gutting fish?' Chaucer persisted. 'Fast with those little blades of theirs? I just don't want to end up on one of their slabs, that's all.'

Walworth hesitated. This wasn't going well at all. 'Signor

Divaldi,' he smiled at the painter, 'would you excuse us? Affairs of state, you understand.'

'Of course, signor.' The Italian bowed and wandered away, muttering. That was another half-vat of Chinese white wasted.

'You're being irrational, Chaucer,' the mayor said when he had gone. 'London is the strongest city in the country; nay, Europe; possibly, the world. Do you seriously believe that a handful of Kentish rabble—?'

'You know the story of Troy, Master Walworth?' Chaucer interrupted him.

'The what?'

'*The Iliad.* Homer. Troy was a strong city too and it withstood the Greeks for ten years before they crept into the place in the belly of a wooden horse.'

'Wooden horse?' Walworth threw his arms wide. 'What are you talking about?'

Chaucer closed to the man, looming over him as he sat on his throne. 'Your Billingsgate gutters. The men who light the torches of an evening. The hewers of coal and the drawers of water. In short, Master Walworth, the people of London – *your* people. How far can you trust them? When they see John Nameless's army staring at them from across the river, will they rally to you and fight to the last man? Or will they throw open the city gates and say, "Come on in"?'

A sudden silence hit the Guildhall and William Walworth's mouth hung open, picturing the scene. 'Well,' he said quietly, 'put like that, we'd better go and see Sir Robert Knollys.'

Whenever anyone was in doubt, they went to see Sir Robert Knollys. Veteran of Crécy, Poitiers and Nájera, close friend of the late Black Prince, master of five hundred Genoese crossbowmen, his grand house stood like a fortress in Seething Lane on the slopes of Tower Hill, the river sparkling in the summer sun behind it.

Lombard Street was, as ever, a melee of bankers and merchants, their clerks laden with manuscript scrolls, but they all stood aside as the mayor of London's gilded carriage rattled over the cobbles, jarring Walworth's teeth as it always did.

Sensibly, Brembre and Chaucer rode behind, the clatter of their horses' hoofs echoing around the heart of the city.

It was difficult to gauge Robert Knollys's age. His beard was forked and as silver as Chaucer's but, since he was bald as a badger, it was not easy to pinpoint a decade. Because of his reputation, Chaucer knew that the man had to be nearing sixty, yet he moved like a cat and his eye and his hand were equally steady.

'A rising, you say?' He fixed that eye – and the other one – on Chaucer now.

'Rebellion, sir,' Chaucer said.

'You actually used the word "revolution" earlier, Chaucer,' Walworth reminded him. And the three of them began babbling again over semantics. Knollys held up his hand.

'Hoo!' he shouted and his audience chamber fell silent. 'They killed a man?'

'Yes, sir,' Chaucer said. 'One of my fellow pilgrims.'

'For what reason?' Knollys asked.

'He appeared to be about to refuse to swear fealty to them.'

'Fealty?' Knollys chuckled. 'You can only swear fealty to a liege lord. Chaucer; you know that. Are these riff-raff claiming that status?'

'Sir.' Chaucer looked deep into the knight's eyes. 'In all honesty, I don't know what they're claiming. All I know is that they have been whipped up with the radical rantings of one John Ball, a hedge priest who claims that no man is another's master . . .'

'Hmm,' Knollys sneered. 'Bedlam-without-Bishopsgate is full of people like him.'

'I believe they have burned Rochester Castle, sir,' Chaucer persisted.

'Rubbish,' Knollys grunted. 'Johnnie Newton would never surrender Rochester – I'd stake my life on it.' He looked at the three anxious faces in front of him. 'Gentlemen,' he said, 'this is not the first time the men of Kent be up in the Weald and I doubt it will be the last. My guess is that they'll empty every cellar between Rochester and Maidstone and they'll go home when the barrels are dry. You won't see them again, Master Chaucer. And if you do, there are five hundred Italian crossbowmen within my walls here who'll make short work of 'em. Now, be about your business, gentlemen. Walworth, you have a city to run. Brembre, there's money to be made. Chaucer . . . er . . . write a poem or something. And see yourselves out.'

The pair brushed past a lackey waiting in the shadows who bowed as they passed.

'What is it, Ludovico?' Knollys was pouring himself a large Rhenish.

'A letter, sire, pressed into my hand at the gate.'

Knollys paused, then took the parchment. This was the second letter he had received in the last four days without a seal or ribbon. The hand was neat and careful. 'Thank you, Ludovico. Er . . . send the capitano to see me, would you? I would like a word.'

'Signor.' Ludovico bowed and slid behind the arras.

Knollys took a deep breath and tore open the fold. By the candle's flickering light, he read the scrawled words. 'Look to yourself, minion. It is your time. The crows take the eyes first, I am told.'

He blinked, then crossed the room, pulling open a drawer as he did so. He held up the first letter, the one that had come days before. 'We know,' it said. 'Chandos talked. And what he talked of, it will cost you one hundred nobles to hear. Leave it on St Augustus's Day at the Dog in Dowgate.'

Knollys shook his head. Johnny Chandos had been dead for ten, no, eleven years. And yet . . . and yet. He held up the two letters. Different hands, certainly. Three in all, because the most recent had been addressed and written by two different people. One letter demanded money. The other threatened death. Could Chaucer be right? This was a world gone mad.

'Bugger all.' Chaucer shrugged and was happy to take a swig of Harry Baillie's ale, especially as it was free. The questions had been fired at him faster than Hardesty's arrows could fly, but the one answer did for all.

'Really?' John Gower was one of the many who crowded around the comptroller. They had all hoped for some reassurance from the powers that be.

'Brembre didn't believe it. Walworth dithered. Knollys didn't seem to know what day it is. He refused to believe that Rochester Castle had burned down.'

'But we saw the flames,' Madame Eglantyne seemed lost without her Woo-Woo and her voice was a shadow of its former rather hectoring self. Her nun nodded by way of support.

'It's no good going to the King,' Maghfield grunted. 'Even if he would see you, Chaucer.'

Geoffrey Chaucer was affronted. He had gone off in search of help and it wasn't his fault if everyone in a position of power was a dimwit. But, say it how you liked, the fact remained that he *was* the Comptroller of the King's Woollens and Court Poet. He opened his mouth to protest, but Maghfield was not to be stopped.

'He's a fourteen-year-old boy who's barely finished shitting yellow.' Although the nuns closed their eyes in horror, no one could argue with that – he had a way with words, did the merchant venturer.

'In short, people,' Chaucer wiped the froth from his moustache, 'we're on our own.'

'Harry,' Gower said. 'You know the pilgrim's road better than any of us. How long would it take for the rabble to reach us?'

'Er . . .'

'An army's only as fast as its slowest member.' Tom Hardesty was using a borrowed knife to whittle a new bow for himself, planing and smoothing the golden wood lovingly. 'Did anybody see any children with the peasants?'

Everyone looked at everyone else. 'I think I did,' said a voice from the back, which could have been the miller's. 'Poor half-starved things, they were. Couldn't do much in the way of marching.'

Madame Eglantyne raised her head and spoke with something of her old asperity. 'Let them eat cake,' she said, coldly. 'If it's good enough for cattle . . .'

'Madame Prioress . . .' Father Ambrosius was appalled and crossed himself lavishly.

'We're in no position to feed the five thousand,' Harry Baillie said hurriedly. It was hurting him that he had undertaken to feed the pilgrims for nothing while they awaited developments. A load of starving children was out of the question – after all, he already had five of his own.

'Make that twenty thousand,' Hardesty corrected him. 'And if Rochester's gone, add ten thousand more. If there are children with them, they'll make no more than ten miles a day. If they rose at dawn this morning, they'll be in Southfleet tonight, Dartford tomorrow night. There may be an advance guard of men on stolen horses but there won't be many. Shooter's Hill by cock-shut on Saturday. They won't be here in numbers until Sunday.'

'Well, I'm not sitting around to have my throat cut,' Maghfield said, getting up from his stool. 'I'm going home.'

'Where's that, Master Maghfield?' Chaucer asked, 'if you don't mind my asking.'

'Colchester. If needs be, I can get a ship from Ipswich. They know how to put down vermin in the Low Countries.'

'And we,' Madame Eglantyne stood up too, a shadow passing over her face as she made her instinctive gesture to clutch the departed Woo-Woo to her chest. 'We are for Stratford-atte-Bow. We'll be safe in sanctuary. That rabble won't dare attack a house of God. Come, sister.'

The prioress's nun gathered her rosary and Bible, her embroidery and her wools, and stood with her. She hadn't had to make a decision in her life and didn't intend to start now.

'With respect, madam,' Hardesty put down his knife and blew a piece of sawdust from the bow, 'if they've taken the castle at Rochester, they won't be able to leave the cathedral alone. Willian of Perth's shrine alone . . .'

'He's right,' Baillie said. 'All right, the old bugger – oh, saving your presence, ladies – was a miserable Scottish baker, but after robbers killed him on the road, he performed the odd miracle or two. Am I right, Father Ambrosius?'

'Indubitably,' the priest said.

'Worth a small fortune, that tomb,' Baillie went on. 'The gold and silver alone.'

'And a bunch of Benedictines won't make much of a stand against the rebels,' Hardesty prophesied.

'We have no saintly relics at my priory,' Madame Eglantyne

said. 'Not since we lost the Saviour's . . .' and she mouthed the next word, looking furtively at her nun, who tried to pretend she had gone deaf, '. . . foreskin,' she gulped, closing her eyes like a frog with an unexpectedly large moth, 'to the Bishop of Winchester. We will not be a target for anyone. Master Yeoman.'

'Madam?'

'Will you act as escort for me and for my nun?' Her voice trailed away and there was a tear in her eye. 'I've already lost my Woo-Woo and I'd feel more comfortable if a man of your integrity and prowess would guide us across London.'

'It will be my pleasure, ma'am,' he said. 'Master Baillie, I'd be grateful for the loan of a billhook. Then I'll be back.'

'Back?' Gower repeated. 'Why, man?'

Hardesty looked around him. 'This place is defensible,' he said. 'A bit of work here and there, trenches, revetments. Oh, it's not the Tower, but it'll slow the rebels up for a day or two. Besides,' he looked out of the Tabard's windows, 'nobody takes my weapons and says run; nobody. John Nameless and I have a score to settle.'

So, that, too, was settled. Each pilgrim made his or her own decision to go or to stay. Harry Baillie, the waddling Mistress Baillie and their people had little choice; the Tabard was their only home. Maghfield collected his baggage and had a minion saddle his horse. In place of his mighty falchion, he carried one of Harry Baillie's cook's knives stuck into his belt – it wasn't much, but it was something. The nuns made their way north-east across the bridge, the broad-shouldered yeoman at their side.

'Well, good luck, Geoff.' John Gower shook his friend's hand. 'See you next year, eh? When all this nonsense is over?'

'Count on it, John,' Chaucer said and watched his fellow poet wheel his horse away and clatter out of the Tabard yard.

'Where away, Master Chaucer?' Father Ambrosius stood back as the comptroller hauled himself into his saddle.

'Home,' the poet said, 'to the Aldgate. I fancy there's more chance of survival surrounded by walls ten feet thick of stalwart stone than a wooden inn, no matter what the yeoman's take on its defensibility.'

'*Pax vobiscum*, my son.' Ambrosius made the sign of the

cross and Chaucer thanked him, making, like the rest of the world it seemed, for the bridge.

Harry Baillie stood at the door of his tavern, counting the pilgrims as they left, cursing under his breath the ones who stayed. It was taking bread out of the mouths of his children; his profits were all to Hell in a handbasket. The remainers didn't know that he never paid a thing in advance, so all the inns they wouldn't be staying in this year were the ones which had none of their money. Harry Baillie was even richer than he had been when they set off and, in all conscience, that was rich enough. But even so, he managed to make them feel guilty, and they felt guiltier still when they saw his wife, clearly about to give birth in the next day or so, staggering past them with mounds of bedding in her arms. She stopped every now and then to arch her back and press her hands into it, to relieve her burden. They weren't to know that Barbara gave birth as easily as she shelled peas and had never had a backache in her life. The Baillies were a team and she knew what was needed and when.

Finally, it seemed to Baillie that he had shamed all that he was going to shame, and he now had seven pilgrims under his roof; not a bad number, and he could still turn a good profit at that. Hardesty still had to come back, but he would get more than his money's worth out of him, what with improvements to security which would be good for years to come. He was about to close the door, when Maghfield's friend, the other Flemish merchant, came hurrying down the stairs, his bag over his shoulder.

'Going home, Master . . . Er . . .?' He could never remember everyone's name, let alone the foreign ones.

'I've been thinking it over, Master Baillie,' the man said. His accent was almost negligible but very definitely Flemish. Probably also planning a bunk to the Low Countries. Baillie was relieved – one less to ask for a credit towards next year. 'I have my wife and children at home and I should get back to them. Our Walbrook house is . . . well, not fortified, but we have men there, working in the outhouses, you know. Not enough to repel that mob we met, though. I should be with them. Organizing, you know the kind of thing. Women' – he paused respectfully as Mistress Baillie squeezed past him in the narrow passage, carrying two buckets of water and with a small child in a sling on her back – 'women need us men to tell them what to do, do they not?'

Baillie gave a nervous laugh. Barbara Baillie was an understanding sort, but when she was near her time, her temper could be a little short.

'So, I should return home. Indeed, Master Baillie, I *must* return home. When you have calculated the refunds due to us all because of the *force majeure* which we encountered, you can send it to my man of business in the Royal Exchange.'

'Erm . . . Act of God, surely?' Baillie murmured.

'Act of God? Thousands of armed peasants? I think not, Master Baillie. However, I am not in a hurry for my refund. Shall we say . . . week Tuesday? Start of business? Good day to you.' And the merchant tipped his hat and was gone, out into the yard to where his mare stood patiently waiting, another woman to be told what to do.

There was never a good time for a horse to throw a shoe, but trotting through Southwark in the dead of night was worse than most. Tom Hardesty had not intended to stay at the Stratford priory for long, but Madame Eglantyne had had other ideas. First, she had had to assemble her sisters in the chapel to tell them of her horrendous news, of the horror that she had faced. The yeoman was trotted out to vouch for her tale and Hardesty had never had so many women twittering over him in his life. Then he had been given a square, if uninteresting, meal, while Madame Eglantyne took a bath, one of the two she indulged in every spring, and changed into a fresh though identical habit. Only her golden bracelet could not be replaced. That was unique, a memory of things past.

With just a hint of her blonde hair showing beneath her veil, she had put on another gold bracelet to replace the one the peasants had stolen and was carrying in her arms an identical lapdog to the one last seen disappearing into the throng.

'This is my Foo-Foo, Master Hardesty,' she purred. 'Foo-Foo, this brave man brought your mama safely home.'

Foo-Foo looked less than grateful for that. The repellent little creature rolled its eyes and bared its tiny, needle-sharp teeth at the yeoman, snapping and yelping as its doting mistress clasped it to her bosom. Hardesty looked at the dog with disdain – he routinely used such animals for target practice when he ran out of rats and was unimpressed by its golden collar. After all his feting, he could hardly refuse to kneel for a quick spot of Compline, so it was dusk before he set out.

As his mare plodded through the darkening streets, the merchant began to wonder if he had made the right decision. The honest truth was, he didn't really want to go home. But now, finally, as proper dark fell, late, as the year neared its turn, he was outside his house, his horse now taking her own path to her stable, glad to be back to the quiet of her stall. He slid from her back and was about to start to remove her saddle and her bridle when a groom appeared at his elbow.

'We weren't expecting you, sir,' he said, tying his points in some confusion. The kitchen maid who was responsible for their being untied in the first place slid off in the shadows back to her room in the garret, scurrying past the rows of silent looms.

The merchant turned to speak to the groom but, suddenly, was so tired he couldn't think of a thing to say and just grunted to the man and turned for the house. He was surprised to see so many windows lighted; his wife's frugality leaned in many directions, but the profligate use of candles was her main concern of the moment, especially with the lighter nights. Up with the cock and bed with the moon was just one of the old saws from the old country which she trotted out when anyone was up too late. Up with the cock, indeed, thought the merchant. That'll be the day.

He pushed open the door and the candles lit in every sconce were not the only things to amaze him. Somewhere, from above his head, a sweet voice was singing. There was no instrument – there were no instruments in the house – but the words rang softly down the stairs. He stopped dead in the brightness of the hall and listened, his nerves on edge. This was a moment which probably would never come again; this sparkling room, this music.

'Madam, you are of beauty so fine, and known all the world around. For as crystal glorious you do shine, and like rubies are your cheeks so round . . .' The song dissolved into laughter.

The merchant grimaced. Not great poetry, but what a pretty voice. But where . . .?

'Master Gillis, Master Gillis,' a voice was suddenly in the hall with him, not singing, but shouting. Running feet were everywhere. His man of business was in front of him, shaking him by the shoulders. 'Master Gillis. How did you know?'

Gillis blinked. 'How did I know what?'

The steward looked at the cook who looked at the between maid. Their eyes were wide. The singing had stopped and somehow the candle flames themselves seemed still.

'Your wife, Master Gillis. The mistress. We can't find her anywhere. She's . . . gone.'

From overhead came another peal of laughter and Arend Gillis sank down onto one of the many uncomfortable chairs his wife insisted on littering around the hall. He looked up with haunted eyes at the steward and another old saying from the old country stole into his head.

'Be careful what you wish for.'

Tom Hardesty led his limping horse along the river's bank, the London clouds scudding under the moon high above. Something spooked the animal and it jinked and whinnied, throwing back its head. Hardesty caught the bridle and steadied the horse, stroking its nose and whispering soft words. Beyond the jetty, where the rowing boats clunked together on the ebb tide, he saw a bundle of cloth in the water. It was caught up in the mooring ropes, pulled this way and that by the mystifying eddies of the Thames. At first, the yeoman thought nothing of it, then *something*, and he never knew what, made him look again, this time more closely.

He knelt on the slimy planks of the jetty and prodded the saturated bundle with his billhook. Slowly, out of the darkness, a hand came up, white in the night and, as he peeled back the cloth, a face. It was the face of a woman, the mouth clamped shut, the dead eyes half open. Someone had cut her throat.

# FOUR

Jack Chub sat in the smouldering outbuildings of Rochester Castle that evening, nursing his aching feet. 'Nobody told us we'd have to march bloody everywhere,' he grumbled to Will Lorkin, dozing alongside him, his head resting on a pile of priceless manuscripts, singed at the edges and already illegible.

'Decent wine, though,' Lorkin yawned. 'From the cathedral cloisters, this lot come.'

''Ere,' Chub sat upright, dipping his bleeding toes into a bowl of holy water, 'did you get anything from that tomb? Tomb of Whatisface the Baker?'

'William of Perth?' Lorkin never missed a chance to pass on his knowledge. 'Nah. No chance. Wat and his mates have had that. Away on their dancers with anything valuable.'

'Yes,' Chub shrugged. 'That's how it goes, don't it? All that "when Adam delved and Eve span" bollocks. I don't see we're any better off, to be honest, even though we're risking a noose, not to mention Hellfire and damnation, for doing what we're doing.'

'Ah, you don't want to be so negative, Chubby. Rochester was just the start of it. Wait till we get to London.'

'London?' Chub reached for another bottle of the monks' wine. 'Who said anything about that? I heard from a knarre who used to chop logs for Wat Tyler's old mum, we're going south today, to Maidstone.'

Chaucer left the Tabard with mixed feelings. He had slept in Harry Baillie's beds from time to time and had been unimpressed. Unimpressed too by the 'sundries' on his bill the next morning. On asking, Baillie's factotum had explained, with a straight face, that the word covered anything not on the basic tariff. On being pressed, he admitted that it covered sheet, pillows and mattress, Harry Baillie taking 'bed' to mean quite literally the wooden and string structure and 'breakfast' the dry biscuit left on the nightstand. So, the Comptroller of Woollens was not anxious to avail himself of the Tabard's hospitality again. For all Harry Baillie had promised that everything would be free, Chaucer suspected that his definition of the word and Baillie's probably differed by a country mile. He had left Bertha stabled at the Tabard, because he would have to go back eventually, if only to pick up his bag, and he ambled home, his head full of images he would rather not have; the spurt of the blood from the franklin's head, besmottering his beard and the front of his threadbare coat. The eyes of the crowd, like wolves in the thicket, burning in unison at their prey. And he heard their chanting, like the voices of the dead. He shivered as he turned in at the door at the foot of the stair leading to his room.

Alice, who was coming down the stair, jumped visibly. 'Master Chaucer!' she said, her hand to her throat. 'I wasn't expecting you for . . . don't tell me that Harry Baillie left you all high and dry!'

'No, Alice,' Chaucer said, suddenly more tired than he could say. 'No, he didn't. But as to what did happen, do you mind if we talk about that some other time? I'm for my bed, if it's all ready for me.'

Alice patted his arm. 'It's all ready, Master Chaucer,' she said. 'Aired and made, perfect for tired bones. Up you go and I'll bring you something to drink, shall I? A nice Rhenish that's seen a hot poker. Honey? Nutmeg?'

Chaucer could have cried. The shock of the Canterbury road had been rather more than he had realized and these small kindnesses were almost more than he could bear. He wasn't sure that his voice would not give him away, so he nodded and toiled his way up the stairs.

Alice swung away into her husband's inn. 'Doggett,' she said, grabbing his arm and pulling his ear down so he could hear her whisper. 'The old bugger's back early.'

Her man stood upright. 'Again? What now?'

'I dunno, but something's shaken him. I'd got the room all ready for that priest who was asking for a bed for a night – when was he expected? Did he give you a time?'

'Tomorrow. We'll have to watch the door. If it wasn't that Chaucer had connections, I'd chuck the old bastard out. Do you *know* how much money he owes me?'

Alice patted him; it was her reflex gesture when men got excitable and it had got her out of a lot of trouble over the years. Into a lot as well, but she always drew a veil over that. 'He owes you a bit more now,' she said, apologetically. 'I promised him a posset of Rhenish. Can you . . .?' She looked up at him, with what she hoped was a winning expression.

He looked down at her and sighed, then smiled. 'Go on, then. The fire's hot in the kitchen, there's a bottle open over there.' He smacked her rear as she passed him and chuckled. Alice wasn't perfect, but he knew he could do a damned sight worse.

Upstairs, Chaucer breathed in the smell of old books, all sixty of them, old paper and fresh, clean sheets. The scent of a June afternoon lingered over the bed, the bee-loud, honey-heavy scent of the rosemary over which the sheets had dried. He slid out of his road-dust and into a clean nightshirt from his press and was almost asleep when Alice came into his room, his warmed wine in a tankard wrapped in a cloth. She tucked him in as she might a child, put the drink on the nightstand and went down the stairs, cursing him mildly for being an inconvenient old fool.

The next morning seemed to come in a flash. Chaucer always slept well on pilgrimage and so he wasn't surprised to find it was past dawn when he opened his eyes. What was surprising was that he recognized the room, from the books on the shelf to the cracks – like a mad map of an unknowable country – on the ceiling. Then, he remembered. He was home because of a horde of knarres roaming the countryside. He shook his head and stretched, sliding out of bed gingerly, so as not to jar his back. He went over to the window and pulled back the heavy curtain he drew across even in summer, to keep out the early sun and the sounds of a great city awakening.

Chaucer was feeling his age that morning. The ride back to London had been a little quicker than either he or Bertha would have liked. The mare was short coupled and stocky with a straight shoulder which made for a short-striding, choppy ride that left him half crippled by the end of the day. So different from the ambling palfreys of the merchants and Madame Eglantyne, who had no doubt spent the night without so much as a twinge. Bertha's uneven step seemed to have made his eyes and ears go a bit funny, too. There was a rushing noise in his head that sounded as though he were by the sea, a kind of surging roar, but very far away. He could see what looked like a wavering line of smoke, but more solid than any smoke he had ever seen, on the horizon, sharp points and glints of light flashing from its midst.

He stepped back a pace and rubbed his eyes. Then he covered his ears and filled his cheeks with air, trying to clear the wax which Bertha's uneven legs had shaken free. He fumbled in his purse for his spectacles, then spent a moment or two straightening out the flimsy wires that hooked them over his ears. Then he looked again and his heart almost leapt from his mouth. The sea and the smoke were nothing of the kind. They were people, shouting people, waving implements and fists in the air and chanting, chanting words he did not want to hear.

Backing away from the window, he scrabbled on the floor for where he had left his clothes of the night before and, still tying his points, ran as best as his knees would allow, down the stairs, almost cannoning into Alice, a bowl of porridge in her hands.

'Must go,' he gasped. 'Take cover. Tell Doggett.' And with that, he was gone.

Still holding her porridge, Alice went back into the kitchen and started eating the oatmeal, hardly noticing. 'Doggett,' she called. 'If that priest comes by today, tell him the room's still vacant, if he's interested.'

A booming reply told her that her husband was in the cellar.

'I don't know. He's finally gone mad, I suppose.' She looked down at the bowl on the table and pulled a face. She didn't even *like* porridge.

As he hurried away, Chaucer caught sight of Ludlum, the Aldgate keeper, his shoulders broad, a crossbow slung over his back. His lads, doughty knarres all, were shoulder to shoulder with him. All right, so there was an army of peasants marching across Goodman's Field, swarming around Gracechurch and the White Chapel. But if anybody could handle them, it was Ludlum and his lads. No place here for a Comptroller of Woollens.

As Chaucer hurried through familiar streets to the Tabard, he could still hear the mob behind him. Were they getting louder, or was it just that the sound had got into his brain and was playing tricks? The cobbles underfoot were making his back twinge again but he hardly noticed. He needed to be back in the Tabard, with people he trusted and who knew what they were facing. He hoped Hardesty had finished his bow and a whole quiver-full of arrows beside. They would need that and more.

At the corner of Gropequaint Lane and Candlewick Street, just before he got to the bridge, as he paused, hands on knees, to draw breath, he heard a voice from just above his head.

'In a hurry, Master Chaucer?' The clipped, precise vowels belonged to a Flemish merchant, and without looking up, Chaucer knew which one.

'Master Maghfield,' he said, straightening with care. 'I thought you had gone home.'

He noticed that the venturer had replaced his falchion, dangling from his hip as he looked down at the comptroller.

The merchant gave a barking laugh, with no humour in it. 'I did, briefly, Master Chaucer. But it seems that my wife had taken the opportunity to go and visit her mother in Uxbridge while I was away on the pilgrimage. The house was empty; even the servants have taken themselves off. I wasn't sorry. I was tired and didn't want conversation. But, this morning . . . well, I thought I would return to the Tabard.'

'And there are thousands of peasants approaching from the east,' Chaucer pointed out.

There was another bark of laughter. 'And that, too, Master Chaucer. You are correct. That, I presume, is why the servants had vanished. As we seem to be having a quiet moment . . .'

Chaucer stood upright finally and looked up into the merchant's face, shielding his eyes in the morning sun. 'Hmm?'

'About the money that you owe me.'

'About it?' Chaucer hedged.

'Well, more about the repayment, really.' The merchant was smiling, or was he? It was hard to tell with the sun behind him.

The loan wasn't big, but Chaucer would rather not repay it unless he absolutely had to. It had long been his habit to hang on to what money came his way – comptrolling and poetry were not known for their high remuneration and, with thousands of peasants on the rampage, who knew what the future held? He patted his purse, which felt different, somehow. He looked down. In his haste to dress, he had his purse on inside his hose – he looked as though he had some enormous mormal on his thigh.

Maghfield touched his mare with his spurs and she jinked into a canter. 'I'll see you at the Tabard, Master Chaucer,' he said over his shoulder. 'When you have adjusted your dress.'

The yard at the Tabard was, if anything, busier than ever when Chaucer, his purse extricated from his hose, arrived, somewhat hotter and sweatier than he had intended. The grooms were stabling horses, the potboys were carrying baggage and Harry Baillie was losing his temper as only he could. To the untutored eye, he seemed to be his usual genial self, standing in the doorway of his inn, his hands folded complacently over his aproned paunch. But closer to, he was a man on the edge. His wife was upstairs in the best bed, surrounded by the best midwives money could buy, all exhorting her to push, for reasons he couldn't fathom. His second-best bar parlour was full of men from various inns along the route to Canterbury, sent, ostensibly, to make a bargain with him for payment for perishable goods obtained for non-existent pilgrims. His yard was full of people and horse shit. And now, just to put the gilt on the gingerbread, Geoffrey Chaucer was edging through the crowd, no doubt intent on a refund. It was really too much. Harry Baillie straightened up, patted his apron into place and adjusted his hat. He was going to tell Geoffrey Chaucer, once and for all by Our Lady that—

'Master Baillie! Master Baillie!'

The voice from above him was urgent and he spun round. 'What?' He knew what, but was playing for time.

'Master Baillie. It's the mistress . . .'

With a glance over his shoulder at the rapidly approaching Comptroller of Woollens, at the milling crowd, the horses and their shit, Harry Baillie conquered his fear of childbed and fled up the stairs. 'I'm on my way,' he called, his voice all but drowned out by the cries of his latest offspring, furious as all his children seemed to be, at being propelled into a world in such turmoil.

Chaucer, reaching the door in time to see Baillie's heels disappear into the dark at the top of the stair, looked around him in confusion. It was true that he and Baillie didn't always see eye to eye, but for the man to flee in such a manner was nothing but downright rudeness. He looked for someone to complain to and managed to grab a passing potboy by the ear.

'Why did Master Baillie run away from me just now?' The poet's knee-jerk decision to leave his Aldgate fastness for this hellhole was making him testy.

'He didn't . . .' The potboy was finding it hard to think with his head wrenched to one side.

Chaucer gave him a shake and the lad cried out in protest. 'Don't backchat me, boy,' Chaucer said. 'I asked you . . .'

The reasonable tones of John Gower cut through the boy's protests. 'Don't take it out on the boy, Geoff,' he said, gently removing the poet's pinching fingers from the boy's ear. 'Master Baillie is about to become a father again' – he cocked his own, unpinched ear – 'or, perhaps I should say, has become a father again, if the sound of a good pair of lungs from upstairs is any guide.' He nodded to the potboy who shot off in the direction of the cellar, glad to gain the quiet of the underground fastness where he spent most of his time.

Chaucer took the stance of any man baulked of a good rant and tutted extravagantly and changed the subject. 'I am here to warn everyone . . .' he began.

'. . . of the horde of the peasantry heading this way?' Gower checked. 'Yes, we know. Why do you think *I* came back? The brethren along the river are up to their knees in rumours. I've sent Marian and the children to her mother's in the West Country. Everyone has a different story – I would be intrigued to hear yours. Everything has been a little garbled, thus far. And of course, we mustn't forget Tom Hardesty's body.'

As far as Chaucer could remember, the yeoman was a well set-up chap, but nothing to make him more important than a rabble heading this way at the speed of the slowest man, intent on murder and mayhem. 'I . . .' he was still uncomfortably aware that he had almost made himself look somewhat stupid by haranguing a man whose wife had just that second given birth, so he stopped for a little think. 'What about Tom Hardesty's body?' he asked, eventually. 'He looked quite healthy, as I recall. Has he been hurt in some way?' He looked around vaguely, as if he could in some way assuage any injury.

Gower was briefly puzzled then realized the problem. 'No, Geoff. I mean the body that he found. A drowning, in the river.'

Chaucer shrugged. There were drownings in the river every day. Some sought the kind embrace of the water when life was not so kind. Others – the majority, he suspected – simply fell in when the worse for drink. There had been a case not long ago when a ferryman had missed his stroke and was drowned. So he didn't really see the excitement, not when there was an unnumbered horde of furious peasants heading their way.

'Don't shrug, Geoff!' Gower was rather disconcerted – he had always assumed his friend to have more compassion. 'A soul has been sent to heaven before its time. Surely, that is worth more than a mere shrug?'

Chaucer looked at Gower with haunted eyes. 'There are peasants, John, you do know that, do you? Thousands, tens of thousands, of them, massing to the east. I saw them, out of my very own window. Imagine it; more people than we have ever seen before in one place; disgruntled, angry people with sharp implements and murder in their hearts. And you take me to task over a *shrug*?'

Gower was a patient man and he remained so now, but only

by the merest whisker. 'It's not the shrug per se,' he said, moving Chaucer out of everyone's scurrying way by putting an implacable arm around his shoulder and moving him in the direction of the best parlour. 'It's your casual acceptance that a body in the Thames is not news.'

Chaucer stopped suddenly and they both almost fell over. 'I've seen the damned river almost bobbing with bodies, John. That's the point I think I was trying to make.'

'I see that.' Gower got them underway again. 'But this body was rather different, Geoff. Tom Hardesty found it trapped under a jetty, a woman with her throat cut.'

Chaucer couldn't shrug again, Gower's grip was too tight. 'Suicide,' he said, the shrug in his voice instead of his shoulders.

'I don't think so, Geoff,' Gower said. 'Her head was all but off her shoulders. No suicide can cut that deep. Especially not a woman.'

Chaucer was intrigued in spite of himself. It was still hard to know how anyone could care about one death when there were almost certain to be hundreds in the near future, but he had always liked tales of bloody murder. 'What did Hardesty do with the body?'

Gower laughed and patted his friend on the shoulder before letting go. This was more like the Geoff Chaucer he knew. 'Well, you know Hardesty already, I think, even after less than two days. He brought her back here, of course. To the Tabard.'

Chaucer stopped again, aghast. 'Here? But . . .' he looked around, frowning. 'People *eat* here. Drink. Sleep. Surely, a body from the river with its head all but off can't be kept *here*?'

'Do you know,' Gower said, 'that could be Harry Baillie talking, if you add a few obscenities I doubt you are that familiar with. But, a long rant cut short, she is out in the stable, wrapped in an old carpet, to try to reduce the . . . well, not to put a fine point on it . . . smell. River mud and week-old flesh is not an aromatic feast, as I am sure you can imagine.'

'Hardesty carried her here?' Chaucer was aghast. It sounded an almost unbelievably unpleasant chore.

'He and his horse. The creature had cast a shoe so wasn't

fast enough to get away, but it was an eye-roll away from panic when it got here. All the horses are spooked, that's why the stable yard is in such chaos. Some are having to spend the night outside.'

'I wondered why it was *quite* so bad.' Things were beginning to fall into place, one by one. 'Is there any way to tell who she is?' Chaucer was feeling his inner storyteller take over.

'No. I don't know if you have ever seen a body which has been seven days in water . . .'

'You keep saying "seven days",' Chaucer pointed out. 'Is there any real way of knowing?'

Gower nodded. 'I thought that, but one of Baillie's stable lads – you know the one, about a hundred years old at first glance, perhaps only ninety when you look closer – he used to be a waterman and says he can tell how long a body has been in the water in increments of an hour. After six days, it's a bit less precise, or so he says. But he has come out at a week or thereabouts. That's in the water, and assuming she went in more or less at the point of death. So, add last night into the sum and I suppose . . . well, let's call it a week, for simplicity's sake.'

Chaucer suppressed a shudder. He had once forgotten a piece of cheese which he had been nibbling on when writing a particularly poignant part of *Anelida and Arcite*. In the excitement of the muse's visitation, he had put the cheese under his pillow, and the horror of putting his hand into its maggot-eaten remains a week later had stayed with him since that day. So a seven-day body – he hoped he would be able to avoid having to see it; imagining it was turning his stomach.

Gower had never seen a man turn green in front of his eyes before, but he did so now and changed the subject, within its limits. 'We can't tell who she is, no,' he said. 'Her clothing might mean something to someone, but we haven't had them laundered yet.'

'*Laundered?*' Chaucer was horrified. 'Who would you ask to do that foul job, in the name of all that's holy?' His memory took him back to the sweet-smelling laundry at Clare last summer, and the soft rounded arms of Joyce, his old love, smoothing the linens with her stone, sprinkling them with perfumed waters. It seemed a lifetime away.

Gower looked surprised. He had assumed that Chaucer knew all about Barbara Baillie, for whom no job was too big, too small or too gruesome. 'The lady of the house, of course. But then she was laid low with her pains and hasn't been back downstairs as yet.'

Chaucer's eyes nearly popped out of his head. The world was not just upside down but twirling round at random. 'I heard the cries of a newborn as I set foot inside this inn,' he said. 'Surely . . .'

'Mark my words,' Gower said. 'The woman will be downstairs and pouring ale before this morning's out. Nothing keeps Mistress Baillie in bed for long.'

'Har har.' A passing potboy couldn't help himself, with the master safely upstairs for now. 'Certainly not Master Baillie, from what I hear. Why . . .'

'About your work,' a voice came from nowhere, simultaneously with the sound of a stinging slap around the head. 'Master Baillie can acquit himself perfectly well in bed or anywhere else, if it comes to it.'

The potboy turned with a horrified look on his face. 'Mistress Baillie!' he croaked. 'I . . . I wasn't expecting . . .'

'No one ever is,' she said, following up the slap with another. 'Now, about your business.' She turned with a sweet, hostess's smile to the two poets. 'Gentlemen, welcome back to the Tabard. It's an exciting day, one way and another, is it not?'

Chaucer bowed and Gower smiled. 'Indeed it is, Mistress Baillie. I understand you . . .' Gower had never been called upon to congratulate a new mother within less than half an hour of the birth, not even his own wife. He was sure there was probably a form of words for it, but couldn't quite call it to mind.

She beamed. 'A bonny, bouncing boy,' she said. 'He is at the breast as we speak. I shall call him Geoffrey John.' She saw their startled glances. 'Little Geoffrey has a wet nurse, gentlemen. Though Master Baillie and I work for our livings, we are not animals, you know. He is the very spit and image of his father – he has his nose, poor little chap.' She thwacked

Chaucer on the chest to share her amusement and almost knocked him flying. 'Master Baillie is having a lie-down. Childbed always takes him like that. As a rule, I don't pander to him, but I fancy he'll have a lot on his plate, come sundown.' She smiled again at her guests. 'Well, I mustn't tarry. I have linens to wash, as I understand. Poor soul. And those potboys – give them an inch and they'll take a mile.' She squinted over Chaucer's shoulder into the bright yard outside. 'Now, who's that coming?'

The men followed her gaze.

'Oh, for the love of God. It's that "By Our Lady" nun and her hangers-on. And another dog, as I live and breathe.' And she bustled off, muttering imprecations under her breath.

For a moment, Chaucer and Gower stood silently, recovering from the whirlwind that was Mistress Baillie. 'Apparently,' Gower said after a minute's pause, 'she is always rather quiet when she has been delivered.'

Without another word, the men scurried off to the best parlour – after Mistress Baillie, it was essential to have a brief rest before dealing with Madame Eglantyne.

'In the name of God, go!' The archbishop's man held out his crozier in front of the mob. They filled Christ Church Great Gate, the stone carvings of archbishops long dead staring down at them in disbelief. Stone roses bloomed in the curves of archways and fox-faced devils leered down at them. The bolder of the rebels leered back.

'Where's Sudbury?' Nameless called, sitting his stolen palfrey at the head of his men.

'If you mean the archbishop, he's not here.'

'Sacristan,' Nameless leaned forward in the saddle, 'we have no quarrel with you or your monks. You're like us, downtrodden minions. Our quarrel is with his High and Mightiness.'

'And who are you?' the sacristan asked. All his life he had trodden these hallowed stones, the ones where the rabble now stood. He had splashed through the puddles of the Dark Entry on his way to the great cathedral, its ancient stones grey in the winter snows or gilded in the summer suns. If this man had no quarrel with him, then the feeling was not reciprocated.

'I am Wat Tyler,' Nameless said, 'and you'll all know that name soon enough. We're coming in.'

The sacristan and his monks closed ranks, their black and white robes a wall, thin and feeble against the multitude. Many were bowed and white-haired. One or two hobbled on sticks. They were no match for the men of Kent and everybody knew it.

Tyler threw up his arm, turning in the saddle to yell at the people at his back. 'This is a house of God,' he said. 'You will respect it. We will leave our weapons at the door.'

There was general grumbling at this, but the sacristan was astonished to see men unbuckling knives and swords, resting pitchforks and billhooks against the cathedral's tracery.

'We've brought no alms either, sacristan,' Tyler grinned, 'if you'll excuse the pun. I hope you'll forgive that.'

Whatever the sacristan's view, the monks were happy to have their lives left to them and they dutifully moved back to let Tyler dismount and enter the cathedral precincts. Some of the peasants, their eyes raised to heaven via the glories of the fan-vaulted canopy, made for the chapel of the Blessed Trinity. Many of them fell to their knees, as pilgrims had done for centuries, the wool of their worn hose scraping on the ancient stones.

Blue Tooth was there first, scowling at the chair of St Augustine that stood in a shaft of sunlight. He grabbed a priest who was scurrying past. 'What's in there, parasite?' he asked.

The man crossed himself and whispered, 'That is the reliquary of the Holy Blissful Martyr,' he said. 'It contains the scalp of St Thomas himself.'

Blue Tooth laughed. 'Pity it doesn't contain Sudbury's,' he said. 'Had he been here, parasite, there'd be another martyr for poor deluded souls to pray to. Open it.'

The priest was horrified. 'I cannot, sir,' he said. 'It is holy beyond our understanding.'

'Bollocks!' Blue Tooth sneered, the crowd at his back getting larger. 'You mean you haven't got a knife to gouge out the lead seal. I can help you with that.' And in a second, there was a blade in his hand, glinting at the priest's throat.

The man shrank back, terrified. Suddenly, a powerful pair of hands pushed Blue Tooth forward so that his head smashed into a marble pillar and blood ran again in Becket's cathedral. The man fell with a groan and Wat Tyler stood over him, snatching up his secreted dagger. 'I said "No weapons",' he said. 'I said, "You will respect this house of God." Here, priest,' he turned the knife in his hand and held it, hilt forward, to the man of God. 'Turn this into a ploughshare. Those of you who wish to pray here,' he called to his people, 'do it. The rest, outside with me. We have places to be.'

The best parlour was cool and quiet and Chaucer sat on the bench under the window, leaning back, eyes closed, trying to take himself back to a time when there wasn't a rat of fear gnawing at his throat. Only a day or so ago, the thought of spending time with Madame Eglantyne would have had him scurrying for cover, but it held no terrors now. He would even pay back the money he owed to Maghfield – he had it in his purse, after all – or withstand the smell of the miller. He would do all that and more, if he could believe that the threat of armed insurrection was just a nasty dream he had had, snuggled in his feathers at the Aldgate. He smiled as he sat there; better still if he could still be in his bed, waiting to set off on his pilgrimage to the Holy Blissful Martyr. Briefly, and deeply, Chaucer slept, flinching now and again as a muscle twitched.

'Is Master Chaucer quite all right, Master Gower?'

The ringing tones of the prioress filled the little room and drove out any serenity it had managed to hang on to.

Gower lowered his voice to a mere husk, hoping she would do the same. 'He's taking a nap, madame,' he said. 'He had an early morning.'

'Early morning?' the woman's voice cut the air like a diamond cuts glass. 'We all had an early morning, Master Gower. My priory is up and awake well before dawn or I would want to know the reason why. Matins waits for no woman.'

If the prioress's nun had a comment to make, she kept it to herself as usual.

Gower smiled, as best he could. He was not an unkind man, but there was a streak in him which occasionally caused him to speak his mind rather too freely. He fought against this now; although Madame Eglantyne was a perfectly noxious woman who thought that the world revolved around her and her equally noxious dog, she was, when all was said and done, a nun. 'Have you brought the sisters with you, madame?' he asked, hoping that the answer would be no. If even one of them was like her prioress, it just didn't bear thinking about.

Madame Eglantyne's sniff could have been heard in the White Hall. 'I have not, Master Gower,' she said. 'I asked them to accompany me, of course. But they preferred to travel south-west, to the priory at Elstow. It's entirely up to them, of course,' she went on, though her face was saying something altogether different, 'but, speaking for myself, I would sooner sup with the Devil than spend a night under the roof of That Woman.' She drew up her substantial bosom as she spoke and tucked Foo-Foo more comfortably under her arm.

Gower tutted sympathetically, although he had no idea at all as to what she was talking about. The nun continued to look non-committal, though there was something in her eyes that told the perspicacious poet that she wouldn't have minded the comforts of Elstow Abbey one little bit.

'They'll be travelling for days, no doubt, and when they get there . . . well!' The prioress's eyes rolled and she leaned in closer to Gower, spraying him with angry spittle, '*She* will no doubt make them welcome, if she has room amongst all her guests. Elstow Abbey,' she said, somehow making it sound like a curse, 'is home to every wanton in the county, in my opinion. And that of the bishop, as if that makes any difference to *her*.' She set her mouth and looked again at Chaucer, who made sure his eyes remained closed. 'Are you sure Master Chaucer is all right?' She nudged her nun. 'Go and poke him. See if he's still with us.'

Chaucer yawned extravagantly and sat up, looking about him as if bemused. There were some things he had done in his life he wasn't proud of, some things he had connived at that he would, in hindsight, rather not have done, but allowing himself to be poked by a nun was not going to go on that list.

'Oh.' Madame Eglantyne sounded somewhat disappointed. 'You are alive.'

'I did say he was,' Gower muttered, and had the pleasure of seeing the nun smile behind her hand.

'He looked dead.' Madame Eglantyne didn't like to be wrong and dismissed the whole episode as if it had never happened.

'Madame Eglantyne!' Chaucer scrambled to his feet and went over to kiss her hand, trying to ignore the snarling dog inches from his face as he did so. 'What brings you here?'

'Thousands of peasants,' she said, curtly. 'As I imagine applies to you and Master Gower here as well as . . . the throng in the yard.'

'It is rather busy, isn't it?' Chaucer agreed. 'And Mistress Baillie has just been delivered of a son, so it's quite an exciting day.'

The prioress struggled with her inner woman. Babies were, by definition, almost as cute as small dogs, and innocent, to boot. However, there was only one way that they could come into the world and that was by the same passage as a man's . . . even in her head, Madame Eglantyne had to struggle with the words . . . *membrum virile* . . . had entered. Possibly more than once. So, on that score, babies were not good at all. However, there was a new soul in the world and so, as a good Benedictine, she should go and make sure that it knew all the rules, from the earliest moment. Gesturing to her nun, she left the room, calling for Mistress Baillie to assure her that all would be well. As the woman in question was at that moment in the cellar, broaching a barrel of sack with a spike and a mallet, the words fell on deaf ears, but at least the prioress had left the room and Chaucer subsided on his settle with a sigh.

'Never mind, Geoff,' Gower said. 'It could be worse.'

'Could it? Yes . . . the miller could have come back with her, for example. What made you think of him?' Chaucer asked.

Gower laughed. 'It was that sudden smell. It reminded me . . .' He looked up at the figure which had suddenly loomed dark in the bright doorway. 'Ah. Good morning, Master Inskip. I didn't realize you were here as well.'

Chaucer closed his eyes and wished again he had taken his luck with the peasants.

'Ar, yes, masters. Her Holiness goes nowhere without me these days. Too many of them common men on the road. She fears for her chastity, she do. It'll be the rape of them Sabine women all over agen. So I come along as well.' He looked around. 'What does an honest man have to do to get a drink around here? I'm as dry as a nun's . . .'

Gower and Chaucer, as one man, leapt for the door into the second-best parlour.

'Stay there,' Chaucer said, over his shoulder, 'and we'll get something sent in.'

'It's on Geoff,' Gower added. 'Least he can do.'

And after a small scuffle in the tight space, they were gone, leaving the miller to whatever thoughts he could muster, and some considered flatulence.

The sun was high in the heavens as Ezekiel and Hannah broke their backs in the fields along the river. It would be a good harvest this year, God willing, but even so, the weeds must be kept down. They were the devil's children, Ezekiel's old papa had taught him and his papa before him. The harvest came from God; the weeds from the Other Place.

'Who are they, Zeek?' Hannah was standing to ease her back and wiping the sweat from her forehead.

He straightened too and saw what she saw. An army of people were marching along the road, some breaking off to fill their caps from the river. They had jingling bells and flags. There were men, women and children, but mostly men.

'It's them,' Ezekiel growled. 'The rebels we heard about.' He dashed across to his billhook and laid it against a tree stump. Across in Dickon's strips, everybody was watching them too, wondering, worrying. Instinctively, Hannah summoned her chicks to her and the little ones, still all snot and curls, huddled against her kirtled skirts. Dickon sprinted through the corn shoots and stood elbow to elbow with Ezekiel.

'What do you think, Zeek?'

Ezekiel shrugged. 'We've got nothing worth taking,' he said. 'They'll pass us by.'

'His Lordship, though,' Dickon scowled. 'They'll go for the manor house.'

'That they will,' Ezekiel nodded.

'He's our lord,' Dickon reasoned. 'We should do something about this.'

Ezekiel squinted at the man, bright in the sun. 'What, you and me, do you mean?' he chuckled. 'Me with my bill and you with your sickle? That'll stop them, all right.'

'It's our duty,' Dickon insisted.

'Don't duty me, Dickon West,' Hannah broke in. 'From what I've heard, that's what those rebels are all about. They say we don't owe anybody our duty.'

'But they're the devil's disciples, Hannah,' Dickon said. 'They want to turn the world upside down.'

'Well, let 'em.' The woman stood her ground. 'I've got my babies here. So have you, Dickon. I'll not see them trampled underfoot for His Lordship.'

'Would you join them, then?' Dickon asked her. 'Follow mad old John Ball?'

'No, she wouldn't,' Ezekiel broke in. 'We're none of us going, not to defend His Lordship, nor to join that rabble. The Lord will keep us safe. All we have to do is keep our heads down. This is not our fight.' He looked Dickon in the face. 'And it never will be.' He got back to his weeding. 'Better the devil you know, I say.'

# FIVE

Tom Hardesty was hard at work at the front of the inn where it faced onto the old Roman road of Watling Street. His mouth was full of nails, so he nodded to Chaucer and Gower as they stepped out of the door, their steps guided by the smell of the miller and the distant cooing of the prioress from a room above the parlour. Harry Baillie had tumbled down the stairs, his childbed vapours extinguished by Madame Eglantyne, and was ordering the grooms and potboys in the yard. The air of general chaos was only reasonable in this world so suddenly turned upside down, but both poets were in need of some relative peace and quiet so the road, busy as it had become with trundling carts and scurrying people, was preferable to anything to be found inside.

Hardesty was hammering planks of wood over the windows on the ground floor and a couple of grooms were lugging a trestle over so he could reach the upstairs dormers in good time. He worked with the economy he brought to everything, the hammer tapping twice on every nail with deceptive ease, the nails spat one by one into his waiting hand. The two poets, neither of whom had done a hand's turn of hard work in their lives, stepped back in admiration.

'Mind where you stand, masters,' Hardesty advised, having finally spat out the final nail. 'These carters are none too careful where they drive today.'

Chaucer looked at the boarded windows. 'Do you think this is necessary, Master Hardesty?' he asked. 'Surely, an armed man at every window would achieve the same thing?'

Hardesty looked around him. 'Armed men at every window would indeed do the trick, Master Chaucer. Do you have any about your person? Because, at the moment, they don't seem to be here.' He stood on tiptoe to see further. 'All armed men, raise your hand.' He waited. 'Hmm, it looks like just me, Master Chaucer. Master Maghfield is handy with a sword, but not with a bow, I think. And if we are resorting to hand-to-hand combat, with the exception of the miller, I think we could all say goodbye to our life. Because,' he leaned nearer, 'I don't know whether you have spotted this, Master Comptroller, but we are outnumbered by hundreds to one. Thousands, even, by nightfall.'

Chaucer looked down contritely and noticed for the first time that his shoes were on the wrong feet. Happily, only he would know that the one he wore habitually on his left foot was the one with the wine stain. But even so – he had become very casual in his dress in his panic, and the thought depressed him.

'So,' Hardesty said, scooping up another handful of nails, 'if you would let me get on, gentlemen? Or help, perhaps?'

Gower smiled and patted the man's shoulder. 'You wouldn't want us near you with a hammer, Master Hardesty,' he said. 'I have never knocked in a nail in my life and don't think now is the time to begin. Geoff?'

Chaucer shook his head. 'Oh, no, no. I remember once Philippa asked me to put up a picture of Our Lady and I took out a chunk of wall. Apparently,' he looked at Gower, who was more likely to be innocent of such things, 'some kinds of wall cannot take a nail.'

'I rest my case,' Gower said, and Hardesty tossed the nails into his mouth, arranging them in line with his tongue. 'We'll leave you to it, Tom, shall we?'

It was perhaps fortunate that the nails prevented the yeoman from speaking clearly and so, unembarrassed, the poets walked around the side of the inn and back into the stable yard.

The stable yard had calmed down a bit from when Chaucer had first arrived, though there was still bustle as more and more people arrived. Some Chaucer recognized from the pilgrimage, but it looked from their dress as though many were family of the grooms and potboys who worked at the Tabard. Harry Baillie would certainly have something to say about it when he discovered what was happening and at least a serious docking of pay was in the future of many of his employees, but these were unprecedented times and there were no rules to follow, whatever Madame Eglantyne might think.

A faint whiff of something almost unbelievably vile overlaid the general melee and, for once, it wasn't Inskip the miller. It was sweet, heavy and cloying, but with a dark edge to it that caught the edge of the tongue. A couple of horses, tied to the rail at the far end of the yard, were pulling on their reins, their eyes rolling.

Gower, whose life in general had been more sheltered than Chaucer's, wrinkled his nose. 'That smell . . . is it . . .?'

'Yes,' Chaucer said. 'It's the smell of death, the smell that comes when you have a week-old body marinated in river water. We'll have to get it moved, John. It's spooking the horses, if nothing else. And this place will be too full by nightfall to have a dead body taking up a stall.'

'Moved? We?' To Gower those were the two main questions raised by the comptroller. 'Why does it have to be us? Hardesty brought it back here, let him move it.'

Chaucer raised an eyebrow. He knew his friend to be a compassionate man, though too outspoken for his own good on occasion. He put this down to the fear of both the unknown and the taint of the death that would come for them all, every man jack of them, soon or late. 'I know the sexton at St Olave's,' he said. 'If we send one of these lads, with a coin or two, we can have the poor soul put in their crypt, until things blow over. Then she can be given a Christian burial.'

Gower raised his own eyebrows and Chaucer saw an argument or two coming.

'I think that sounds like a good plan, John; the only possible one, if I'm honest. We get rid of a smell which, if we don't, will start a stampede. The poor woman will be in a proper, consecrated place, in a winding sheet and not . . . what did you say? An old carpet? And if it's the coins that bother you, I don't mind providing those.'

'But . . .' Gower was not an overly religious man but he knew what was right. 'What if she was . . . well, *felo de se*?'

'I thought you said that her head was almost off.' Chaucer's patience was wearing thin.

'It is.'

'Then it isn't suicide, John. It's murder and there's no two ways about it. But, much as I hate to say it, we will never find the culprit, because how do you begin to look when we don't know who the poor woman is.'

'The clothes may tell us something,' Gower ventured.

'They may, I suppose. If she is the kind of woman who goes about with her name and address embroidered on her shift.' Gower looked so crestfallen that Chaucer took pity on him. After all, he had not seen the body and Gower had – it was not likely to be a sight that any man would quickly forget. 'This is what we'll do. I will send a lad' – he looked about him and beckoned to a snot-faced child, with rough red hair above a face shining with the excitement of it all – 'this lad, in fact, with three coins,' he foraged in his purse, his every move followed by the child's slightly piggy eyes, 'one for . . . what's your name, lad?'

'Nick,' the boy said. 'Well, my mother calls me Nicholas.'

'One for Nick, here. And two for the sexton.' He turned to the boy again. 'Do you know St Olave's Church?'

The boy nodded, pointing in what Chaucer knew was the right direction, which was at least a start.

'Go to the church, then, and tell the sexton that Master Chaucer, the King's Comptroller of Woollens – make sure you tell him that – has a body he needs to be laid out in the crypt . . .'

'Oh, not that stinky one in the stable?' The boy wrinkled his face. 'He won't want that, smelling out his church.'

'Possibly not,' Chaucer said, wondering if his choice of Ganymede had been the right one after all. 'But on the other hand, Nick, my dear boy, if he doesn't take this body, you will not be getting your coin. Did I mention that?'

The boy set his mouth in a mutinous line, but shook his head, then nodded it.

'So, are we agreed, Nick, that the sexton doesn't need to know the state of this body, only that the poor lady is dead and we need her laid out decently? Are we agreed?'

Another nod, this time more vehement.

'Tell the sexton – make sure he takes the coins, mind – tell the sexton that we will bring the body to him before Nones. Have you got that?'

'Yes.' The boy stood upright in front of the poets, his chin lifted, his eyes bright with determination. If possible, his hair glowed redder and stood up more crisply. 'Go to the sexton. Give him two coins. Tell him Master Chaucer wants to lay out a body in his crypt and it will be with him by' – he paused for the first time – 'by Nones.' It wasn't his business if this man wanted to talk gibberish, but he didn't want to look silly. 'What's Nones, when it's at home?'

'It's the time of a service,' Gower said, glancing up at the sky. God, the youth of today! 'Quite soon, in simple speech.'

'Right.' Nick clenched his fist around the coins and set off at a trot.

'Do you think he'll do it?' Gower asked.

Chaucer watched as the boy ran, twisting and turning, through the crowd and out through the archway to the street. 'I believe he will,' he said. 'And the good news is, he at least turned the right way. So,' he rubbed his hands together. 'Now we need someone to move the body. And I think I have the very man.'

'They're coming! They're coming!'

Little Ned had never been so excited in his life. He couldn't remember the first word he had spoken or the first step he had taken, those things that were the milestones of the grown-ups around him. But this day, he would remember, he knew, all his life. His grandpa told him stories about the time that Edward, the Black Prince, had ridden through Cray's Foot on his way to the wars, leopards and lilies flashing in the sun, the prince's entourage, huge men on huge horses going to kill Frenchmen – everybody's ambition. But old grandpa would be even more excited to see what Ned had seen today. The lad wasn't quite sure how old he was, but it was probably six. Grandpa was a thousand, older than that man Methuselah that the priest talked about sometimes. He must find him, Ned knew. He must tell his grandpa and everybody would rejoice.

Grandpa was dozing under the broad spread of a sycamore tree. He and Ned shared the watching of the sheep – one, because he was too old to do anything else; the other because he was too young. Ned shook the old man and Grandpa did what he always did, pretended to be asleep.

'Granpa, Granpa, they're coming!'

Grandpa knew that. He had seen them before Ned had, the little column on the road winding over the packhorse bridge. He estimated there were forty of them, riding swayback nags that would never have passed muster for the Black Prince. The banner of St George floated at their head and they looked like supplicants on their way to a shrine, rattling their drums and shaking their tambourines.

Except they weren't. Grandpa's eyes weren't so old that he couldn't make out the grim faces of the leading horsemen, nor the swords at their hips and the bows slung across their shoulders. As a young man he had fought in France and had seen these men before, or at least their equivalent. They were the Jacquerie, the free-booters in their brigandines and kettle-hats. Their sole purpose was rape and pillage. And God help anyone who crossed them.

Grandpa sat up as Ned knelt beside him and they both watched the men on the road.

'Not much of an army,' a voice behind and above them said. It was Martin, Ned's big brother, whose voice was breaking, along with his mother's heart. Soon only little Ned would be her chick – all the others would have flown the nest.

'That's just the advance guard, boy,' Grandpa said. 'If the rumours are true, there'll be thousands behind them.'

'Making for Blackheath, I reckon.' Hal was the eldest of his generation, a man grown now to replace his dad who had gone of a fever three years since. He sat down next to his brothers.

'Why Blackheath?' Martin sat down cross-legged next to Grandpa.

'Open ground,' Grandpa nodded. 'If those rumours are true, they'll need open ground to pitch their tents.'

'What are they going to do, Grandpa?' Martin asked. At his stage in life, with spots and sudden yearnings and a new awareness of girls, nothing much made sense. And thousands of people on the road made less sense than anything else.

'Take what they claim is theirs, boy,' Grandpa said. 'Somebody else's. What that "else" is doesn't matter much. Just as long as it doesn't belong to them.'

'They're fighting for a cause,' Hal said. There had been a time when he had never crossed his grandpa; it would never have occurred to him, but now things were different. It was a brave new world and the King was younger than he was. Time for everything to change; Father John Ball said so.

Grandpa looked at his eldest grandson and saw the lad's father in him. It had only seemed yesterday that he had taught them both how to fire a bow. And now, his boy was dead and the world had gone mad.

'Hoo!' A voice from the road hailed them and a knot of horsemen broke away from the little column and cantered up the rise, scattering sheep in all directions.

'Martin, Ned,' the old man said, 'get them tetherers before we lose them. Hal . . .' But Grandpa caught the look on his eldest boy's face and didn't like what he saw there.

'No,' the boy said. 'No more orders.' He got to his feet as the horsemen reined in.

'Is Blackheath yonder?' one of the riders asked.

'It might be,' Grandpa grunted.

'It is,' Hal said. 'Two miles as the crow flies. Are you the rebels?'

The riders laughed. 'No, lad,' one of them said. 'We are the Commons of England – and, judging by your smock and your sheep, you are too. Here!' He threw a gilded brooch to Hal, who caught it neatly. Gold twirled around a silver crown crusted with precious stones. 'That came from Canterbury,' the rider said. 'One of the little baubles the Church buys for itself from the tithes we pay. Take it. Sell it if you like – you'll never have to work again, I promise you.'

'Tell me,' Grandpa said, shielding his eyes from the glare of the sun, 'the man you took that from,' he pointed to the brooch, 'Did he part with it willingly?'

There was a pause and then all the riders burst out laughing. 'What do you think, old man?' one of them said.

'I think you're all murdering bastards,' Grandpa said flatly.

Martin and little Ned were on their way back now, the sheep herded and safe. The leading horseman bent low over the saddle. 'Be thankful you've got this little one with you,' he grated. 'His young eyes don't need to see what I would do to you otherwise.' He sat upright. 'You, lad,' he called to Hal. 'There's more where that came from. In London. Will you come with us?'

The old man staggered to his feet. This wasn't happening.

'Gladly,' Hal said, and stuffed the bauble into his jack. 'Martin? Going my way?'

The younger boy blinked. He looked at his grandfather, old before his time, bowed down by the crippling grind of the years, the poverty, the merciless winds and the rain. And he looked at the horsemen in their stolen finery, wine sacks bulging at their saddle-bows and silver rings on their fingers.

'Yes,' the boy blurted out. 'Yes, I am.'

The horsemen wheeled away, the shepherd lads running down the hill after them to join the others on the road.

'Where are they going, Granpa?' little Ned asked, bewildered by the last few minutes.

Grandpa looked down at his youngest grandson. There was a tear in his eye. 'I don't know, Ned.' He patted the boy's golden curls. 'Unless it's to Hell.'

The boy looked up at his grandfather, the Granpa who knew everything. And he saw that the old man was crying. Then he looked down towards the road. His brothers and the horsemen had gone now, lost in the trees that fringed the sheepfolds. But little Ned wasn't looking for them. He was looking at what was coming out of the woods to the south-east; a giant multitude, more people than he'd ever seen before, more people than could possibly live in the world. He covered his ears with his hands because suddenly, and he didn't know why, he was afraid of the noise they made. He had heard about this noise before, he remembered. He had heard about it from the priest who had told him all about old Methuselah. The priest had been talking about something called damnation and the legions of the damned who lived in Hell – that was what Granpa had said.

And little Ned knew that he was looking at those legions now.

'Master Inskip?' Chaucer's voice was so smooth it put honey to shame. The miller was laid out on a bench in the

second-best parlour, which had emptied, bit by bit, as his
farts had grown both louder and more insupportable. He
opened one eye and looked up at the comptroller but otherwise didn't respond.

'Master Inskip? May I ask you a favour?' Again, there was
no response. 'I'll pay.'

In one boneless movement, the miller was on his feet, his
hand extended. 'It would be my pleasure, Master Chaucer,'
he said. He looked around. 'It looks like everybody's gone
anyway, so there's naught to do here. I was having a nice chat
to . . . somebody. Can't remember his name. But he seemed
pleasant enough. He was telling me Mistress Baillie has
called her new babby Inskip. Nice, that. Ain't it? But . . .'
He looked back at Chaucer, his hand still out. 'What is it
you want me to do?'

'It's not a pleasant task,' Gower felt it only right to point
out.

'Won't bother me,' the miller said. 'I know what you're
thinking. You're thinking that a miller just deals with flour,
nice clean stuff, flour. But you'd be wrong.' His low brow
furrowed as he thought back to what he had just said. 'My
flour's clean enough, I don't mean it ain't. But the rest of the
job, you'd be surprised. Rats in the wheat. Mice in the barley.
Shit everywhere, sometimes. I has to sift it out and sometimes
there's more shit than grain. And if it's raining . . . well, I
suppose you've only seen rat shit in a house, dry and hard,
you think. You should see it in the rain! And maggots? Don't
get me started on maggots. You has to kill the rats, see, and
if one drags itself off, if you ain't clubbed it right,' and he
mimed a clubbing with such relish the poets almost heard the
thud and the squeal, 'if you don't club it *just* right, the bastard'll
crawl behind a sack or summat and there, what have you got?'
He didn't wait for a reply. 'You've got a swarm of maggots
and blowflies before you can wink.'

Chaucer and Gower were speechless, and both were prom-
ising themselves they would never eat another piece of bread
as long as they lived.

'So don't talk to me about not pleasant. Not pleasant is
meat and drink to me. Ar.' He had reminded himself that he

had had a drink on the go when he fell asleep and looked under the settle. 'Some bastard's stole my drink!'

'When you have finished this little job,' Chaucer reassured him, 'I will buy you another.' He caught the look in the man's eyes. 'Or two.'

'And pay me, though.' The miller's rheumy eyes were cunning.

'Of course.' With a sigh, Chaucer rummaged for another coin from his already discernibly slimmer purse.

'So, what's this job, then?' He looked from one to the other, an eyebrow raised in query.

'Do you know about the body that Tom Hardesty found in the river?' Chaucer asked.

'I should think every soul with a nose knows about that'n,' the miller said. 'Stinks to high heaven.'

'Yes, she does, poor soul,' Chaucer agreed. 'We need to move her. The sexton at St Olave's has agreed to take her.' He was avoiding Gower's eye as he spoke; he could always tell when Chaucer was lying. 'So, if you could take her, with proper solemnity, if possible, to St Olave's, then that would be very kind of you.'

The miller looked suspicious. 'Kind, yes. But you *are* still paying me?'

'Yes, yes, for the love of God, yes.' Chaucer was beginning to wish he had stayed out of this altogether. 'So, you'll do it?'

'Yes.' The hand shot out and stayed out until the coin was firmly pressed into the palm. 'I'll borrow the muck cart. It can't smell any worse and she won't, neither. It might even fool the sexton, if he thinks it's the cart and not the corpus.' And the miller walked off into the mill of the yard, shouting to a boy to shackle his horse into the traces and disappearing finally into the charnel house of the end stall.

After a moment, Gower spoke. 'I know he's doing the right thing,' he said, 'and it's not a job I would like, but . . .'

Chaucer finished the thought, '. . . but if I never spend another second of my life with that man, it would be a blessing devoutly to be wished.'

Gower smiled and pressed his hands together in mock prayer. 'Amen,' he intoned. 'Amen!'

Chaucer spent quite an active afternoon, contrary to his usual practice. At about this time, had things gone according to plan, he and his fellow pilgrims would have been approaching Rochester ready to spend the night in – hopefully – a clean and tidy room in an inn, perhaps the Bishop and Chorister. The worst that could happen was that he would have to share a room with John Gower, but that held no terror. Had it been simply an ordinary day, he might have spent the afternoon writing before the open window of his room, having comptrolled a few woollens in the morning. He would have heard the sounds of the busy Aldgate coming up from below his feet, the sound of Alice on the stairs, bringing him drinks and small morsels to eat. She spoiled him, he knew that, but then, he was an exemplary lodger and had, after all, the ear of the King and any number of important city merchants. He was a man to be spoiled and kept in with.

But this Saturday, things were different. He couldn't find a single place where he was not being trodden on, gouged, or similarly knocked about. Outside was impossible; Tom Hardesty had requisitioned as many willing lads from the stables as possible and they were shoring up the outer boundaries of the Tabard with what timber they could muster. Puzzled horses were finding their mangers removed and the hay dumped unceremoniously on the ground as the wood was taken off to strengthen a gate or a gap in the wall. The cook was reduced to using one knife – and that not even his favourite – as an attempt was made to arm all those who had not got weapons of their own. Despite the heat, blazing fires burned in every grate. Tom Hardesty had himself once gained entry to a besieged manor down a chimney, so he knew that that was a weak spot which could be plugged in only one way; certain death by roasting, should anyone be foolish enough to try it. And, he pointed out, it would be necessary, as events unfolded, to be able to pour boiling water down on the attackers, should lead be unavailable.

Chaucer had gone to Harry Baillie and begged to be told

which would be his room, but Baillie had shrugged, muttered something which Chaucer, fortunately, had been unable to catch, and scurried off to the kitchen. He had sent boys out to scour the neighbourhood for what food they could get – preferably on credit, hard cash if necessary – and the pantries had filled nicely, though, as the cook pointed out, there was no dish on God's green earth that included some of the ingredients together. But beggars could not be choosers, and Baillie told him to be grateful and use up the ripe things first, no matter how odd the combination. No one would be asking for their money back, in these upturned times. The cook sat, twirling his one remaining knife and cursed Harry Baillie up hill and down, but still . . . green onions and mulberries . . . how hard could it be? After a moment, he threw the knife into the top of the scarred, stained table, put his head in his arms and wept.

Finally, Chaucer managed to find Tom Hardesty taking a moment's ease on a bench under the shade of a newly constructed parapet.

Chaucer sat beside him and smiled. 'You've done wonders, Tom,' he said. 'Who would have thought it possible?'

Hardesty looked around him and wiped the sweat from his brow with his sleeve. 'It's not bad, Master Chaucer. I would have liked to be able to construct more brattices, but we have to cut our coats according to our cloth, don't we?'

Chaucer had next to no idea what a brattice was, but he knew it wasn't an item of apparel. He had a vague idea that it might be something to do with fishing, but dismissed the idea as unlikely. He had practised this conversation with the yeoman several times as he had dodged lengths of wood and scurrying people that afternoon but, now he was here, decided to go straight in with no preamble. 'So, Tom, the woman in the river?'

'Yes, indeed, poor soul.' Hardesty crossed himself and bowed his head momentarily.

'Master Gower and I were wondering . . . well, *I* was wondering . . . why you brought her here?'

Hardesty was puzzled. 'What else was I to do with her? My home is far from here and I couldn't leave her to the fishes.'

Chaucer was disposed to ask why not, but decided that he had better take the more sympathetic route. 'Of course not, of course not. I was just wondering why . . . well, to be honest, there are bodies in the Thames all the time. Sometimes you can see a couple caught in the eddies under the bridge on any one day. So I . . .'

'You wondered, yes.' Hardesty's voice was cold.

'I wondered if you knew her, perhaps. So you wanted her to be . . .'

'What? More comfortable? Alive? Master Chaucer, let me tell you something, and I shall tell you this just this once. Ask me again, and you will get a black eye if I am in a good mood, much worse if I am not. I do not know this poor creature. I saw her, caught in the jetty, her poor eyes gone to the fishes, her nose, her lips to the eels. I saw her there, her throat ripped open like a deer's by dogs. I couldn't leave her there. I thought . . .' he bowed his head again, then continued in a softer voice – 'I thought of my mother, my sisters, my sweethearts. What if the same thing happened to them and they were left to rot under a pier until their arms and legs broke away, their head dropped to the bottom of the river and they all, in their parts, were swept out to sea, to the Black Deeps and beyond.' He looked into Chaucer's face with his honest eyes wet with tears. 'You have a wife, Master Chaucer?'

'I do, my dear Philippa.'

'Is she here?' Hardesty looked around, as if Mistress Chaucer might suddenly pop out from behind one of his hastily contrived wooden buttresses.

Chaucer laughed. 'No, no. Philippa lives in a very important household, many miles to the north-east of here.'

Hardesty had been told of these things and now, as then, he found it very bizarre. He blinked and said, 'Well, then. If your . . .'

'Philippa.'

'. . . Philippa had been in the water, would you not want someone to find her and make sure she had a Christian burial?'

Chaucer knew when a man had him over a barrel and he gave in gracefully. 'I would, Tom, of course. I hadn't thought of that.' He waited a moment, before adding, 'So, you're sure you didn't know her?'

'Your black eye is postponed, Master Chaucer, until I am so annoyed that I need to hit someone. For now, good day. I have an inn to make safe for what looks like every waif and stray in London and beyond. If you can wield a hammer, find one. If you can't, kindly excuse me.' And the yeoman was gone, leaving Chaucer on his bench, feeling lower than a worm.

'Um . . . I'm sorry to bother you at this hour, Sir Robert.'

Robert Knollys was used to being bothered at all hours, but rarely by the Lord Mayor of London, whose cap was awry and whose entourage was bristling with more weaponry than the old man remembered at Crécy. It was, indeed, late, the moon flitting in and out of the clouds that scudded over the turrets of his mansion and the curtain wall of the Tower beyond.

'I assume you have a reason?' Knollys clicked his fingers and a liveried lackey poured him a goblet of Romonye. He didn't offer one to William Walworth. 'Sabbath and all.'

'This was stuffed under my door earlier this evening.'

'What is it?'

'A letter. A warning. I don't know. All I know is that whoever placed it on my rushes got past at least twenty guards and several stout doors.'

Knollys took the scrolled parchment – letters were beginning to haunt him, one way and another – and reached for his spectacles, their oak frames decorated with gilt studs in the French style. He clipped them to his nose. 'Oh, these things are useless!' he snapped. 'I can't see much more than my own moustache. Read it to me, Walworth.'

The mayor cleared his throat. 'Lord of Gomorrah, beware . . .' he began.

'Who?' Knollys stopped him.

'Me,' Walworth said. 'Gomorrah was one of the cities of the plain—'

'Yes, yes,' the old soldier snapped. 'I know my Bible, sir. At least whoever wrote this is not calling you a Sodomite. Read on.'

'John Sheep bids John Nameless, John the Miller and John Carter to stand together in God's name. He bids Piers Plowman go to his work and chastise Hob the Robber. Look you shape to one head and no more.'

Knollys snatched the parchment back and angled it to the light of the nearest candle. 'Gobbledegook,' he muttered. 'Who are these people?'

'Well, I've made various enquiries. Talked to some of my people . . .'

'Billingsgate fish-gutters, you mean?'

'My mayoral staff.' Walworth stood on his dignity as only a fishmonger could.

'Well?' Knollys sipped his wine. 'What did they tell you?'

'John Sheep, they believe, is John Ball, the Hellfire preacher who has been roaming Kent of late. You may remember his trial.'

'No,' Knollys said. 'I don't.'

'Miller and Carter are generic names, aren't they? Everyman. The mob. The great unwashed.'

Knollys slammed down his goblet so that the candle, the lackey and William Walworth all jumped. 'That nonsense we heard from that fellow Chaucer has rattled you, hasn't it? Peasants on the road, indeed! Look here,' Knollys peered as best he could and hoped that he was pointing to the correct line. 'Piers Plowman – that's that rubbish by that idiot Langland, isn't it? And as for Hob the Robber – must be Robin Hood, an elf who lives in a wood. You're jumping at shadows, Walworth.'

'My people,' the mayor stood his ground, 'believe that Hob the Robber is Sir Robert Hailes, the Lord Treasurer.'

'Bobby Hailes?' Knollys frowned. 'Why him, for God's sake?'

'Because, Sir Robert,' Walworth shrieked, 'Sir Robert Hailes was the one who brought in the poll tax, about which these wretched peasants are complaining about.' Walworth was aware that the sentence had got away from him somewhere in the syntax, but hoped Knollys wouldn't have noticed.

There was a silence for a moment, whether caused by Walworth's dodgy grammar or not, he would never know. 'All that may be true,' Knollys said at last. 'But they are the deranged ramblings of a lunatic.'

'Be that as it may,' the mayor said. 'A lunatic can kill a man as easily as anyone. And if that happens to be me, we need to do something about it.'

'We, Walworth?' Knollys repeated. 'We? Don't build up your part, man. You have guards enough.'

'I'm not sure I do, Sir Robert,' the mayor's lip quivered. 'There is a mob of these people, to the east of the city now, the sweepings of Essex. And my people tell me that John Sheep, also known as John Ball, was released from Maidstone gaol yesterday. He's on the road, Sir Robert. He's on the road.'

Knollys gulped his Romonye as the words of his own letter came flooding back to him – 'Look to yourself, minion. It is your time.'

John Gower lay sleepless. He was not a man who suffered from sleeplessness as a rule but if he did, he could usually drop off in minutes by reciting some of his poems to himself. He used to say, when the man himself was not present or was out of earshot, that if he needed to sleep even quicker, he just recited some of Chaucer's poetry. But tonight, he was beyond all help. The problem lay in many directions.

First, and perhaps foremost when he first lay down to sleep, he had the most terrible indigestion. The meals at the Tabard were usually something to look forward to and many was the grand house which had tried to poach Baillie's cook; what that man could not do with a sturgeon wasn't worth talking about. But supper that night, as Baillie had explained, standing on the table at the top of an almost impossibly crowded room, and declaiming so everyone could hear, even those designated a seat so far below the salt that they were outside in the yard, had been cooked to conserve the supplies and make sure everyone could eat. As far as Gower could tell, the meal had consisted of oats boiled up with the sweepings of the fish market and a sprinkling of mustard. He had forced it down, but had been within an inch of going home and taking his chances with the mob and the monks. And now, he was belching regularly every minute, and with each eructation came the memory of some fish nightmare. And there wasn't even an R in the month. He was a dead man for sure.

Secondly, with no announcement from Baillie this time, everyone had had a rather nasty surprise when they went up to their rooms, at cock-shut, to conserve the candle stocks. The bedsteads – some of them rather fine testers, others simple cots – had, whether fine or simple, gone towards Hardesty's fortifications. There was not a stick of wood in the place except for the tables and benches – Baillie had put down his foot on that score. But, although the landlord was mortified to see his own mother's birth- and deathbed fall to Hardesty's axe, he could see the logic that a palliasse on the floor was as much a palliasse as it was when strung on a bed. So, everyone was sleeping on the floor, old or young, limber or gouty. But that wasn't the worst thing, not by a country mile.

Thirdly, most of the guests at the Tabard that night were sleeping with more people than they had ever slept with before. The lucky ones – the prioress being one, and her nun by mere proximity another – had two people in their bed and another one or two against the wall on piles of straw. At least they were all women. The unlucky ones were laid like piglets at the teat, rolled so close that to turn over took planning and the agreement of every bedfellow. Gower had not too bad a bedful, he had to admit. He was towards the middle, which had its problems but was far better than being on the edge, where rolling off onto the boards was a constant threat, not that it was far to fall. To his left, he had Ambrosius the priest, who had arrived after supper was over and, from the grease stain on his habit, had been wise to do so. He had been annoying at first, as he muttered himself to sleep over his rosary, but was soon sleeping like a baby, but without the concomitant threshing and whimpers. To the priest's left was a merchant who Gower didn't know, but who had nonetheless tried to sell him some shares in a cargo of a ship expected any moment from the Levant. Who was to *his* left, Gower had no idea, but his thoughts were with him as every now and again there was a soft thump and a muffled oath.

The problem lay to his right. At first, he had been pleased to see that his bedfellow was to be Geoffrey Chaucer and they had lain down together in total amity. They had murmured together about their poetry, planning what they would write to mark these times in which they were living. A slightly sour note was struck when the priest broke from his devotions to tell them that they should never plan for tomorrow, that every moment was a gift from the Lord and that, without His Grace, they might not see the dawn. That had silenced them for a moment, before they carried on, but without the innocent pleasure they had enjoyed before. Soon, their conversation had petered out and Chaucer fell asleep. Gower, in the half-light, had looked at his friend fondly, as the cares of the last few days fell away as his eyes closed and his mouth fell open, pouting like a child.

Then, it began. At first, the noise was intermittent, like distant waves on a shingle beach, but snapped off at the end of each rush of pebbles with a grunt. Then, the waves seemed to get nearer, the sea more angry, whipped up as if Poseidon himself were orchestrating each inrush of salt-laden water. Then, worse, silence fell and the world seemed to hold its breath, along with Geoffrey Chaucer, Comptroller of the King's Woollens. Just as Gower began to fear that his old friend had suddenly died in his sleep, the noise began again, but much louder and nearer, and so it went on until eventually it seemed to fill the world. Gower tried everything. He pinched his old friend's nostrils closed, but that just made things worse when he let go. He gave up a few precious digits of space and turned him over. For a few blessed minutes there was peace, before he was off again.

Gower closed his eyes and resolutely began quoting himself in desperation. He may have got the odd word wrong here and there, but in the privacy of his head, who was to know? And if it stopped him throttling Geoffrey Chaucer, then it was probably worth it.

# SIX

'Bit strong, Will,' Jack Chub hauled the sack of wine across his shoulders. 'Killing that merchant like that.'

'Now, now, Chubby. What did John Ball say only yesterday – "Stand together in God's name". That's what we've got to do. Anyway, he had it coming. Him and all his kind. He looked at me funny and I just lost it, that's all. Anyway, he was a bloody Fleming, wasn't he? A foreigner. They've got no right to be here.'

'S'pose.' Chub shrugged.

'Anyway,' Lorkin said, grabbing a ham from a market stall and taking a bite. 'We're drinking Romonye now. Eating ham.' He waved his booty in the air. 'Today, Maidstone. Tomorrow, the world.'

The pair trudged over the bridge, bringing up the wake of the marching, singing peasants. 'Did you hear, by the way,' Lorkin asked his friend, in a spray of half-chewed pig. 'When we've finally found Sudbury and cut his bollocks off, John Ball's going to be Archbishop of Canterbury.'

'Yeah,' said Chub. 'And I'm gonna be the Black bloody Prince.'

Surprisingly, John Gower and most of the guests at the Tabard did get some sleep that night and woke, if not refreshed, at least wondering what breakfast might bring. Bearing in mind that they had gone to sleep thinking they might all be murdered in their beds, dawn was a welcome sight and spirits were unexpectedly high.

Chaucer sat on the same bench under the parapet that he had found the afternoon before and ate his oatmeal with an effort. Alice made his with milk at the Aldgate, and dotted it with sugar plums in season, or even bilberries or raspberries when she could get some. Sometimes, and he looked wistfully in the direction of the Aldgate, beyond the tumbling river under the bridge, she would crumble just a little raw sugar over it, if a ship had just come in. Some of the captains paid her husband in sugar for their drinks and whatever other comforts he could provide, and Alice would sneak some to her favourite lodger, as he fondly considered himself to be. But this was oatmeal, oatmeal in the wild, feral oatmeal, with no domesticated comforts like fruit or sweetness. But he was hungry and suspected he would grow hungrier, so he persevered.

For some reason that Chaucer couldn't fathom, John Gower was a little less friendly than usual that morning. His nod when they woke and dressed in the crowded room was a little frosty, Chaucer thought. But everyone was a little introspective these days, and who could wonder? The world seemed to have gone mad and all a man could do was to take one step at a time and try to reach the end of his days without being hanged by a band of men with ideas above their station. Chaucer found his heart was beating a little faster than was strictly comfortable and, to add insult to injury, he had finished his porridge. He slumped a little on his bench. Life was cruel.

And suddenly, it got crueller.

'Master Chaucer.' The comptroller was suddenly aware that he was not alone on his bench. 'I meant to speak to you yesterday, but what with one thing and another, we didn't seem to get the chance.'

Chaucer summoned up a smile. 'Master Maghfield. How nice. I was just wondering how you were.'

Maghfield leaned forward so he could look into Chaucer's disconsolate face. 'I am *very* well, Master Chaucer. How kind you are to ask.'

Chaucer could never quite fathom what was unusual about Maghfield's speech. He didn't have an accent as such, at least, not like some of the other merchants, more recently come from the Hanse or the Levant, but there was something a little stilted about the words he used, something unreal about him, even when he was being apparently friendly.

'And how are *you*, Master Chaucer?' He clapped a hand like a ham down on the poet's knee. 'Are you keeping well? Not too worried about all this . . .' he waved his hand around, encompassing the Tabard and its new population. 'All this nonsense we have at the moment?'

'Well,' Chaucer saw an opening and sprang for it like a greyhound from the slips. 'It is a worry, Master Maghfield. I am far from my wife and children. Any moment, I may need to take my chances with the mob and go to their aid.'

Maghfield's friendly hand clasped Chaucer's knee, if not to the point of pain, then at least discomfort. 'I believe I knew about your wife, Master Chaucer. But children . . . no, I don't believe I was aware you had children. How old are they now?'

'Ooh, now, let me think.' Chaucer was not about to let this merchant know that his son Thomas was knocking fifteen and was already built like a drayhorse. 'Little Agnes is rising ten.' That sounded better. 'I may need to fly to her side at any moment. She is currently with . . . a very good family in . . . Oxford.' Chaucer would be the first to admit that he had not been the most attentive of fathers, but he was almost sure that was right. 'So, of course, I am making sure that my purse has spare cash, so I may . . .'

'Fly to her side, yes.' Maghfield let go of Chaucer's knee and threw an arm around his shoulders, an action which made Chaucer's bowels go to water. 'Master Chaucer, this is what I will do for you. You will pay me back the debt you owe and if you need to fly to young Agnes's side, I will make you another loan. At an interest rate which reflects the state of the world, of course.' He smiled again at Chaucer and clutched him tighter to his side. 'How does that sound? Hmmm?'

Chaucer swallowed the enormous rock that seemed to have taken residence in his throat and said, 'That sounds very generous, Master Maghfield. Very generous. Umm . . . how much was it?'

Maghfield let him go and rummaged in the front of his houppelande, bringing out a small book. He leafed through its pages, muttering to himself, then spread it on his palm and impaled it with a meaty finger. 'There you are, Master Chaucer. All correct, I believe, with date and interest up to last week. So, of course, there will be a minor adjustment when it comes to the final figure.'

'Ah,' Chaucer cried. 'Alas! I have forgotten my eyeglasses. In the excitement, Master Maghfield, as any man might.'

'Eyeglasses?' A voice came from the parapet above. John Gower was taking his turn at beating the bounds. 'Here, take mine.' And a pair of spectacles dangled in front of Chaucer on a fine cord.

'How kind,' Chaucer murmured and settled them on his nose. 'Now, let me see,' he took the book from Maghfield. 'Where . . .?'

Maghfield's finger stabbed the place.

'Goodness.' Chaucer was a little horrified. 'As much as that? But . . .'

Maghfield looked down at him. He could have made two of the poet and had enough spare for a schoolboy or two. 'I'm feeling magnanimous, Master Chaucer. Let's say half today, shall we?'

Chaucer felt hope leap.

'And the rest next Sunday. If we're spared.'

'If we're spared,' Chaucer muttered, reaching for his purse. 'Yes.' He wondered if it were a mortal sin to perhaps hope, just a little bit, that he wouldn't be among the lucky ones.

As the morning wore on, the day seemed to hold its breath. Although the Tabard was full almost to bursting, even so the silence seemed to envelop the inn and its environs so that a man could almost hear his own heart beating. June was often stifling in London, the smell of the people, the animals, the streets themselves forming an almost visible miasma, but in these strange times, it was impossible to recall whether it was ever this silent, this hot, this . . . the poet in Chaucer searched for a word, but could only come up with 'expectant'.

He knew that when people looked at him, they did not see a man of action. They saw what he probably was these days, a petty bureaucrat, a bit overweight, a tad slovenly in his dress when Alice didn't take him in hand, possibly a little boring, even. But he had seen some sights in his life, had been in spots which might even, to the casual observer not involved, have been tighter than this. But he hadn't been in his forties then. Twenty years ago – no, more – he had found himself cut off from the others in enemy territory. He'd always rather liked the French – good food, good wine, good God . . . thoughts like that were treason, surely? They could get a man into trouble. There'd been a girl involved, of course, a pretty little thing from Retters. But then, Geoffrey Chaucer was a pretty little thing then too – sixteen, blond, handsome. Certainly, the lovely Lady Blanche had thought so, but Chaucer was a little uneasy around the older woman, especially when the husband of that older woman was Lionel, Duke of Clarence, son of the King, et cetera. No – better stick to a girl of his own age.

And stuck young Chaucer had, rolling in the hay one long summer's night with . . . what *was* her name? So he had been otherwise engaged when du Guesclin's patrol had found him. All right, so Bertrand du Guesclin wasn't Constable of France then, but he *was* the most terrifying man Chaucer had ever met. The English hated and feared him in equal measure and there he was, sitting cross-legged on his saddle, picking his teeth with his poignard. Yes, Chaucer was a page. In the service of the royal family. Would the King bail him out? Pay his ransom? It wasn't for Chaucer to say. Would that, du Guesclin wondered, be a possibility? Or would Chaucer end up just being a page in history, a footnote in that rubbish Jean Froissart was writing? If so, du Guesclin would finish things now. Did Chaucer have a preference? Sword? Axe? Crossbow bolt? It was all one to du Guesclin. No, the page had assured him – the King would stand surety for him. No need for all this talk of execution.

In his more flamboyant moments, Geoffrey Chaucer wondered how he would have measured up to Bertrand du Guesclin. In his mind, at the Tabard that day, he saw himself crossing blades with the greatest swordsman in France, batting aside his futile iron, driving every Englishman's nemesis to the ground. All without breaking into a sweat. And of course, du Guesclin was dead now, having chanced his arm once too often. On the other hand, he had got back most of the territory that King Edward and the Black Prince had pinched in the first place.

Chaucer sucked in his increasing girth, straightened his back and held his chin high. He'd be all right. When the King's officers had come to collect him all those years ago, with the £10 ransom in their purses, he had given them some guff about attempting to capture du Guesclin, but he'd been hopelessly outnumbered. Girl? No, of course not; Chaucer's mind had been on higher things. Haystack? Certainly not; a page in Duke Lionel's household wouldn't be seen dead in a haystack. He drew the poignard from his sheath and weighed it in his hand. Then he threw it into the air and promptly dropped it with a clatter. Damn! Never mind. As far as those riff-raff on the road who were making for London knew, he was still the man who had locked horns with the great du Guesclin and had lived to tell the tale. He just had, somehow, to make sure the peasants knew that story and didn't ask too many questions about it.

Chaucer was so deep in his thoughts that he hadn't heard the bustle that was Mistress Baillie approaching like a whirl-wind from the direction of the wash-house in the corner of the yard. In fact, he didn't know she was there at all until a swathe of wet linen suddenly wrapped itself around his head. Wrenched from his introspection so abruptly, he could only manage a stifled yelp.

'Master Chaucer!' Strong hands were there, unwrapping the wet linen. 'I'm so sorry. I was just flicking the water out and I let go. I am *so* sorry, let me . . . no, don't . . . there we are!' And with clucks and pats, the woman had his liripipe arranged and his beard smoothed down before he could properly realize what was going on.

He took a deep breath. 'Mistress Baillie. I was a bit surprised there, for a moment.' Chaucer had a horrible thought that perhaps he had screamed like a girl, but his hostess was too polite to mention it.

'Of course you were, Master Chaucer,' she said, picking a rogue rosemary leaf from his hair. 'I wouldn't wash on the Lord's Day as a rule, of course. I have had my lecture from Madame Eglantyne and yet another from Father Ambrosius, but needs must. We can none of us stand on ceremony in these times, can we?'

'I understand, Mistress Baillie,' Chaucer said, trying to look more nonchalant than he felt. A yard or two of best cambric suddenly impeding one's breathing will always bring a man up a little short. 'How kind of you to take on guests' washing at a time like this. Should you not be resting more?' He had never been present at the births of any of his children and had no regrets on that score. He felt sure he remembered, though, that Philippa had at least lain down for a day or so.

'Resting?' She looked puzzled for a moment and then laughed. 'Because of young Geoffrey John currently bawling his lungs out upstairs? No, indeed, Master Chaucer. Nothing to rest over. He slipped out as smooth as an eel. No, I promised I would wash the clouts of that poor soul from the river, and so I have. They took some pounding, but I think I have them tolerably clean.'

'Oh.' Chaucer tried not to look too horrified. 'So . . . these all belong to her, do they?'

'They do.' She held up a chemise and looked at it critically, holding it up to the sun. 'They are not cheap clothes either, Master Chaucer. Not gaudy, you understand me, nothing to attract attention.' She leaned in and whispered. 'She wasn't a whore, is what I'm saying. She was a decent body, money enough but not to squander, that's the kind of woman I think she was. A bit like my good self, probably.' She let another gale of laughter ring out. 'Though I would like to see the man who could slit my throat and throw me in the river!'

Chaucer managed a weak smile. So, not just a slap round the head with a soaking cloth, but a slap round the head with a soaking cloth worn by a corpse of a murdered woman after a week in the Thames. Though he had to hand it to Mistress Baillie; she certainly was death to stains.

'Would it inconvenience you if I spread my laundry here? It's the sunniest spot at the moment and I want to get it dry as soon as I can and packed away. I don't know if we will ever find out who the poor soul was, and this silliness will only make it worse.'

Chaucer had to mentally doff his cap to any woman who could call the impending arrival of tens of thousands of armed peasants 'silliness'.

'But I don't want the family, when and if they are found,

to not have something to remember her by. Besides,' she wrinkled her nose, 'the smell was beginning to turn my stomach. And the things that fell out of the folds! Master Chaucer, you wouldn't believe—'

'Yes, Mistress Baillie, thank you.' Chaucer had about reached his limit on the gruesome detail front. 'I wouldn't mind at all if you spread them here. I am moving anyway. I need to have a word with Tom Hardesty.'

But Mistress Baillie wouldn't let it go. 'This, for instance. What do you make of it?'

Chaucer didn't want to make anything of it, but he looked anyway. There was a patch of beige in the woman's palm, once wet, now dry. It looked reassuringly unlike an unpleasant denizen of the deep. The poet-comptroller frowned and held out a tentative finger. 'It's paper,' he said. 'Cheap parchment. Must have been in her placket. Look – ink lines. If only we could read it, eh?'

'Ooh, yes,' Mistress Baillie enthused, her eyes damp with romance. 'It could be a love letter from a man she had forsaken. She had broken his heart and he killed her for it?' She beamed at Chaucer with all the enthusiasm of a young girl deep in calf love rather than a mother of six. 'What do you think?'

Chaucer thought it sounded like one of John Gower's less likely plots, but it wasn't his place to say so. 'We'll never know,' he said. 'Now, if you'll excuse me, I really *must* see Master Hardesty.'

Despite the fact that she and her romantic notions had held him up, Mistress Baillie was grateful that the annoying creature was moving on. He could no more take a hint than could her day-old son. Sitting there, hogging the sun, selfish old wandought. She was spreading her washing on the bench almost before he had stood up, putting the parchment into her own placket for later musings, and soon the garments of the dead woman were splayed in the sun, the thinner fabrics almost dry as soon as they touched the hot wood. Mistress Baillie fingered the fine cambric of the chemise. If they didn't find her family, that would make a fine addition to her wardrobe; she had long ago ceased to be squeamish, as anyone must living with Harry Baillie.

'Thank you, Master Chaucer,' she sang out to his retreating back. 'You are such a gentleman, sir. So thoughtful.' She raised an eyebrow at one of the stable boys as she made her way back to the fastness of her scullery. It wasn't just Master Baillie who could sweet-talk the men who, directly or indirectly, put the food in her children's mouths.

Tom Hardesty seemed to be everywhere and yet nowhere. Everyone Chaucer asked had certainly seen him, often within the last few minutes, but he was never actually there. So Chaucer took to wandering about aimlessly, several times coming close to being brained by planks of wood and falling hammers but, finally, he heard the man's voice, coming from somewhere overhead.

Looking up, he could see the yeoman's sturdy legs and feet, planted as firmly as any ox in any furrow as he leaned over the wall of the yard, in shouted converse with someone in the street.

'We're full.' The man left no room for compromise and he spoke nothing but the truth.

Although the man in the road outside was shouting, his words were too muffled to be heard.

'I'm sorry,' Hardesty said. 'I know you were on the pilgrimage and I know that Master Baillie offered everyone the option . . .'

The shouting grew louder, but no more comprehensible.

'It's no good yelling.' Chaucer couldn't help but be impressed by the yeoman's even temper. He had been working with untrained hands to help him for almost two days straight. He had dragged a rotting corpse from the river and brought her back to the Tabard because it would be wrong to do otherwise. He had not raised his voice, as far as Chaucer could tell, though he had grown a little testy, possibly, when more or less asked point-blank if he had killed the woman himself – and who wouldn't? Chaucer would have suspected him more had he not got a mite annoyed. He had eaten the vile food they had been given with equanimity and, while he ate, he whittled arrows, trimmed goose feathers to fletch them and had a rapt circle of youngsters at his feet, all attempting to do the same.

He was an example to everyone. Chaucer beat down the cynic inside that said that perhaps Thomas Hardesty, Yeoman of the Shire, might be just a little too good to be true.

'It's no good yelling,' the yeoman persisted. 'I can't let you in.'

Silence was the only response and Chaucer heard Hardesty sigh.

'Master Gillis . . .' So *that* was who it was, the other Flemish merchant who had been talking shop with Maghfield. 'Master Gillis, if you could just tell your daughter to stop crying . . . Master Gillis, this is a low trick.'

Chaucer smiled. So, Hardesty *did* have an Achilles' heel. But then he was the same himself – he never could withstand women's tears. His own Philippa had often begged with tears in her eyes and he was usually helpless before them. He could count on the fingers of one hand the times he had not given in.

Hardesty straightened up and called down to his men on the gate, 'Let them in. They are friend, not foe, and they have brought food and weapons.'

Every man had his price, Chaucer knew. And if the food was edible, so much the better, though if he knew his yeoman, it would be the weapons that had won the day.

Hardesty had put two of the strongest of the lads in Baillie's employ on the gate and, as they struggled to open it, Chaucer could see why. Hardesty had used two huge staples on each upright, near the top, and two heavy chains, with a weight on the end, had been added on pulleys to the underside of the parapet. So to open the gate, not only the weight of the wood had to be moved, but also the weight and friction of the chains. There was a thick wooden bar across, top and bottom, which had to be slid completely to the side before the gates would move. If the mob reached the doors, then there were ladders of varying heights so that men could climb up and add their weight to it as well. To Chaucer's only semi-tutored eye, it looked as impregnable as it could possibly be, given the materials to hand.

Eventually, the door was open far enough for Gillis and his children – a boy and a girl, not that different in age from

Chaucer's Thomas – to slip inside. He turned to the lads and they opened the gate a little further, to allow Gillis's mare and the cart she was pulling through.

'Not the horse,' Hardesty said, firmly. 'We have no room for more horseflesh. Unless you are willing for it to be our suppers, Master Gillis.'

Gillis looked up at Hardesty, shielding his eyes from the sun. 'This horse has carried me for many miles, through snow and—'

'Papa,' the lad said, his voice a breaking squeak. 'You know you bought that horse only last week, to go to Canterbury. She doesn't even have a name. It isn't worth the argument.' He was already undoing the traces and took the weight as the trap fell forward. 'Let her go.' He slapped the mare on the rump and, with rolling eyes, she trotted out through the gates, which ponderously shut on her.

'That will come out of your allowance!' Gillis said, through gritted teeth. 'Do you think I am made of money? Why, I should take my belt to you, you ungrateful—'

'Master Gillis.' Hardesty slid down the ladder with the ease of a sailor on the rigging. 'If this is to be your attitude, I will be asking you to leave.'

Gillis looked him up and down. Now he was inside, he had no intention of talking to the help. It was Harry Baillie or no one for him. Chaucer kept back in the shadows beneath the parapet. He wanted none of this argument. He had had enough of merchants for one day.

'Now, look here . . . Harding, is it?' Gillis set his mouth and lifted his chin. He could not have failed to notice that he was six fingers shorter and a good half-hundredweight lighter than the yeoman, and hadn't faced up to anyone likely to hit back in years. Save one, but he kept his tangles with that person to himself.

'Hardesty.' The yeoman cracked his knuckles but kept his smile in place.

'Look here, Hardesty, then,' Gillis said. How these knarres thought their names mattered a jot, he couldn't really see. He had had a difficult night, what with the servants running off with no warning, his son as awkward as all get out, his daughter either singing like a lunatic, crying or . . .

There was a wail from somewhere to his left, rising through the scale to a full-out scream.

. . . screaming. He turned, ready to snap. 'Magge! What have I said about the screaming?'

But the girl had stopped the noise and was pointing at the washing spread on the bench. Her finger trembled and her mouth hung open, unable to make a coherent sound. Her brother stepped forward and picked up a piece of cloth, turning it over before holding it out to his father.

'Papa,' he said. 'Don't shout at Magge. Look; it's mother's surcoat. I recognize this stitching. Look.' He held it out again, but his father didn't touch it. 'You must remember. Magge used the wrong thread and Mother' – his eyes darted around the crowd which was gathering, attracted by the girl's scream – 'Mother was annoyed, do you recall?'

Arend Gillis blinked at his son, still not taking the proffered garment. What had he come to, he and his family, that, even in this moment, when his heart was in his mouth and his wife was missing, his son would be too ashamed to say in front of strangers that his mother had taken the skin off her own daughter's back for using the wrong thread on an invisible seam? He licked dry lips and croaked, 'Is she here?'

Chaucer stepped forward and took the man kindly by the elbow. 'Come with me, Master Gillis. And you, children,' he beckoned them to follow. 'Let's see if we can find somewhere quiet.' He looked around and realized there was nowhere quiet, that there might never be anywhere quiet again. 'Quieter, perhaps I should say.' And, with pulls and pushes and gentle words, he ushered them away, like a hen with chicks, to find somewhere to pass on his news.

It took a while for Magge Gillis to become quiet. Her brother Audric, from the lofty pinnacle of his fifteen years, comforted her with an arm around her shoulders. Chaucer couldn't help but notice that her father didn't touch her, not even with a fatherly pat. Eventually, though, her sobs slowed to a gulp every minute or two and, finally, she was quiet, though her eyes were red and her top lip unattractively covered in snot. In fact, Chaucer could not chase away the unkind thought that, as teenage children went, these two would win a prize at any fair as the ugliest pair in the county. Taken feature by feature, nothing was that awry – Chaucer had seen worse on any walk down any street on any day in London – but there was just something about the way they were put together which made them hard to look at for long. The girl had what on any other head would be flaxen plaits, one on each side of her rather beefy cheeks. But the hair was like straw in more than just its colour – it looked as if it might snap should anyone be unwise enough to fondle it, and the scalp was thick with loose skin flakes like snow. Her nose was so far beyond retroussé as to be porcine. The boy's face was a mask of spots which, glancing at his father's pocked complexion, was both hereditary and hopefully fairly transient.

But it was not the time for personal slights. These children were poor motherless mites, unless the surcoat hem was lying and it was another woman waiting to be claimed in the crypt of St Olave's. But it seemed unlikely. The surcoat was not that old and, judging by Master Gillis's carefully mended hose and the children's clothes with their much-let-down hems, their mother was not a woman who would give away clothes with more than a day's wear left in them. And yet, the clothes were of good quality and the family was clearly well-to-do. Chaucer knew that there was a story in this room with him, just waiting to unfold.

'I don't want to upset you further,' he said, in gentle tones, 'but when did you last see your mother, your wife?' He nodded to Gillis to include him but that looked difficult – the man was looking out of the window into the crowded street, his mind clearly elsewhere. 'Master Gillis?'

If the man heard, he gave no sign.

'Master Gillis? Can we talk? Would you rather the children were . . . not here?'

Gillis turned sharply, as if Chaucer had given vent to a loud 'Hoo!'

'What?'

'The children? Do you mind if they stay?'

Gillis stared at them as if seeing them for the first time. 'Children?' he said. 'I don't consider them children. They have

been working for their place at my table since they were ten.
My wife . . . well, she wanted them to be independent. To live
the kind of life she lived as a girl.' He looked again, at his
daughter's red eyes, her snotty nose. 'They can stay.'

'Magge? Audric?' If they weren't children, then they could
make up their own minds.

They looked at each other, as they constantly did, for
reassurance. Then, Audric answered for them both. 'Yes,
we'll stay.'

'So,' Chaucer asked again. 'When did you last see your
mother, your wife?'

'Last Sunday,' Magge said. 'She came into my room after
I had gone to bed to remind me I hadn't fed the sow.'

'That was your job?' Chaucer was something of an innocent
when it came to the care of pigs, but when he had lived in
houses where the animals were kept, it was the job of the
lowest kitchen maid to do that.

Magge sniffed unattractively and scrubbed at her nose with
her sleeve. 'Mother believed in hard work. She said that when
I had a home of my own, I would understand what I would
be asking the servants to do.' She scrubbed her nose again
and looked down. 'Mother had some very firm ideas.'

Chaucer patted her arm. He was beginning to thoroughly
dislike Mistress Gillis, *de mortuis nihil nisi bonum* notwithstanding. 'So, you fed the sow on Monday morn—'

'Oh, no, Master Chaucer!' Magge was horrified. 'I fed her
on Sunday. Mother would not have allowed me to put it off.
I got up and fed her. It's not so dark at ten of a summer's
night. I didn't mind.'

Chaucer had to take a moment to compose himself. It may
well have been that these people loved the dead woman, though
it was hard to imagine that being so. But still, blood is thicker
than water, he thought as he continued. 'You were very brave,
going out at night like that. Tell me, Magge, what was your
mother wearing when you saw her on the Sunday night?'

The girl shrugged. 'I don't know.'

'Do think,' Chaucer said. 'Was it the clothes . . . well, the
clothes you recognized outside?'

'It was too dark to tell,' the girl said simply.

Before Chaucer could speak, her father turned and said, simply, 'My wife, Master Chaucer did not believe in waste, so candles were for emergencies. Clothes were to cover the body for modesty's sake. Food was to keep the body alive, not for pleasure. I don't need to tell you, with my children here, what her views were on procreation. You are being polite, but it would save us all a lot of trouble if we just accept, here and now, that I would be surprised to find that my wife had a friend in the world.'

Chaucer was thinking fast. There were words to speak to the bereaved and in his time he had spoken them often; too often, he sometimes thought. But none of them would come to his lips. He realized he was still patting Magge's arm and stopped, lest it should be misconstrued. Finally, he thought of something to say. 'Perhaps Mistress Gillis felt the strains of running a household onerous,' he said. 'Perhaps it made her . . . testy, sometimes.' He looked into the flinty eyes of the remains of the Gillis family and his heart quailed. 'I've . . . I've seen it happen to the most loving of women.'

'In that case, it would be a shame,' Gillis said. 'But in the case of my wife, she had not a loving bone in her body. She bore me two children because to not do so would have seemed to others a dereliction of duty. She kissed neither at their begetting nor their birth and, they may correct me if I err, she has never kissed them since. Or me.' Gillis gave a wintry smile. 'I know that you now think I killed my wife. I am assuming her death was not natural because had it been, someone would have been with her, would have recognized her, would have brought word. So she was found, her body hidden, perhaps. Buried in a shallow grave?'

Chaucer gave nothing away.

'But I assure you, Master Chaucer,' Gillis went on, 'I did not harm my wife. You would have to care to murder someone, and I didn't . . . don't. I didn't hate her either, as I am sure you suspect. I simply . . .' he shrugged. 'Didn't care, one way or another. She had ceased to hurt me. I gave her enough money to run the house, and she ran it. Although I have always suspected she didn't spend what I gave her, that if we search the house we would find quite a little hoard.'

'You might,' Chaucer said, 'if the peasants don't find it first.'

Audric gave a hoot of laughter, almost the first noise he had made. 'I hope they do,' he said. 'It would serve her right.' He dropped his eyes and looked at the others from under his lids. 'I know where it is,' he said, his voice almost a whisper, as if his mother was listening.

His father's eyes almost popped out of his head. 'Where is it?' He looked at Chaucer with his piggy eyes, set just that bit too close together. 'It is my money, after all, Master Chaucer!'

Chaucer couldn't miss the avarice in the man's face. Before his wife went too far, they were probably a proper pigeon pair.

'She had forgotten she had told me to clean out the fireplace under the copper.' Audric turned to Chaucer. It was important, he felt somehow, that this man be given all the details he knew. 'It goes right back, Master Chaucer, and I am the only one who doesn't mind climbing inside. It's a tight squeeze and Magge doesn't like small spaces.' He squeezed her hand as she looked down, new tears flowing. 'She came into the wash-house and . . . I kept quiet. There were ashes on the floor I hadn't swept up and I . . . anyway, I kept quiet. But she didn't notice the ashes. She went straight to the chimney breast and I heard a stone scrape. Then I heard a chink and then I heard' – he raised his eyes in disbelief at his own words, but said them anyway – 'I heard my mother laugh.'

'You may be the only one alive to have heard that sound,' Gillis said, his voice flat.

Audric, with the ingenuousness of his age, nodded. 'I wasn't sure it was her, Papa, when I heard it. But it was.' He got back to his story. 'When she had gone, I finished sweeping out the grate and got out and looked to see what could have made the noise. It must have been a stone in the chimney-piece but I couldn't tell which one.' He darted a look at his father. 'I didn't dare spend too much time. She would have come to see what was taking me so long cleaning out the fire. Father, it could be a *fortune*, could it not?' His eyes were bright and the family resemblance grew stronger.

The men sat silent, each doing sums in his head. Chaucer

had never run his own household. Since their marriage, he and Philippa had always lived in other men's houses, either together or singly. Even now, in his little room above the Aldgate, Chaucer didn't have to spend money on anything above his food and drink – and often, as Doggett would have said had he known his thoughts, not even that. Pennies, halfpennies, farthings, leopards and helms – they were all one to Chaucer. Not until nobles and marks kicked in did Geoffrey Chaucer take notice and that was only wearing his comptroller's hat. So he had no idea how much a house would cost to run. He thought he had heard that a labourer got 2d a day, which sounded quite reasonable, in the scheme of things. So . . . his comptroller's mind was working overtime . . . so, assume that servants in houses got less, because they got their food . . . but then that food would have to be bought . . . so let's say 2d each and there were five servants . . . call it a shilling . . . and . . .

Gillis waited patiently as the man counted on his fingers, his eyes rolled up and his fingers twitching but then said, 'I think you exaggerate, Audric. Your mother's housekeeping was one pound a week and, although I know she saved some pence from it by cheese-paring, that couldn't possibly be a fortune.'

'Did she have money when you married?' Chaucer asked.

Gillis looked staggered and it was a moment before he could reply. 'Of course she did,' he said, frowning. 'Otherwise . . . why would I have married her, Master Chaucer?' He shook his head, unable to take in the sheer ignorance of the man.

Chaucer realized his mistake as soon as he spoke. Of *course* she had brought money. What bride didn't, above the ranks of the hoi polloi? He had meant did she keep it and, of course, as soon as Gillis spoke, he realized how stupid a question that would be.

'I hope, Master Chaucer, that you were not suggesting she had squirrelled away her own dowry?' Gillis laughed for the first time since he and the comptroller had met. Possibly for the first time in years; the sound was certainly rusty with disuse.

'Ha ha,' Chaucer joined him, hoping his laugh sounded more genuine to other ears than it did to his own. 'What an idea!'

'When Fye and I came here from Bruges, we had nothing *but* her dowry. I had been brought up a weaver, but it was not a natural skill for me.' He held up his hands, the fingers short and thick with just a single ring, a wedding band, thin and mean and embedded in the flesh. The greenish tinge on his fourth finger gave away the fact that the ring was copper, not gold. 'I don't have the dexterity. My fingers are strong but clumsy. My father was at his wits' end because I spoiled so many bolts of cloth. So he made a marriage bond with Fye's father, one of his oldest friends, and' – he dropped his hands into his lap, twisting his ring round and round – 'here we are.'

There was little to say after that. Magge was still steeped in her own tears and Audric was slumped in the same ungainly pose he had been in since Chaucer had taken them aside. He let a few moments pass and then cleared his throat. 'I don't think it is safe just now for you to visit your wife's remains,' he said, softly. 'She was taken with all ceremony to the care of the sacristan of St Olave's.' There was no need for these people to know about the dung cart and the old piece of carpet, even though they had no love for the woman. 'As a rule, she would be buried by now but' – he waved his arms eloquently to the four corners of the compass – 'what with one thing and another . . .'

'I don't want to see her!' Magge's cry was heartfelt and Chaucer was quick to reassure her.

'Your mother has been dead a long time,' he said. 'I don't think it would be wise to see her, even if you wanted to. Remember her as she was.'

All three of the Gillises looked at Chaucer with horror in their eyes.

Poet though he was, Chaucer knew when he was beaten and left with no more words. He settled for a murmured, 'I'll leave the three of you alone. To mourn.'

# SEVEN

The deer heard them first, ears twitching and noses in the air as they grazed in the woods of Shooter's Hill. The June heat was softer here, dampened by the leafy canopy, and their muzzles as they raised their heads, dark eyes watchful, were moist with the richness of the grasses of summer. They were used to the thud of galloping hoofs, the jingling of bells and the braying of horns. Pilgrims passed this way in the summer, hoping that the Holy Blissful Martyr would hear their prayers, cure their maladies, and show them just a glimpse of God's grace. Huntsmen came this way too, looking for the deer as they grazed, driving them out of their dells and glades, forcing them into the open to be mauled by hounds and riddled with arrows.

But this was different. There were horses, yes, but few of them and they weren't chasing deer. There was the occasional blast of a horn, but it was not to drive prey onto the high ground. Or was it? The deer could not understand what was happening but two great multitudes of men, more than they had ever seen before, were marching towards each other. They linked arms as they crashed through the undergrowth, trampling the grass and bracken, snapping off small coppiced trees. There were women with them, carrying packs on their backs, all they owned. And children, scampering around their elders, laughing and rolling in the summer greenery. It was like a holy day, yet better than a holy day, because there were no priests with them. No knell of doom, no tocsin bell, just thousands on the march to a brave new world that their leaders had promised them.

When the two multitudes first saw each other, they stopped, each mob swaying like a prizefighter, sizing up the other, reckoning the odds. A lone horseman trotted forward on a chestnut cob and sat staring at the uplifted faces in front of him.

'John Sheep?' he called out in the sudden stillness.

From the other side, another horseman came forward. He was small, hunched, his face purple from a recent beating, his lip cut and swollen.

'John Nameless?' he croaked, wincing as his lip stung him like a fresh blow.

Nameless smiled and swung down from his saddle. The other man needed help. They stood facing each other.

'No need for nameless now,' the younger man said. 'I am Wat Tyler. And you,' he knelt on the lush, deer-cropped grass, 'are Father John Ball.'

The man smiled, despite his pain, and held out a hand. The two men hugged each other and a roar erupted from the two armies. Men ran towards each other, slapping backs and dancing with delight.

'There,' the old man pointed to the grey city wobbling in the summer heat across the fields. 'There's Elysium, Wat. London. It's yours.'

'No,' growled Tyler amidst the cacophony. 'It's ours.'

John Gower raised his face to the warming sun. After another night in Chaucer's bed, he was beginning to feel a little fragile. He leaned his back against the ancient stone of the Tabard's stable wall and let the sounds drift off and away. The warmth of the sun at this time of year never left the wall, radiating slowly overnight and still there in the morning. He was missing his family more than he had expected, but he knew they were safe and that was the main thing. He deliberately let his muscles relax, feeling his fingers sink into his thighs, his shoulders droop, his knees splay slightly, his feet roll out onto their outer edges. Even his toes felt loose and floppy and, eventually, he slept. There was something about his posture that made everyone avoid his special, sunbathed corner; they could all tell a desperate man when they saw one. In his dreams, he was setting off on a pilgrimage, hopeful and happy. His family had waved him off. His face was set towards the shrine of the Blessed Martyr. There wasn't a sound except the jingle of bits, the clop of hoofs and somewhere, someone, singing sweetly. He smiled in his sleep and all was right with the world.

Someone was shaking his arm. Gower frowned. The idiot!

If he wasn't careful, he'd have him off his horse. And shouting. Someone was shouting in his ear. Why couldn't people just be quiet? A pilgrimage should be a reverent thing, not some kind of rough-house. He shook his arm fretfully, but the shouting continued and he slowly turned his head towards it.

He flinched. His assailant appeared to be a hydra, a many-headed monster of a thing, with hundreds of heads, all with eyes bulging, mouths flying with spittle. They were all shouting his name, urgently, louder and louder. And they were pulling his arm off, right out of its socket. Who . . .?

'Master *Gower*!'

John Gower sat up, his eyes rolling in all directions. They finally settled on the person sitting next to him and he drew back with a start. He also instinctively covered his nose. The woman sitting close by him on his bench gave off a stench so strong that it was almost visible. He knew the face – and the aroma – and searched his mind feverishly to try to place it. Then, he suddenly remembered and clamped a hand over his purse. With sudden serendipity he also remembered her name. 'Nell, isn't it?' he said, in tones reminiscent of a gentlewoman taking nourishing broth to one of the poor of her parish. He brushed her hand from his sleeve. 'How can I help you?'

'Master Gower,' she wheedled, 'they won't let me stay here, and me a poor widder with no family, all me babbies—'

'Don't try that again,' Gower snapped. 'I know you almost fooled me once, but you won't do it twice. I know your game and want nothing to do with you.' He wrinkled his nose and flapped a hand in front of it. 'I would love to know how you get any clients, though.'

She drew herself up. 'I *beg* your pardon, Master Gower,' she said, spitting just a little on the 's'. 'I do *not* have clients.'

Gower slid along the bench a little more, putting some space between the two of them. She kept pace with him as though they were tied together.

'I grant you,' she said, vehemently, 'I *grant* you that perhaps my story of the fire and the babbies is not quite the whole truth, but I do *not* have clients. I have gentleman friends, yes, that I won't deny. Gentlemen of discernment, some of them.'

Gower couldn't help but notice that her speech had become

less laden with the eccentricities of the commonality. He began to take more notice of her. Yes, she was filthy – there was absolutely no way of denying that. She had approximately a third of the teeth God gave her and her hair crawled with nameless things. And there was always, over and above anything else, the smell. He couldn't help looking at the rogue breast which, as was its habit, had escaped from her bodice. It hung, flat and grimy, down the front of her girdle and lay in her lap, like a pet.

She followed his gaze and, with a tut, flicked it back in with a practised hand. 'Me dugs have seen better days,' she said, lapsing back into her patois, 'but I've a few tricks up me gown'd put hairs on yer chest. Go back to Mistress Gower with a few surprises for her, eh?' She nudged him with a sharp elbow. 'Eh?' Her hand was out, claw-like, for anything he was prepared to pay to make her go away.

Gower shifted along the bench a little further but still she clung to his arm.

'I know you don't think a lot of me, Master Gower,' she said, thrusting her face close to his, her eyes gleaming mischievously as she saw him flinch. 'But I am a human being too, just like you are. There are thousands of men on the road and they aren't as picky as you. Any woman without a man to shield her will be on her back as soon as look at you, and left for dead, I shouldn't wonder. I may not have always been choosy enough, but I still have the right to say no, if you please.'

Gower was struck by the sudden dignity of the woman. 'I know you do. But I don't know how I can help you.'

'Ask that Baillie oaf if I can stay here. Not in a room. I know better than to ask for that. But I've come all the way from Dartford. A stable, perhaps. I don't mind the company of horses. And they don't mind me, before you say anything.'

'I wouldn't dream of it!' Gower was outraged, as a man must be whose words have just been taken out of his mouth. 'I'll speak to Master Baillie. But I can't promise anything.' He slid along the bench again but overshot the end and fell in an ignominious heap on some straw cleaned out from a rather neglected stable.

She leaned over the edge and looked down at him, her few

blackened teeth on display in her wide grin. 'That's very kind of you, Master Gower,' she said. 'Very kind.' To say a proper thank you, she sat on the end of the bench and threw her skirts over her head, to give him a glimpse of what could be his, should he say the word. And then, with a hop and a skip, she was gone.

John Gower lay back in the gently steaming straw, his eyes closed, and groaned aloud.

'Who's that, Will?' Jack Chub was trying to fit the spectacles he'd lifted from the manor house at Snodland onto his nose. For the life of him, he didn't know why excessively rich people wore these, but all the best linen and cutlery had gone by the time he'd got there and he was having something. He couldn't wear them for long because they made him feel a bit giddy, but he was determined to persevere. When he had learned to read, they would probably come in handy. Looking about him, the banner that danced above the knot of horsemen cantering up the hill looked more wobbly than the wind could explain; he shut one eye, but that didn't make much difference, so he pushed the spectacles to the end of his nose and tried to look nonchalant and studious.

'Dunno.' Will Lorkin was squeezing more moss into his Cordovans to stiffen the toes. 'What's this toe length, then, Jack, d'you reckon? Seven, eight inches?'

'Boasting again,' Chub grunted.

'I hear your average Crackow is twenty inches.' Lorkin was ever an arbiter of high fashion, especially since the footwear had cost him nothing.

'Crackow?' Chub frowned. 'What's that, then?'

'It's a place,' the wider-travelled Lorkin informed him. 'Where they make such things. It's in Bohemia or somewhere.'

'Oh.' Chub gave the spectacles up as a bad idea that would never catch on. He snapped the embellished oak side pieces off and stuffed them in his jerkin, throwing the lenses down in the grass. 'That knarre's carrying a flag of truce. Don't know the other banner, though.'

Lorkin looked up for the first time. 'Ah, that's foreign, that is.'

'I didn't know you was so up in the armorial rolls world, Will,' Chub sneered.

'Well, it won't matter soon, will it? There won't *be* such a thing as a coat of arms soon. Either that, or we'll all have one.' Lorkin bent down and snatched off his right shoe with a muffled oath. He shook out the moss and a disgruntled woodlouse trundled away. Chub tried not to laugh as his compatriot carefully sorted through the vegetation and restuffed his toes.

'Amen to that,' Chub said, kindly ignoring the livestock incident. That's what friends were for, to not notice when you looked a fool.

The horseman with the unknown device reined in his courser where the gorse bushes ringed the hill. What he saw before him would have unnerved a lesser man. Thousands of peasants, in every colour of stolen fabric, outsize liripipes and ill-fitting shoes, sat munching their bread, their cheese, their meat. Most of them had never eaten so well in their lives. Here and there, the cross of St George floated over their heads, as well as the bannerets and guidons of half the aristocracy of Kent. A lesser man would have been unnerved.

'I am Bertucat d'Albret,' he announced in fractured English. 'I am commanded by your King to ask you why you are all on the road, disturbing the peace of his realm.'

There were jeers and jibes. Those nearest spat at the horse's legs. A solid frame pushed through the crowd and a man stood there, like an ox in the furrow, arms folded.

'Are you the leader of this rabble?' d'Albret asked, his hand resting on his hip as his horse shifted. The knot of horsemen at his back moved in closer.

'I am Wat Tyler,' the leader said. 'The land we stand on is common land, open to all of us. As to the road, granted it's the King's highway, and we beg leave of His Grace to use it to get to London.'

The jeers had stopped and the mob was silent now, watching d'Albret and his reaction.

'Let me ask you again,' the messenger said. 'Why are you marching on the capital?'

Tyler smiled. 'Unlike you, condottiere,' he said, 'we are not mercenary soldiers. We don't march anywhere, still less ride. We walk. And we are walking to London to deliver His Grace the King from the evil counsellors who surround him. Such men are traitors, not just to His Grace, but to the people of England.'

'The people of England!' It was d'Albret's turn to spit and the peasants nearest to him were on their feet in an instant, shouting and jostling. Wisely, the condottiere pulled his horse back and wheeled away, his cavalcade cantering after him. There were cheers as Tyler laughed and made his way back through the crowd.

'There you are,' Lorkin said. Sitting where he and Chub were, he had just made out the conversation. 'I said he was foreign, din' I?'

'Wat put him in his place, though, didn't he?' Chub chortled. 'Turned as white as his flag of bloody truce at the end there.'

'He did, Chubby.' Lorkin finished relacing his shoes and stood up. 'Now. I think I'm ready. Fancy a carole?'

Chub grunted and looked up at him. 'Why would I want to dance with you?' he asked.

'Because I've got the shoes for it now. Anyway, look around you. What have we got? One woman for every twenty men? I've already tried that fat one over there and the one with the wonky eye. Beggars as we once were, Chubby, we still can't be choosers.'

Chub thought it over. His friend, as was so often the case, was not wrong. He had himself tried it with the woman with the wonky eye, having mistaken her somewhat skewed expression for a bit of a come-on. Fortunately, her aim was also rather off to the left, so he had escaped with everything intact but . . . even so. Coming to a decision, he held out his hand and was hauled to his feet. With an extravagant bow, Lorkin led him into the thick of the crowd, dancing a very passable step to an estampie played in the silence of his head.

In his life, a lot of things had happened to Geoffrey Chaucer, some good, some bad, some his fault and some the fault of others. But none had surprised him as much as Madame Eglantyne dashing up to him as he was retying his points having emptied his bladder in a quiet corner of the stable yard and shouting, 'Master Chaucer! Please hold my Foo-Foo! I am feeling faint!'

Chaucer was not the most manually dextrous of men but on this occasion he managed to grab the dog without undue incident and also lower the prioress onto a low wall, where she sat with her head lolling disconcertingly on her elegant, aristocratic neck. There was no sign of her sister nun, usually trailing behind like a shadow.

The dog stared balefully at Chaucer with its protruding eyes and, every time the comptroller put out a hand to pat the prioress consolingly, gave vent to a warning growl through its tiny, needle-sharp teeth. Chaucer was beginning to wonder how long this stalemate could possibly continue when, suddenly, the woman looked up at him, her eyes filled with tears and wailed, 'I can't go on, Master Chaucer. I simply can't!'

Before Chaucer could reply, her head lolled again and her eyes rolled alarmingly in her head. He looked round and called over a stable boy who seemed momentarily not to be employed in some exacting task for Hardesty. He held out the dog and nodded to the boy to take it. 'Come along, lad, it's only a dog. It won't bite.'

The boy gave him a puzzled look. 'Of course it will, Master Chaucer,' he said, speaking nothing but the truth. 'It might not be big, but it's the nastiest-tempered animal any of us lads've ever seen. We've had rats here with nicer natures.' The staff at the Tabard had all had Baillie's usual lecture on how to treat the guests, but most of them had decided for themselves that for the pittance he paid them, he could whistle. So he stepped back with his hands behind him and swallowed hard. He was a nice boy and being rude didn't come naturally, but everyone has a limit and he was at his. 'Hold the dog yourself, begging your pardon, Master Chaucer. I've got the midnight to dawn shift on the eastern parapet tonight and, if I have to go to my Maker, I don't need to be chewed by a dog no bigger than a rat before I do.' He backed away further and then ran off round the corner of the nearest stable.

Madame Eglantyne raised her head and howled her distress.

'Even my Foo-Foo, my beloved, is rejected by the sweepings of the gutters. I cannot *bear* it, Master Chaucer! I simply cannot *bear* it!'

Ignoring the dog's threats, Chaucer sat beside the prioress and patted her arm. 'Pray do not distress yourself, Madame Eglantyne,' he said. 'Whatever can be wrong to cause you such misery?' Even as he spoke, he rolled his eyes at his own stupidity. The woman was sleeping in a crowded room in an even more crowded inn. Her nuns had gone elsewhere rather than follow her lead, her only companions now a near mute and a dog which looked as if it had been skinned. Thousands of peasants with murder in their hearts were sweeping into London and would carry all before them. It was the coming of Doom, the end of days. Though Chaucer doubted that the woman was quite as chaste and pure as she liked to make out – there was that bangle to take into account, for a start – being the plaything of a ravening mob was probably not what she would choose as a future event. But his question, once asked, could not be taken back, so he sat quietly as Foo-Foo chewed wetly on the end of his liripipe and waited for her reply.

Eventually, she blew her nose on a scrap of Valenciennes and sniffed. Looking down at her hands, she murmured something that Chaucer didn't quite catch, but it seemed rude to ask her to repeat herself so he simply continued to pat her arm. Then, raising her chin, she spoke more clearly. 'I have not always been a good woman, Master Chaucer. No!' She held up an imperious hand, becoming more her usual self by the second. 'No, do not gainsay me!'

Chaucer hastened to make some gainsaying noises, deep in his throat.

'I must tell you what has distressed me.' She gazed into his eyes and he felt himself lean back, trying to put some distance between his face and hers. 'You are a man of gentle upbringing, Master Chaucer, I can tell that. So I will not tell you the details of my . . . wickedness.'

Chaucer managed to hold in his deep sigh of relief and patted more assiduously.

'Suffice it to say that the event took place when I was a

much younger woman, very green in judgement, and it would certainly never be allowed to happen now.'

She shut her mouth like a trap and Chaucer believed her; who would be able to get past Foo-Foo, for a start?

'But . . .' and she dropped her voice to a whisper and in her anxious, darting eyes and trembling mouth, the poet could briefly see the girl she had been, the girl who had done the wrong which so angered this woman. 'But . . . someone knows. I have received a missive' – she clapped a hand to her bosom – 'a missive which I keep here, in my bodice, close to my heart where no one will find it. It tells . . .' she lowered her eyes again and blushed. 'It tells of the event of which I spoke.'

Chaucer couldn't help but feel that this was possibly an overstatement.

'An event which I thought only I and one other knew of.'

Chaucer could see the chink here and pounced on it. 'So, presumably,' he said, 'this missive is from that person.'

She reared up and Chaucer only just missed getting his nose broken. 'It is indeed *not* from that person,' she said, sharply. 'It is from someone evil, someone who wants to make my life a misery, wants to drive me to despair.' She looked up, her nostrils flaring. 'And wants money, too, of course. But, as a nun, of course, I have no money.'

Again, the bangle flashed across Chaucer's line of sight and he smiled blandly.

'The animal who wrote this letter asked that I leave one hundred nobles at the shrine of Mary Matfelon in Whitechapel. But with all this' – she waved her arm – 'unpleasantness, I have been unable to do so.' Her resolve crumbled and she wept on Chaucer's shoulder. 'And now, Master Chaucer, and now, all the world will know of my sin.'

Chaucer was not good with weeping women, but her grip was like iron and so he had to stay there, between the Scylla of Foo-Foo's growls and the Charybdis of Eglantyne's tears.

'Me?' Nicholas Brembre positively shrank back into the shadows. 'Why me?'

'Because,' William Walworth sneered, 'you're one of the

richest men in London, a former mayor, and you're supposed to carry some gravitas.'

'Well, d'Albret here got nowhere with them,' the merchant pointed out, flapping his hands so that the sleeves of his houppelande bounced up and down.

'If I'd had a hundred men at my back . . .' the condottiere growled. 'No, make that fifty, I'd have dispersed the bastards.'

'With respect, Sir Bertucat,' Brembre was a man with his back to the wall in every sense, 'this is not the battlefield of Nájera and Edward the Black Prince is no longer with us.'

Everybody crossed themselves.

'Precisely,' Walworth snapped. 'With even more respect, Sir Bertucat, perhaps a military man was not quite the right person to send. We need someone of a more . . . civilian persuasion. And that's you, Brembre.'

'What if they take me prisoner?' the merchant babbled.

'Don't flatter yourself, Nicholas,' Walworth said. 'Even though you're one of the richest men in London, I'll wager the Kentish riff-raff don't know that. Wear something scruffy. Take some apples with you – chuck 'em around. These people, like everybody else, will have their price. Find out what it is. Promise them the earth, but for God's sake, keep your fingers crossed. Their demands may be unreasonable.'

There was a silence. Brembre tried one last ploy to avoid the inevitable. 'What about Chaucer? Why don't we send him?'

'Chaucer?' Walworth frowned. 'He's a nonentity. *And* he's an awkward one; he'd probably go over to the rabble.'

'You might need this,' d'Albret had unhooked his sword and offered it, hilt first, to the man who had once been Lord Mayor. Brembre shuddered. 'I have a feeling I'll need more than that,' he mumbled.

In the event, he didn't have much more than that. Nicholas Brembre, with just ten men riding with him, cantered up Shooter's Hill the next morning as the June sun warmed the earth. D'Albret had told him what to expect, but even so, Brembre wasn't ready. The camp of the peasants seemed to have no end; their tents and makeshift huts stretched across every open space and, no doubt, some of them slept in the trees.

A huge flag of St George lifted in the morning breeze in the centre, and it was here that the rabble brought Brembre, his flag of truce hoisted high, the leopards and lilies of the King alongside it. If anything might save his life today, it was these two pieces of cloth.

The tent under the cross was no ramshackle make-do. Brembre recognized the devices stitched to the sides as the coat of arms of the Blundells, knights of the shire for Kent, with whom he had often had dealings. Outside its entrance flap, a little man sat on a stool, peering up at him.

'Are you from the King?' he asked.

'I am,' Brembre said, holding his horse steady and trying to work out the best way to run, should he have to.

'I am Father John Ball,' the man said, but he wore no habit and his head was not tonsured. The merchant had heard the name. John Ball was a madman who seemed to believe the nonsense that Jack was as good as his master; there was no reasoning with people like that. They probably believed the world was round.

'His Grace the King,' Brembre said, 'would like to know why you see fit to march in such numbers on his capital.'

Before Ball could answer, a younger, larger man burst out of the tent. 'I am Wat Tyler,' he said. 'My people have elected me their leader.'

'Elected?' Brembre repeated. Did a peasant even know what that meant?

'I told the mercenary thug who came before you,' Tyler said, swigging from an ale-sack, 'we march on London to rescue His Grace from evil counsellors.' He clicked his fingers and a minion scuttled to his side with parchment in his hand. At a nod from Tyler, he passed it up to Brembre.

'What's this?' the merchant asked.

'I assume you can read,' Tyler scoffed. 'It's a list. A list of the evil counsellors I spoke of. From John of Gaunt to the humblest lick-spittle at the King's court. They are condemned to hang. All of them.'

Brembre ran his eye down the list. All the great and good

of the royal court were there, dukes, earls, knights, friends of
his, acquaintances and then, a mere three names from the
bottom, his own name jumped out at him.

'You can keep that,' Tyler said, 'as a warning to them. I
have other copies. Master . . . er . . .?'

'Chaucer,' Brembre said quickly. 'Geoffrey Chaucer,
Comptroller of the King's Woollens.'

There were hoots of derision.

'Can't we talk about this?' Brembre asked, knowing full
well what the answer would be.

'Indeed we can,' Tyler said. 'When London's burning and
these men are twirling from the end of their ropes. Until then,
Master Chaucer, be grateful that you came under a flag of
truce and that I am an honourable man.' He clicked his fingers
again and another lackey stood at his elbow. 'Write down his
name,' he said. 'Geoffrey Chaucer.' He smiled up at Brembre,
'Don't take it personally, Comptroller. You're just a pawn in
a greater game, that's all. And I intend to sweep the board.'


Harry Baillie had always considered himself to be a reasonable
man and, except where money was concerned, few would
disagree. He would argue for days about a mis-accounted
farthing – mis-accounted in the wrong direction, that was – but
in most other things, he could take the world or leave it alone,
its choice. His children tumbled around his feet, his wife had
him in the palm of her hand. There were many families in the
environs of the Tabard who ate each day courtesy of the unsung
charity of Harry Baillie. But he was beginning to feel a little
trapped. The walls of the Tabard had always been the walls
of his castle, as far as he was concerned but, now they were
beginning to resemble an actual castle, he was not feeling
happy.

He had talked with his wife when he could catch her standing
still, which was seldom. It was fruitless trying to talk to any
of his guests; from the highest to the lowest, they were all in
a lather about the peasants. Those who could wield a hammer
did; those who couldn't, made encouraging noises at the others.
Where all the wood had come from, Baillie hated to consider,
but he could see arguments with his neighbours ahead,

stretching to the crack of Doom. He had definitely recognized part of the Widow Watkins' stable door being added to a buttress. Happily, she was addicted to the cook's saffron buns, so she should be easy to appease. Not so some of the others; money would have to change hands and Harry Baillie shuddered.

He made his way through what he thought could quite rightly be considered a throng to the yard and called out, 'Master Hardesty? Master *Hardesty*! Are you there?'

A muffled shout came from near the door and Hardesty, covered in sawdust but looking happier than a man in his position had any right to look, popped out and waved at Baillie.

'Two seconds,' he shouted back, and ducked behind a baulk of timber. In rather more than two seconds, he was back, dusting off his shoulders and shaking his head, running his fingers through his hair.

'Sawdust gets everywhere,' he said. 'How can I help you, Master Baillie?' He looked around him, hands on hips. 'I'm rather pleased with all we've accomplished in so short a time, aren't you?'

Baillie felt his wind leave his sails in no uncertain manner. It was difficult to complain when the man had included him in the achievement, he who had not so much as handled a nail. He nodded and smiled, looking around him, as if assessing the situation. In fact, all he could see was chaos and desolation. Always assuming that in a perfect world the peasants left them all alone, this would take years to put right. Though, on the brighter side, they wouldn't want for firewood for many a long year.

'You have done a very . . . thorough job, Master Hardesty. I will give you that.' It was faint praise, but it was clear that Hardesty didn't feel damned by it. He smacked his open hand on a solid bulwark made of the headboard of Baillie's very own bed and smiled a satisfied smile.

'This will stand for a thousand years, Master Baillie,' he said, proudly. 'I don't care to blow my own trumpet as a rule, but we are as safe in here as . . .' The yeoman was briefly stuck for words but Baillie was there to help.

'Rats in a trap, Master Hardesty. I think that may be the

phrase you seek.' Harry Baillie was not normally quite so restrained, but he had his position to consider and his staff were watching. There was nowhere left in the Tabard where you could have any privacy, not even for a minute. 'It's all very well to stop people getting in, but you must surely realize that we may need to get out. We have enough food for . . .' he paused and looked around him. Ears were cocked, waiting to hear the bad news. As everyone knew, the way to hysteria was through a man's stomach. 'Enough food for the rest of today,' he whispered, 'assuming not everyone is in an eating frame of mind. If we don't get more before tonight, there will be anarchy inside these walls as well as out.'

Hardesty's face was as open as the sky and usually as sunny, but a storm cloud gathered now. 'Master Baillie,' he said, his voice tight with annoyance. 'Do I look like a stupid man to you?'

Baillie had always hated rhetorical questions but this one seemed quite easy, as rhetorical questions went. 'Of course not, Master Hardesty,' he announced. 'All I want to know is . . .'

'I know what you want to know,' Hardesty said, grabbing the host's sleeve and pulling him behind a buttress. In the confined space, both men had to crouch, so Hardesty's dramatic outflung arm didn't have quite the panache he could have wished. Also, Baillie's blank face was something of a disappointment. Hardesty tried again and this time pointed with the other hand as well. 'Do you see it, Master Baillie?' he asked, into the ringing silence.

'Erm, a wall?'

Hardesty was both proud and annoyed. Proud that it looked just like an ordinary wall. Annoyed that he had spent days protecting the property of a man who clearly had no more brains than God had given to the average sheep.

'No, Master Baillie.' Hardesty decided to let pride win the day. He knocked on it and on the wall to one side of it. They sounded the same to Baillie, but to Hardesty it made all things clear. 'It is a sally port, a hidden exit. All castles have them, many fortified houses too. It is a secret entrance and exit. It isn't wise to use them too often, and the fewer people who know about them, the better. But it would be the direst folly to build without one.' He led the way back out into the sunlight. 'Let me know when you need to go and get more food and I will teach you the trick of opening it. And also,' the yeoman laughed and clapped Baillie on the back with a blow which would have sent a lesser man flying, 'the way back in. It isn't easy to find.'

Baillie was impressed in spite of himself, but couldn't help one final question. 'What if it is discovered?'

Hardesty cocked an eyebrow and smiled. 'Then we use the more secret one, Master Baillie. But now, if you don't need to ask me any more foolish questions, I must get on.' The sound of falling timbers made his head snap up. A stable lad stood in one corner, looking sheepish and with a pile of planks at his feet. Hardesty set off at a run. 'Have I already told you, boy, how to stack wood? Have I? Well, have I?'

Baillie took the opportunity to step quietly away. Even the bustle of Mistress Baillie would be like a rest cure after this.

They had camped on both sides of the Roman road of Watling Street that ran like an arrow through the heart of Blackheath. The largest tents, the ones with the stolen banners, stood nearest the road and the torches flickered that night as the greatest number of people who had ever travelled together in England looked up at the stars and wondered.

Wat Tyler was no stargazer. The little man sitting alongside him now was a dreamer – he could look for Heaven as often as he liked and he'd never find it. Heaven was here, on earth, and it was made by men; men like Wat Tyler. The rebel leader was surrounded by his cronies as well as John Ball. And the man who bothered him most was Jack Straw, with his dark, watchful eyes and sallow, grey cheeks. Such men, Tyler knew, were dangerous.

'News, Jack?' Tyler lolled back in the carved chair he had helped himself to in Rochester.

'There may be trouble in Southwark,' Straw said, pointing to the rough and ready map on the table in front of them. 'Somewhere . . . here.'

'St Olave's?' Tyler sneered. 'Don't tell me the monks are going to make a fight of it?'

'The Tabard,' Straw said. 'Our friend has sent word. A group of them are fortifying the place.'

'Fortifying an inn?' Tyler scoffed. 'Come off it.'

'There's some knarre with them who knows one end of a bow from another. Seen service in the wars, they say.'

'A quarter of my men have too,' Tyler told him. 'Like yours from Essex, I'm guessing.'

Straw nodded. 'He won't slow us up for long,' he said. 'I'll wager he's just playing for time.'

'We won't give him that,' Tyler said. 'We'll bypass the place. Aim for the bridge. He'll be shooting at shadows.'

'You might want to reconsider that,' Straw said. 'Got that list, Father John? The list of the damned?'

John Ball shuffled in the pile of parchment on the table, peering at a page or two in the guttering candlelight before finding what he wanted. He passed it to Straw who checked it, passed to the second page and gave it to Tyler.

'Sixth from the bottom,' he said. 'A man you've promised to hang.'

Tyler peered at it. 'Geoffrey Chaucer. I remember him. Came with a flag of truce, shitting himself. What of it?'

'He's there,' Straw helped himself to some more of the Archbishop of Canterbury's wine. 'According to our friend, who, let's face it, doesn't miss much, Geoffrey Chaucer's at the Tabard.'

A dark smile flitted across Wat Tyler's face. 'All right,' he said. 'Maybe we won't bypass the Tabard after all. Do we know who runs it?'

'Harry Baillie, our friend says.' Straw locked his hands behind his head.

'One of us, potentially?' Tyler asked.

'An innkeeper?' Straw muttered. 'One of the people? Don't make me laugh!'

'Fine,' Tyler shrugged. 'Then we'll hang him too.'

The Tabard was as quiet as it ever was that night. The many souls under its roof – some of them, literally; the servants of the guests had been given precarious lodgings in the rafters – had become used to the cramped conditions surprisingly quickly and some had even begun to enjoy it, the proximity of warm and willing bodies being an unexpected bonus for many. Snores ripped through the air, accompanied and often drowned out by farting and the occasional cry of someone in the grip of a nightmare of epic proportions. But, by and large, the Tabard slept and slept soundly.

In the fetid warmth of a stable, Maghfield the merchant venturer sat idly stropping his falchion on a stone which stuck out of the rough wall. Fortunately for him and all the sleepers in the inn, the straw was too damp to catch fire as sparks fell onto it. The edge glinted evilly in the moonlight coming through the top half of the door, open to the sky. Maghfield was not a patient man and he had told himself that, as soon as his sword was sharp enough to cut a moonbeam, he would be going back to his bed, no matter how crowded with life, both human and insect. He was not a man to brood on decisions made – no one in his line of business would live a long and healthy life if they lost sleep over bad choices – but he was now beginning to wonder why he had agreed to this assignation at all. Boredom, he decided. That was why – he was a man of action, and to have spent the last few days pacing the limited space within the growing walls was torture. He would be on his way tomorrow, no matter what was going on outside. There was money to be made wherever chaos reigned – he had lived long enough to know that.

The horse shifted at Maghfield's side and stamped a hoof, tossing its head. Its ears had detected a soft footfall and a smell that made it uncomfortable. Maghfield stood and fondled the beast's ears, crooning softly to it in his native language. The horse rolled its eyes, but was still. From the deep shadow at the horse's head, Maghfield watched intently, listening hard. The door opened and a figure stepped inside. Maghfield stifled a sigh. He had been right; he was meeting with an imbecile. If he wished, the newcomer could be dead at his feet and not know what had hit him. But Maghfield was one who liked to know what was going on, and he felt that this man could have information which would be useful, so he slid his falchion

silently back into the scabbard and stepped forward, his soft
leather boots silent in the damp straw.

'Is that you, Master Maghfield?' The harsh tones could only
belong to Inskip the Miller.

'Yes.' Maghfield's answer was as soft as a breath. 'Keep
your voice down, you oaf. What is the point of secrecy if you
then shout?'

'I ent shouting,' Inskip said, testily. 'This is my normal
voice.'

'Well, whisper in your normal voice, then.'

'There's nobody about,' the miller said. 'But I'll whisper if
you insist. What I have to say won't take but a minute and I
can say it in any voice you choose.'

Maghfield stepped forward, his hand on his falchion hilt.
'Miller,' he hissed between his teeth. 'Tell me what you came
to tell me and let's be gone. My boots are ruined in this straw,
my temper is short, and the little maid who I have paid good
money for will not keep my bed warm for ever. So spit it out
and make it snappy.'

The miller also took a step forward, a snarl beginning to
curl his all but toothless mouth. 'Mind your words, merchant,'
he said, his voice low. 'What I have to tell you will . . .' His
head snapped round. 'What was that?'

Both men held their breath as soft footfalls approached the
stables. The miller looked at the merchant and shook his head,
covering his mouth and wagging his finger. The merchant
made sure his falchion was firm in his grasp and he crept
nearer to the door, standing pressed against the wall and peering
round.

He mouthed, 'It's Ambrosius and that drab.'

The miller signalled with his eyebrows that he had no idea
what the merchant had just said, but moved back further into
the shadows of the stable.

For a moment, Maghfield considered miming, to clarify who
had disturbed them. But then, he decided that he had played
the spy for long enough on this hot and sultry night. He looked
again to see where Ambrosius and Nell had ensconced themselves and, seeing they were intent on each other, he slipped
away out of the stable, leaving the miller behind, gesticulating

wildly and impotently behind his back. As he crept out of the
stables, he glanced back at the interlopers and saw Nell's bright
eyes over the priest's shoulder. One of them closed, slowly and
disconcertingly, in a wink.

The miller, alone in the ammonia-scented dark, waited. He
stifled a chuckle. If his luck were in, he should be set fair for
some fun and games with Nell when the priest was done with
her. He had never met a yellow hood yet who turned down a
chance of a groat or two. And, he smoothed his hair and
twitched his jerkin, especially not with as fine a specimen of
manhood as he. And, in his wide experience of the world and
of the religious in particular, he doubted the priest would keep
him waiting long. He leaned against the wall, folded his arms,
and lost himself in thoughts to keep him in the mood for love.
A slow smile crept across his unlovely face and the world
held its breath.

# EIGHT

The King came down from Windsor that day, his entourage bright with his banners, outriders trotting along both banks of the Thames as his barges butted through the sparkling water, the oarsmen in their deep green velvet keeping time to the beat of a single drum.

Sir Robert Knollys had been sent by the Earl of Salisbury the day before, the old soldier trying to talk sense to the boy without making him shit his breeches. Not that much actually troubled young Richard. He was fourteen and the cost of his haircut alone would keep Wat Tyler in clover for a year. Knollys looked down at the lad now, lolling on his throne at the stern of the boat. When he was little, people said that he had the looks of his father, Edward of Woodstock, the Black Prince. But his clear blue eyes now looked arrogant, his lips thin and sneering. Above all, there seemed to be a perpetual smell under his nose.

'Do they do things differently there?' he asked, looking up from the locket he was holding.

'Where, Your Grace?' Knollys had given up trying to discern any logic in the boy hours ago.

'Bohemia,' the King said. 'Where *she* comes from.'

*She* was Anne of Bohemia, the intended bride of the Lord's Anointed, and he had not met her yet. For a moment, Knollys toyed with telling the lad that Bohemians had faces in the middle of their chests and that they walked on their hands, but he suspected the boy had no sense of humour at all. 'The ladies, I believe, ride side-saddle,' the old man said, 'and, at court at least, they use forks, two-pronged skewers, to pick up food.'

The disgust on the King's face said it all. 'Fascinating,' he said. 'But I meant in the bedroom. Swiving. Is it done in Bohemia as it is here?'

Robert Knollys's children had long ago flown the nest. He

had lost his own virginity when he was a page, before the Flood, and he had no intention of sharing intimate details with his King, especially one whose voice had not yet broken. 'Perhaps Your Grace should discuss that with your Father Confessor,' he suggested.

'Don't be ridiculous, Knollys!' Richard snapped. 'The man's a churchman. Doesn't know one end of a woman from another.'

Robert Knollys raised an eyebrow. Clearly the boy was more of an ingénu than he realized. In the event, a petitioner, one of a clutch waiting patiently at the barge's prow, intervened to save the day.

'Grant mercy, liege lord,' the man said, kneeling before the boy and handing him a scrolled parchment.

Richard clicked his fingers and a lackey took the document and read it. 'Request for crenellation, sire,' the clerk said. 'Stoke by Nayland.'

'*Another* one?' Richard tutted. 'Does no one want anything but lumps of stone on their houses?'

'Status, sire,' Knollys said. 'It means everything to some people.'

'Where are we, Knollys?' The portrait of the pretty Anne had been consigned to a slop bucket. The veteran of Crécy and Nájera scanned the banks on both sides of the river. 'Chertsey, Your Grace.'

'Are we nearly there yet?'

Knollys held up a wetted finger to test the wind. 'We should be at the Tower by nightfall, sire,' he said.

'And then what?' the King yawned. '*More* petitioners?'

'The Archbishop of Canterbury has requested an audience, sire,' Knollys told him.

'Old Sudbury?' Richard sneered. 'He can bore for England, that man.' Something caught the boy's eye along the riverbank where the chestnuts bowed over the water and the sun gilded the great abbey beyond. 'Handful of monks,' he observed as the brethren bowed towards his gilded boat. 'Shouldn't there be more . . . what's the word, Knollys? Adulation?'

Indeed there should. In the old King's day, whenever he rode the river, the banks would be crawling with locals, the great and the good on their jetties, their men-at-arms standing to attention, pretty girls throwing flowers and milky babies beaming for the highest in the land. But today, a few threadbare brothers and the odd peasant. Some of them were waving, cheering feebly, bowing as the King passed by. But there was a sullen cast to their faces, a darkness in their eyes that Knollys neither liked nor trusted. He thought to himself what an easy target the lad who wore the crown made, ostentatious in his velvet, pearls and ermine, a diadem glittering in his golden curls. And instinctively, he edged closer, signalling to his crossbowmen on each side to turn so that their bulk stood between the King and his people.

'It'll be different when we reach London, sire,' he lied, and crossed his fingers behind his back.

It wasn't unusual for Witton Gilbert to get the shitty end of the stick. Fifteenth of sixteen children, he had been the baby of the family for a scant ten months and had no recollection of the experience. He was not only the next-to-youngest, he was also possibly the most ill-favoured of an unattractive bunch. Rumour had it that his mother had once been offered a noble for him by a travelling pedlar, so that he could display him and attract a crowd to which he could sell his wares. While she had bustled off into the house to fetch the lad's spare jerkin and hose, the pedlar had changed his mind, reneged on the deal and hot-footed it down the road.

So Witton Gilbert took up his pitchfork with resignation and regarded the dung pile which steamed gently before him. He always turned the dung pile on a Wednesday – that had been dinned into his head by frequent slaps over the years. Raining? Turn the dung pile. Snowing? Turn the dung pile. Uprising of the peasantry? Turn the dung pile. He had a slight problem this Wednesday which he had never had before. The yard was so full of tethered horses, people, baulks of timber and just general noise and scurry that he wasn't sure where he could turn the dung pile to. As a rule, he would move it a couple of yards to left or right, as appropriate, so the older, riper, rotted straw and horse-shit mixture would come to the top, for the farmers and smallholders to come and take away after a suitable recompense to Harry Baillie. And so the dung pile waxed and waned, and so Witton Gilbert would turn it.

His other problem was that the dung pile was now the biggest he had ever seen it. Despite the horses in the stables being kept in deep litter in these uncertain times – with thousands of men on the march, mucking out a horse was not high on men's priorities – some of the worst of it still needed to be removed; and here it was, warm and rotting in the June sun. The chambermaids had taken the opportunity to empty the pots onto it as well, so the urine running into the gutter was not all equine, as Witton's nose told him. In fact, Witton Gilbert was getting as close to angry as he ever became. His eyebrow knotted and his virtually toothless mouth worked with some silent curses that would have turned milk. He stepped forward and plunged his pitchfork into the heap. His brain was not of the highest calibre and didn't work well when he was upset, but it ran true as an arrow when dung was involved. Get air to it, that was the key. So as long as Witton Gilbert had breath in his body, he would turn that dung pile, come hell or high water. A man did, after all, have his pride.

'It's gnawing away at you, isn't it, Geoff?' John Gower was sipping Harry Baillie's ale as the afternoon sun kissed the new ramparts of the Tabard. 'The murder of Mistress Gillis.'

'Is it that obvious?' Chaucer was munching the crust of bread he had saved from earlier in the day. The evening repast was a bit of a hit-or-miss affair at the Tabard in these turbulent times and so he was getting into the habit of keeping edible morsels close at hand, against the day. 'I thought I was doing a convincing job of making you believe I was focusing on the Armageddon that's coming our way.'

'Oh, that,' Gower shrugged. 'It's been days now and . . . nothing. Somebody will have bought the peasants off. Everyman has his price, after all.'

'What price a pilgrim's wife with her throat cut?'

'Who's your money on?' Gower was swatting away the gnats drawn to his goblet.

'They say there are forty thousand people in London,' the comptroller said. 'Take out the children, the old and infirm . . . what's that leave? Twenty-five thousand? Perhaps more.' It was Chaucer's turn to shrug. 'Could be any of them.'

'Could be the husband,' Gower murmured.

'Arend?' Chaucer frowned. 'Husbands don't kill their wives . . . do they?'

Something in Gower's expression told Chaucer that he thought they did. 'He's a miserable bastard, Geoff. Treats his children like servants.'

'So did Fye, apparently. Odd, that. Maternal instinct and all that. Women are supposed to love their offspring.'

'I got the impression that Fye Gillis didn't love anybody,' Gower said. 'We need to find someone who didn't love her back. She loved money, though.' Gower splatted a gnat on Baillie's table, one of the few still standing. 'But then, show me a Fleming who doesn't.'

'Don't you care for our Walloon cousins, John?' Chaucer asked with a wry smile on his face.

'Wearing my day hat,' Gower said, 'I've crossed swords with too many of them, coming over here, setting up their looms all over the place.'

'Hardly all over the place, John,' Chaucer remonstrated. 'They're mostly outside the walls. Bishopsgate. Portsoken.'

'The Gillises aren't,' Gower persisted. 'Walbrook Ward, aren't they?'

'Needlers' Lane,' Chaucer nodded.

'I don't have to tell you what a dog-eat-dog world the world of the weaver-merchant is, Geoffrey. Arend Gillis will have his enemies, business rivals by the score. If they can't get at him, they can perhaps get his wife.'

Chaucer nodded. 'Of course, there are the children.'

Gower sat upright. 'The Gillis children? Surely not. They seem too . . . cowed, for one thing.'

'Oh, it's unlikely, I'll grant you,' the comptroller said, getting up and leaning over the rail of the landing, scattering the crumbs off his lap onto the boards for the sparrows. 'Only the girl seemed genuinely upset, though. And only because she has no autonomy; without her mother, she is rudderless. But she'll learn, hopefully. The boy, though – he seemed curiously unmoved. More interested in his mother's savings.'

'Chip off the old block,' Gower muttered. 'But is he unmoved enough to cut his own mother's throat?'

Chaucer straightened and looked out over the Tabard's roof to the south, where the strip fields of Southwark lay golden in the summer light. 'We can't see each other's hearts, John,' he sighed. 'That's the pity of it. What we really think. What we're driven to in the watches of the night.' He turned his back on whatever may have been massing in the mists of the Neckinger and trickling, even as he spoke, around the grey stone of Bermondsey Abbey. 'Needlers' Lane,' he said. 'We'll get some answers there, hopefully. Coming?'

Gower looked up at his old friend. 'Two things, Geoffrey,' he said. 'First, how do we get out of this place now that Hardesty's walled us in? And second, I wouldn't, as you now know, pass water on the Flemings if they were on fire.'

There was a less than subtle cough at Chaucer's elbow and Harry Baillie stood there, beaming. 'Sorry, lordings,' he said. 'I couldn't help overhearing that last bit, seeing as we're so overcrowded. As to the second, Master Gower, strictly between us three, I am with you there. But the first, Master Chaucer, I think I may have . . . wait a minute? What's that idiot doing now? I only gave him a job as a favour to his mother . . .' He stepped forward and leaned over the rail. 'Oi, you!' Baillie turned and propelled himself down the stairs at a rate close to suicidal, given their steepness, their fragility and his size.

'That was odd,' Gower observed, getting up and looking out over the yard. 'Is he finding all this a bit too much, do you think?'

Chaucer raised an eyebrow and sipped again at his ale. 'I wouldn't be surprised,' he said. 'I mustn't let him forget to tell me about the first thing, though. What *is* he doing now?'

Gilbert was stopped in his tracks by a sudden shout from the back door of the inn. He turned, leaning on his pitchfork; sometimes his slightly shorter left leg gave him gyp and it was good to relax a little.

'You! Filbert, whatever your name is!' Harry Baillie had better things to do than remember everyone's name. 'What in the name of all that's holy are you doing?' Baillie set off at a smart pace across the yard, minions scattering left and right. 'You can't turn the dung pile in all this . . .' he waved his hands impotently. 'In all this! Stop it!'

'Dung pile'll fester, Master Baillie,' Gilbert ventured. He didn't know much, but he knew for a certain fact that he knew more about dung piles than any innkeeper born. 'You'll get gases, y'see. Her might even blow up.'

Baillie looked sceptical.

'Seen it.' Witton Gilbert knew he was on strong ground. 'Dung pile at the livery in Giltspur Street weren't turned right and her blew up and besmottered everything in half a league with horse shit. The monks at Bart's were proper put out.' He leaned more heavily on his pitchfork. 'All for the want of a bit of a turn.'

Baillie looked at his yard, full of people and their belongings. Some of them he would be quite happy to see covered in horse shit, but in someone else's yard, not here. So he nodded to his dung-pile-turner and said, 'In that case, Gilbert,' the name had come to him in a sudden flash, 'do your worst. But please, for the love of God, don't spread it around. Just turn it gently.' Baillie mimed a gentle twist of the pitchfork and Gilbert looked at him with sympathy. It was a mystery to him how a man could run a great business such as the Tabard but had no idea how a dung pile needed turning. He swung round, pitchfork held low, ready to jab and twist and let the air in.

Baillie stepped back to avoid the man's jabbing elbow and trod heavily on the instep of a passing chambermaid, heading back to the inn with armfuls of clean linen. The woman screamed as though she were being murdered and Baillie turned on her, crossly. 'Don't overdo it, err, there. I know I'm a big chap, but I didn't hurt you *that* much.'

Despite his protestations, the girl continued to scream, the linen dropped in the mire of the yard, her fists rigid by her side, her eyes closed and her mouth a red cavern of sound.

'Come *on*, now,' Baillie said, giving her a shake.

'No, Master Baillie,' said a breathy voice from his other side. 'It's not *her* foot. It's *that* one.'

Baillie turned to follow the other maid's pointing finger. There, hanging out of the dung pile, was a leg, filthy from the dung and the straw but still, very recognizable. It was the leg, stiff and out of place as it was, of Inskip the Miller.

From the back of the crowd which had coalesced around the dung pile at a respectful distance, Chaucer and Gower came forward, using elbows without compunction.

'That's the miller's leg!' Gower said, redundantly.

'And presumably, the rest of the miller attached to it,' Chaucer added. 'Baillie, get young . . . whatsisname here to dig him out. It's not decent, leaving him like that.'

'He's dead, master,' Witton Gilbert thought it only fair to mention. 'That leg's stiff as a board.' He poked it with the blunt end of his pitchfork, by way of demonstration.

'Don't do *that*,' Baillie said, pulling on the man's noisome sleeve. 'Just . . . just dig him out, carefully now, with your hands or something. A trowel? Has anyone got a trowel?'

The crowd stepped back one pace. Their demeanour suggested that, even if they had a trowel, it wasn't going to be used to dig out a dead man from a dung pile. Gilbert stood there looking sullen.

'I'll give you a leopard if you do,' Baillie wheedled.

Gilbert shrugged.

'So will I,' Gower added, nudging Chaucer.

'Yes, all right,' the comptroller added. 'So will I. Just do it, will you? Even Inskip deserves better than this.'

With a flourish, Gilbert brought out a small spade which had been tucked in his belt. For three leopards he was ready for anything. 'Fer tidying, see,' he said. 'When I moves a dung pile.' With surprisingly gentle hands, he scraped the straw and excrement away from the miller's body and stepped back suddenly, crossing himself.

'What's the matter, man?' Baillie said. 'Keep digging.'

Witton Gilbert had not led a sheltered life. In fact, it was fair to say he had seen – and done – things which most men would shun. But this was different. This was in his dung pile. 'Oh, sir,' he said, in barely more than a whisper.

'Oh, sir, look. Someone has nearly cut off the poor soul's head.'

Gower leaned closer and then turned to Chaucer, his face turning a grey-green. Swallowing the bile which had risen in his throat, he nodded and leaned in closely to speak in his friend's ear. 'Yes,' he murmured. 'Before you ask me, Geoff. It's the same. The same as Fye Gillis.'

Chaucer moved over so he was next to Harry Baillie.

'Before we were interrupted,' he said, 'you said you could help me get out.'

Baillie's eyes were fixed on the ragged wound in Inskip's throat, down to the backbone so the head lolled loose, all but cut off. 'Yes,' he said, not looking Chaucer in the face. 'This way, Master Chaucer. This way.'

Gower looked at Chaucer and shrugged. They had already agreed, as far as he was concerned, that he wouldn't be accompanying the comptroller in his quest, and his word was as good as his bond. He turned away to make his point even clearer and Chaucer followed the innkeeper behind a pile of wood.

'Well, Master Baillie?' Chaucer was beginning to lose his nerve. Unlike many in the Tabard, he had not been up on the ramparts, looking out over London to see what was going on. As far as he was concerned, out of sight was almost out of mind and he had almost got used to the sudden jolts as his heart told his head that there were thousands of peasants with murder in their hearts coming closer by the hour. 'I'm sorry. I thought you meant that there was a way out. But I see . . .' He hoped his relief didn't show in his voice.

Baillie smiled a slow smile, the smile of a man with a trick up his sleeve. Without speaking, he pressed a knothole, and a door sprang open in the wall. From the other side, summer sun poured in, dancing with dust motes kicked up from the road outside. 'There you are, Master Chaucer,' he said, as proudly as if he had made it himself. 'It's called a sally port, by all accounts. I daresay you've seen one before, living in castles as you've done.'

'I have . . .' Chaucer still stood Tabard-side. 'Is . . . how do I get back in?'

'Watch as I close it behind you,' Baillie said, airily. 'Master Hardesty says you'll see the latch pop out and you just press it to get back in.' He gave Chaucer a light push between the shoulder blades and he was suddenly out in the road. Before he could turn, the door had clicked shut and there was no way on God's green earth that he would ever find it again. He felt his blood run cold. He was out here. Out on the outside with God alone knew what horrors. He had spent the last days keeping his eyes on the ground, worrying about things within mere inches of his head. But now . . . now, he had no choice. Now he *had* to look. No more turning his back on the misty marshlands of Bermondsey. Now, as the sun burned gold through the purple strips of cloud, he could see the peasants clearly. Their tents reached east and west as far as he could see and he knew there were more at Blackheath and beyond the Aldgate. For all he knew, the entire city was surrounded and death was in the air. Yet, in the camp there was laughter and music – the riff-raff were having a holiday, though there was nothing holy about it. The cross of St George floated wide, along with the stolen banners of Kent. Mother of God, they were playing football!

The city, once he had crossed the bridge, was unnaturally quiet. There had been times when he could barely move for the throng of people in East Cheap. In the market, most of the stalls stood empty, the odd cow's carcass twirling slowly from its chain. Chickens in their coops looked up at him with their wild, inquisitive eyes, wondering if he was the man for whom they would die today. He turned left along the Cheap, past St Michael's Lane and St Martin Ongar. The Ropery lay to his left, between the tall workshops and the river, miles of hemp lying in huge coils ready to be transported to the ships. But the ships at Dowgate and St Paul's rode silently at anchor, their sails furled, their gangplanks up and barred. Grim-looking captains paced their decks, armed to the teeth, watching the river and the land beyond.

The Steelyard was silent. No clanking metal, no roar of furnaces. It was as though Death himself had come calling and had left no one alive. It had been like this, Chaucer knew, in the days of his boyhood, when the Pestilence had claimed its thousands and all that moved on the roads were the dead carts, their ghastly loads slipping and lurching over the cobbles. Even the bells of the great churches were still today, as if time itself had stopped.

Chaucer stepped over the long-dried-up ditch of the Walbrook, making for Bridge Row. Here he met trouble for the first time.

'Where are you going?' A rough-looking man stopped him.

'That's my business,' Chaucer said.

The man chuckled and two others joined him. 'Not any more, matey,' he said. 'This is Walbrook Ward and we're keeping it safe.'

'So am I,' Chaucer said and flashed his royal badge, 'on the King's business.'

'The King?' the man blinked.

'The Lord's Anointed,' Chaucer felt he had to explain, 'runs the country.'

'Not for much longer,' one of the others said.

'I'm surprised you boys aren't at the Old Change.'

'Old Change?' the first man echoed. 'Why?'

Chaucer beckoned him closer. 'The peasants,' he murmured. 'They've taken St Paul's.'

'Never!' all three men chorused.

'I've just come from there,' Chaucer lied. 'Never seen so much gold. Those monks, eh?'

'Right,' the first man said, grasping his halberd. 'Old Change, eh?'

'Better hurry,' Chaucer said. 'From what I hear, old Wat Tyler's got most of it already.'

And he couldn't help chuckling as he heard their feet clattering away to the west.

Needlers' Lane looked as under siege as the Tabard. Shutters were closed and locked, spaces boarded up. There was no one about. He knocked on the door of the Gillis house and workshop. Nothing.

'Go away!' a voice snarled from overhead to his right.

Chaucer stepped backwards and looked up. From between the oak cross-beams an old woman was scowling down at him.

'Good afternoon, gammer,' he touched his liripipe. 'My

name is Geoffrey Chaucer, Comptroller of the King's Woollens.
I'm looking into the death of Mistress Gillis.'

To his slight surprise, the old girl spat volubly onto the cobbles,
narrowly missing the Comptroller of Woollens. Well, that says it
all, Chaucer thought. Did she speak for the whole street? The old
woman disappeared for a moment, then reappeared with a banner
bearing the lilies and leopards of the King. She poked her head
out again. 'There's nothing to steal in this house,' she hissed.
'We're for the King, we are!'

'So am I, madam,' Chaucer said. 'To the extent of comptrolling his woollens.'

'You peasants can bloody well bugger off!' she shrieked,
seconds before she was dragged away by a younger woman,
whom Chaucer hoped would be a little more sane.

'Time for your evening nap, Mother,' she said, pushing the
old woman aside. She hauled the flag back in and filled
the window with her chubby face and ample bosoms. 'I'm
sorry, sir. It's Mother. She hasn't been right since they brought
in the Statute of Labourers and she was a bit iffy before that,
if you ask me. How can I help you, sir, in these strange times?'

'I am Geoffrey Chaucer,' he said for what felt like the
hundredth time, 'Comptroller of the King's Woollens. I am
making enquiries about Mistress Gillis.'

'Next door,' the woman said.

'Yes, I know.' Chaucer didn't want to risk this woman
disappearing too, so he spoke quickly. 'She's dead.'

'Oh.' The woman crossed herself.

'You are . . .?' he asked.

'Oh, mortified, of course.'

'No, I mean, what's your name?'

'Catherine,' she bobbed, catching her breasts on the sill, but
bearing it well. 'My husband Welkin and I are weavers here.
Can I say what an honour it is to make your acquaintance, sir?
We've often received offensive letters from your office. Nice
to put a face to it all.'

'Indeed.' Chaucer's smile was acid. 'But I am here on
another matter. Can I come in?'

'Oh, no, sir, that would be inappropriate. There's thousands
of peasants massing south of the river. And to the east. Probably

to the west, too, I shouldn't wonder. Welkin says I mustn't let anybody in. A woman isn't safe.'

'No,' Chaucer said. 'Fye Gillis certainly wasn't.'

'Dead, you say?'

'Murdered.' Chaucer's voice suddenly sounded very loud in that empty street. 'Found in the river with her throat cut.'

'Well, I never. Still, that's the Flemings for you.'

'They're not all that bad, surely?' Chaucer had always had good dealings with the people of the Scheldt, even if he wouldn't be happy to let his daughter marry one.

'Well, yes, they are,' Catherine said. 'But Fye was worse than most. Beat her kids. Never spoke to us. Had a smell under her nose. And money; obsessed with it, she was.'

'So, there may have been a few who wanted to see her dead?'

'Lord love you, sir, yes. None of 'em'll be opening their doors to you today, for obvious reasons, but there's the Blenkinsops at the sign of the ferret; the Inchbolds at the three chimneys; old Master Fingelhoot at the cordwainers . . .'

'Fingelhoot?' Chaucer repeated. 'That's a Flemish name, isn't it?'

'It is, sir,' Catherine beamed. 'Fye Gillis was so detested, even her own people had it in for her.'

There was a kerfuffle in the house and the woman turned away. 'Mother. For the love of God . . .' the rest of her words were drowned out by the noise of falling furniture. A moment later, Catherine was back. 'Sorry about that, sir. I have to go. And if I were you, I would too. You see, there's a crossbow trained on your back. And old Shattox, him what's holding it, he's a crack shot, he is. Goodbye, sir. Nice talking to you.'

Until Chaucer knew there was a crossbow bolt trained on his back, he had been unaware of the itch between his shoulder blades. But now, he could think of little else. He didn't know whether to turn round and confront old Shattox or to walk away and pretend he wasn't there. He remembered being given advice on just this situation, long, long ago when he was in the household of Lionel of Antwerp. He remembered being told that making the right decision could well be all the difference between life and death. Sadly, what he

*couldn't* remember was which choice to make. He would
have to work it out from basic principles, based on what he
knew. First, and most importantly, the man was a crack shot.
But he was also described as 'old'. But did that mean old,
as in old and decrepit with a shaking hand, or old as in
slightly older than young Shattox, his little brother. And did
a weaver's wife know a crack shot from a hole in the ground?
Had she seen the man in action? Overall, Chaucer decided,
the risk was vanishingly small. He turned his head and found
himself looking into a pair of evil, piggy eyes, set close
together over a beak of a nose. Old Shattox was definitely
old, but there wasn't a tremor to be seen and he had come
up behind Chaucer on silent feet, so he now stood a scant
yard behind him.

'I don't know who you are,' the old man grated, 'but we
don't want the likes of you bothering the likes of us. So pick
up your feet, you over-dressed popinjay, and get out of my
ward and be quick about it.'

Chaucer was somewhat startled to be termed a popinjay. If
he had ever been forced to describe his sartorial style, he
would have probably settled for neat but not gaudy. However,
the crossbow bolt said things that its wielder never could, and
he broke into as near to a trot as was compatible with his girth
and his sense of what was right and proper in the Comptroller
of the King's Woollens. He could see no one, but knew that
eyes would be peering down from every window. Once or
twice, he risked a glance behind him and found to his horror
that old Shattox also had a fair turn of speed. Without seeming
to ruffle a hair, the old man was keeping pace behind him,
stepping silently like a leopard among the lilies. Eventually,
and throwing everything to the winds, Chaucer ran, high-
stepping to prevent tripping in his moss-filled shoes. Sometimes
fashion could be the very devil.

After what seemed a lifetime, hot and out of breath, Chaucer
was at the Tabard, leaning, fighting for breath, against the
wooden walls. He looked around, expecting to see the crossbow
bolt inches from him but no – old Shattox had given up the
pursuit at an unknown point in Chaucer's flight and he was
nowhere to be seen. In the far distance, Chaucer thought he

could hear geriatric laughter, but wondered afterwards whether it was simply the blood drumming in his ears. With people like the old man out there, wandering the streets, he wondered whether the peasants were going to have quite such an easy time of it after all. Superior numbers did not always win the day. But now, to get back in.

Chaucer stood back and looked at the wooden structure in front of him. Hardesty had built right up to the edge of the road and the walls rose sheer into the westering sun. Chaucer shaded his eyes and tried to remember exactly where he had exited. Nothing looked familiar. Then he tried the expedient of putting his back to the wall and sidling along it, trying to find a point of view which seemed familiar. This had no helpful outcome. As he recalled it, the sweat beginning to pool, cold and frightening, in the small of his back, he had come out of the door bent low, to not attract the attention of any wandering scouts from the peasants' camps. So he tried looking at the roadway, for footprints, but although few had passed that way, the dust was still too scuffed to be of any help at all.

He went round to the gate. He was not too proud at this point to let it be known that he couldn't remember a simple thing like the way to get back in through a secret door. He was the cleverest man he knew, by a country mile, and was almost certain that everyone else agreed. Except John Gower, of course. And Nicholas Brembre. But they need never know. He tapped on the gates, where the great walls of timber met in a join so tightly fitted that it was almost indiscernible.

'Hoo,' he whispered to the join. 'Hoo? Can anyone hear me?' He tapped again then applied his ear to the wood. He could hear the low hum of voices, but nothing to suggest anyone had heard him. He cleared his throat and tapped again, calling this time. Surely, someone could hear him. 'Hoo! Hoo, the house! It's Geoffrey Chaucer! Hoo!' He sagged against the door, banging his head on it rhythmically. 'Hoo,' he almost sobbed. 'Hoo?'

A voice from behind him made him jump.

'Master Chaucer? Are you unwell?'

He spun round, almost in tears at the sound of a friendly

voice. Mistress Baillie stood there, a yoke around her neck hung with bags of flour, cheeses and eggs wrapped in straw, her hands carrying two enormous pails of milk.

'I . . . I can't remember how to get back in, Mistress Baillie,' he confessed. There was something about this woman that reminded him of his nurse when he was little, though he could give her a good ten years and then some. 'I . . . seem to have forgotten the magic latch.'

She rolled her eyes, practically the only part of her body not carrying something. 'No magic about it, Master Chaucer. You come with me and we'll soon have you safe inside.' She proffered a milk pail to him and for a moment he thought she was offering him a drink, which he could sorely do with. But before he made himself look more of a fool than he already did, he realized and took it from her, then the other.

'Ooh, that's better.' She flexed her fingers. 'Those things get heavy after the first mile. Now, you come with me.' She scuttled off round the corner and he followed, staggering a little under the weight of the pails. 'Look, see, it's simple. Master Hardesty explained it to me. If you look there,' she pointed, 'and there, you'll see two knots which aren't repeated in the next plank. Do you see?'

Chaucer peered short-sightedly and eventually nodded, just to make the woman move on. One knot was, when all was said and done, very much like another.

'Well, you just press them together, you see, like that,' there was a faint click, 'and the door opens inwards. Clever, Master Hardesty, isn't he? He hasn't much book-learning, but I think he may be the cleverest man I know. I'm thinking of naming my littlest one after him – Geoffrey John Hardesty; what d'you think?' She turned sideways to go through the narrow sally port and stood aside in the cramped space to let Chaucer follow. 'Just slam it to, would you, Master Chaucer? I'd be grateful if you could just help me to the kitchen with the milk, if you can.'

Chaucer was immediately on his mettle. 'Of course I can, Mistress Baillie. Anything to help.'

She turned round to face him with a smile. 'And don't worry,' she said, patting his arm gently, so as not to spill the milk, 'I won't tell them you couldn't get back in.' And, chuckling gently, she led the way to the kitchen through the crowded yard.

Simon of Sudbury was pacing the cold, stone floor of St John's Chapel at the Tower. For all it was June, St John's was always cold as a witch's tit and the Archbishop of Canterbury was in no mood to put up with it. He roared at his sacristan to bring him a toddy of mulled wine – 'plenty of poker!' he shouted at the man's retreating back.

Only God knew what time it was. June's long-lighted day had long gone and the Tower slept. Apart, that is, from Sudbury, his minions and the heavily armed guard prowling the battlements, looking anxiously to the south and east. The archbishop slumped into the sedilia, his special seat in this house of God. He was not a happy man. The peasants had ransacked his own cathedral at Canterbury, jostled his priests. They wanted his head, apparently, because he had had a hand in the raising of the poll tax. Ingrates! They had had thirty years, those greedy, grasping bastards, of high wages far above their worth. And when he had decided, along with Bobby Hailes, to pay their dues via the poll tax, they'd had the effrontery to go on the rampage. They were beasts of burden, for God's sake, life unworthy of life. And now, he realized as he sat there, brooding, they would make for his palace at Lambeth.

And that was not all. He rummaged in his purse, the one heavy with gilt crosses, and pulled out the parchment. It had been there, on and off, since he had received it days ago. The hand was literate, but the spelling odd. In the candlelight from the altar, it flickered in his vision, black lines on the sepia, damning Sudbury to all eternity.

'Bishop, you were then when the deed was done,' it said, 'breaking your vows and hers. Filthy degenerate, unnatural beast. God sees your guilt and so do I. Let the church courts hear of it and the word reaches the Pope himself. Give alms, womanizer, breaker of God's laws. Leave one hundred nobles as your pieces of silver, at the sign of the Sun in Portsoken.'

This was their work; the peasants. Sudbury had no doubt about it. But how did they know, this rabble from Kent, about

that business all those years ago? Why the Sun? Why
Portsoken? Where the Hell, in fact, *was* Portsoken?

'A groat for your thoughts, Archbishop.'

The voice made him turn. 'Bobby Knollys,' Sudbury instinctively got to his feet. 'I was expecting the King.'

'It's late,' Knollys said, lighting another candle and noting
the speed with which Sudbury pocketed the parchment in his
hand, 'or early, depending on your point of view.'

'I know,' Sudbury fumed. 'I've been waiting for the little
shit all day. Did you tell him I need to see him?'

'I did, Sudbury,' Knollys said. 'His Grace's mind is on
other things. His bride-to-be, for instance.'

'Anne of Bohemia?' the archbishop snorted. 'That'll never
happen. What news of the peasants?'

Knollys dragged the Bishop of London's sedilia closer to
Sudbury's and sat down. 'The Essex riff-raff are at Mile End
and the Kentishmen at Blackheath, but I assume you know
that.'

'I do.'

'I've brought the King here because the bastards seem to
be loyal to him. Perhaps he can talk them out of their nonsense.'

'Richard?' Sudbury scoffed. 'Don't make me laugh, Knollys.
I'm still having nightmares about his coronation.'

'He *was* only ten, Archbishop.' Knollys was a grandfather;
he'd learned to make allowances for offspring.

'Well, after tomorrow – or whenever the little snot gets
round to seeing me – it won't matter.'

'Oh?' Knollys raised another eyebrow. 'Why not?'

'Because,' Sudbury hauled up a canvas bag that was lying
at his feet, 'I am resigning my post as Lord Chancellor of
England,' and he pulled out the gold chain of office, flinging
it onto the altar.

Knollys smiled. 'You think the peasants will accept that,
do you, Archbishop?' he asked. 'All, I fear, too little and too
late.'

# NINE

Geoffrey Chaucer had fallen into his bed on Wednesday night and slept like the dead. He had expected to dream after what anyone would consider to be a very difficult day but, if he had, he had no memory on waking. John Gower had gone to bed later than his friend and had lain down next to him with trepidation. If he couldn't get to sleep before the comptroller, he knew he would still be awake at dawn. But, to his surprise, Chaucer slept the night through without a sound. In fact, he was so quiet that Gower poked him in the back several times, just to make sure he hadn't died suddenly in the night. So both men were refreshed and ready for almost anything as they sat breaking their fast on another sunny morning. The sun, though not yet high in the sky, promised another hot day and although it was pleasanter than rain, which they knew would turn the yard to a stinking morass, a cooling breeze would be welcome about now, just to shift the stifling air around a little more. Men grew testy on days like this, and with the miller's body lying in unquiet rest in a stable, it would not be a good idea to let tempers run high. Some of the current occupants of the Tabard had begun to question whether it was safer to be inside with a clearly homicidal maniac, or to be outside, taking their chances with the peasants. Hardesty was doing his best, patrolling in front of the door in case anyone was foolish enough to try to open it. But he was only one man and, forceful though he was, that was unlikely to be enough.

But for now, sitting in a shady parlour, with dust motes dancing in the sunbeams coming through the gaps in the boards nailed over the window, Gower and Chaucer were intent on enjoying the newly made bread, freshly churned butter and slices of home-cured ham that Mistress Baillie had managed to conjure from almost nothing. Granted, the slices were thin and the butter arrived already spread on the bread, but bearing in mind the number she and the cook were having to feed, it was nothing short of miraculous. No one knew what the next meal might bring, but for now, the Tabard's denizens were happily chewing. The well was holding out, so there was no fear of going thirsty.

But eventually, the meal could not be dragged out any further and the miller and his murder had to be brought to the table. Although nothing had been said, Chaucer's position in the King's household had made him a natural choice for deciding on what should happen next. Maghfield – as by far the richest man in the inn at that moment – had been mooted by some, but he had refused their requests. The priest, Ambrosius, had also refused, although the cohort in favour of him was much smaller, being mainly Madame Eglantyne and her silent nun and a rather insignificant little woman who, in saner times, had been a mainstay at every service St Olave's had to offer, saying that he answered only to God and so should everyone else. He had crossed himself elaborately and left the room, muttering about needing to be about his devotions.

Chaucer let it be known that he would wait in the best parlour if anyone had anything to tell him about the death of Inskip the miller. He didn't expect an onslaught, but as the morning wore on, few people had made their way to see him. Baillie had looked in, mainly to wonder aloud when the miller would stop stinking up his stable. He had only just got it usable again after the body of Mistress Gillis had been removed. Did Chaucer, for example, intend to send it to the sacristan of St Olave's, who seemed to be a particularly gullible churchman? Chaucer was not convinced of the man's gullibility; he was, on the contrary, more or less convinced that when the current situation had passed, he would be dealing with a very angry sacristan indeed. But sufficient unto the day was the evil thereof, and Fye Gillis's body could wait. Chaucer fobbed Baillie off with vague pseudo-legalese, muttering 'questio quid juris', and he settled back to the quiet, fly-humming warmth of the June morning.

Chaucer didn't realize he had been asleep until a small noise from the other side of the table jerked him out of his nap. He opened his eyes to find a pair of piercing eyes staring at him from across the table. If he had ever known the name of the man opposite, he had forgotten it now, so he smiled hopefully and waited for him to introduce himself. For a good few moments, the man just continued to stare, but finally stirred himself to speak.

'I've come to confess,' he said, in gentle tones which were at odds with his basilisk stare.

Chaucer stirred himself and prepared for an odd few minutes. The man was sitting down, but even so it was not hard to work out that he was considerably under five foot tall, and if he weighed a quarter of a sack of wool when wringing wet, it would be a wonder. For him to overpower Fye Gillis and cut her throat to the spine would have been difficult, for she was a big woman with strong hands and arms, as her children could attest. For him to overpower the miller would be a total impossibility. The man had been built like a wrestler.

'Confess to what?' Chaucer prompted.

The man rolled his eyes. 'The murders, of course,' he said, with a tut. 'The woman in the river and the miller last night. As well as all the others, of course, the ones you don't know about yet.'

'Ah, those,' Chaucer said, mildly. 'Many of those, are there?'

The man opposite raised a thumb and grasped it with his other hand. 'First,' he said, 'there was Edward of Woodstock; then his old dad, Edward III. Oh, and I nearly forgot – that French bastard, Bertrand du Guesclin. But after them, yes, that woman in the river, and last night, the miller.' He leaned forward, his hands flat on the boards. 'You can't let yourself get stale, you know. You lose the knack, if you do that.' He waved one hand in the air, as delicate as a girl's. 'Artist's hands, these are. They can drain the life out of you like that.' He clicked his fingers and Chaucer jumped. 'You may well jump, Master Chaucer. Oh, yes, indeed you may!'

The little man sat back complacently, his fingers laced across his stomach. Chaucer was a little lost for words. But finally, he said, 'Well, thank you for coming to see me, Master . . .?'

'Gaunt. But you can call me John.'

'Ah.' Chaucer smiled, the very special smile men reserve for those weak in the head but who nonetheless might suddenly

knife them to death. 'Well . . . John. As no one can leave the
Tabard at the moment, consider yourself under house arrest.
And please . . .' he paused.

'Yes? Anything I can do to help, of course.'

'Thank you,' Chaucer murmured. 'Really, too kind. If you
could please refrain from killing anyone else, I would be *so*
grateful.'

'It would be my pleasure.' The little man slid down from
the chair and made for the door with an exaggerated swagger.
'And,' he laid his finger alongside his nose, 'I'll keep this
between ourselves, of course.' He bowed and was gone.

'Of course,' Chaucer said to thin air. 'Let's do that, shall
we?' He closed his eyes and laid his head back on the hard
wood of the settle. They walk among us, he realized, and not
for the first time. He heard the rustle of clothing and someone
cleared their throat. He opened his eyes and started. 'Master
Maghfield. I didn't expect to see you this morning.' His brow
clouded. 'I don't think . . . I don't think I owe you any more
money, do I?' With Maghfield, one never knew.

'Indeed not, Master Chaucer, although, I could check my
book if . . .'

'No, no.' Chaucer laughed, a little nervously. 'It's just . . .
I am a little surprised to see you.'

'I'm here to tell you I was with Master Inskip last night,
Master Chaucer. Of course, I don't know quite when he died,
but I can assure you it was not while he was with me.' The
merchant venturer laughed, slapping the table for emphasis.

'I would not have thought that you and Master Inskip had
much in common,' Chaucer said. 'Though circumstances can
bring us all strange bedfellows.'

'Indeed, Master Chaucer,' Maghfield agreed. 'Who would
ever have imagined, for instance, that you and I would ever
share a bed, and yet we do.'

'That's very true,' Chaucer said. 'These times have brought
us all experiences we might otherwise have missed. I hope
my snoring doesn't cause you too much distress. My dear wife
has often commented, over the years.'

'I fill my ears with wool, appropriately enough,' Maghfield
said. 'It cuts out every sound, from the priest muttering his

rosary to your snores lifting the thatch. But let me tell you about last night, if I may?'

'Indeed.' Chaucer leaned forward, fingers interlaced. 'Where did you meet? Let's start with that.'

'Before we do, let me tell you that it was Miller Inskip who asked to meet and also he who decided where it was to be. But he never told me what he wanted to talk about, because we were interrupted.'

Chaucer held up a hand. 'Let's first establish where.'

'Of course. I am ahead of myself. We met in the stable in which he was found dead.'

Maghfield spoke so plainly that Chaucer was briefly taken aback. 'So . . . you were with him last night in the place where he was found dead?'

'Did I not say so?'

'But . . . you must see how that looks?' Chaucer knew the merchant venturer was not stupid, so he obviously had more to say. But what?

'I do. But as I say, we were interrupted. It was, in fact, not an incident which is easy to tell you about, Master Chaucer, and I am a man who has seen most things and done a good many. As Master Inskip was coming slowly to his point . . . if I may digress here, I think he was beginning to lose his nerve and wish he had not spoken, but I may be wrong and we will never know now. As he was approaching the reason for the meeting, we heard a noise and, after a moment, peeped out to see what or who it was. I won't keep you in suspense, Master Chaucer. It was, to be blunt, Father Ambrosius and Nell, the whore, doing what you can probably imagine, given her calling.'

'Father *Ambrosius*?' Chaucer was appalled.

'Indeed, the very same.' Maghfield sat back and put his hands flat on the table. 'I was, as you clearly are, somewhat taken aback.'

'Father Ambrosius and *Nell*?'

'Yes,' Maghfield said, beginning to get a little testy. 'Would it have been less shocking had it been some other woman? I can't believe you have lived so sheltered a life that you don't know that this goes on, Master Chaucer. Being a man of the cloth does not stop a man having natural urges, I am sure you already know.'

'Of course I do. Of course, but . . . they seem an unlikely couple, somehow. More unlikely than others, shall we say?' Until this moment, Chaucer had forgotten the couple's tête-à-tête in the gardens of the Falcon in Dartford.

'They didn't seem to be having any trouble with the coupling bit,' Maghfield said, with a knowing leer. 'They had been outside the stable – did I say, they weren't under cover, just leaning on the wall under the overhanging roof – for a matter of moments before we looked out to see who was disturbing us, and they were already well into their stride. Father Ambrosius, I might add, has unusually muscular calves.'

Chaucer winced. This was more than enough information.

'Nell winked at me as I made good my escape. I don't expect that Father Ambrosius was her only customer that night, and she was asking me by gesture if I was interested in being next.'

Chaucer, in his role of interrogator, felt he had to ask the next question. 'And were you?'

Maghfield laughed. 'Master Chaucer, although I love my wife, I will not deny that I have had my share of ladies of doubtful character, shall we say? But I have never been desperate enough to sink to the level of Nell. But I believe – if I read *his* wink aright – that the miller was planning to be next in line. He certainly stayed behind when I left the stable.'

Chaucer sat up straighter. 'So, the last you saw of Master Inskip was in the stable?'

'That's right. I went back into the inn and had an ale or two. When I went to bed, you and Master Gower were asleep.'

'I see. And was Father Ambrosius back in his bed?'

Maghfield thought for a moment. 'No. And I don't believe he went to bed all night.' He smiled at Chaucer. 'Or at least, not *our* bed.'

'I see.' Chaucer could see a difficult interview ahead. 'Well, thank you very much for being so frank, Master Maghfield. Blunt, one might almost say. But it has given me a far better idea of Master Inskip's movements last night' – the merchant venturer gave vent to a rather evil chuckle – 'so to speak, so . . . yes, well, very helpful. I wonder if you would be so kind as to ask Father Ambrosius to come in and see me, if you happen to bump into him in the next little while?'

Maghfield got up and bowed low. 'Master Chaucer, it would be my very great pleasure.' And he swept out.

Chaucer had hardly had a moment to collect his thoughts when Father Ambrosius stormed in, his face purple above his drab habit.

'I have just been told by Maghfield to come to see you,' he blustered, stamping up and down the room, his habit flying, his eyes aflame. 'I don't know why a merchant and usurer thinks he can tell me what to do. I am, after all, Master Chaucer, a man of God!' He leaned on the table and thrust his face forward so that Chaucer, short-sighted as he was, could see every vein in his engorged eyeballs. 'Or you, for that matter. Who are *you* to tell me what to do? Servants of Mammon, the lot of you!'

Chaucer kept his voice calm and even. 'Do try to calm down, Father,' he said, gently. 'If Master Maghfield made it sound like an order, I am sure that was not what he intended. It was certainly not what *I* intended. By no means. I simply wanted to have a word with you about last night.'

The priest snapped his head up and flared his nostrils. 'I was in bed before dark, slept through until cock crow! Apart from when your snoring kept me awake!' he snapped.

'Well, you see,' Chaucer said, 'I happen to know that you didn't come to our room last night, and one way I know you are lying is that I know from my friend Master Gower that I didn't snore at all last night. Too exhausted, I suspect, after a rather exciting day, what with one thing and another. But to prevent our getting off on the wrong foot, Father, perhaps we can pretend that you haven't spoken and begin all over again. How does that sound?' He waited quietly until the priest began to look calmer. He hadn't spent much time with the man and had never really taken much notice of him. He simply seemed to be all of a piece with Madame Eglantyne and her nun and anyone in a room with the prioress did have a tendency to disappear. Looked at dispassionately, the priest was not an unattractive man and Nell had done well to enjoy his attentions before she had to deal with the miller. He was tall and straight-backed, with the hair around his tonsure strong and springing, with a tendency to curl. But his face was marred by a truculent expression and a tendency to look under his lids at people – instead of full in the face – made him look untrustworthy. It was a face at odds with his calling and Chaucer feared that he would rise no further than a humble parish priest; this man was no bishop-in-waiting, that was certain. Eventually, the man pulled out the chair pushed under the table by Maghfield and sat down, but on the edge of the seat, one leg curled under, ready to spring away should he need to. Chaucer waited for the man to speak.

'I . . . I spent the night in prayer, Master Chaucer,' the priest said, taking a deep breath and folding his hands together piously.

'Oh, I see,' said Chaucer. 'So, that is what you choose to call it, is it?'

'Call what?' The priest bridled and made as if to go.

Chaucer was at the end of his patience. 'Oh, for the love of God, pardoning me, of course,' he said. 'Don't play the injured innocent with me. You were with Nell in the stable yard last night. You were seen. And heard. Apparently,' he said, with the air of a man delivering a final shot, 'you have very muscular calves.'

'I . . . I was ministering to her immortal soul.' The priest spat it out as if that clinched the matter. 'We were meditating on the Gospel of Luke, the Sermon on the Mount, specifically.'

'I see. Heady stuff for someone of her calling.'

'Nell is eager to learn,' Ambrosius said. 'If someone saw us close together . . .'

'Oh, yes,' Chaucer nodded. 'Very close together, by all accounts.'

'Well, that was why. I was whispering, because it was late and we didn't want to disturb anyone.'

Chaucer nodded again. 'Well, this sounds very convincing, Father Ambrosius, I must say. But perhaps before you go, we could have a word with Nell, see what she says. If you would like to make yourself comfortable . . .' Chaucer went to an

inner door and called through to ask someone to find Nell and
send her in to see him. It didn't take long; Nell liked to stay
where the crowds were, there were plackets to be picked,
purses to be cut, plans to be made for the hours of darkness;
Nell did her best work in crowds.

'You wanted to see me, Master Chaucer?' Her eyes lit on
Ambrosius, sitting sullenly in his chair. 'Oh, Amby! Fancy
seeing you here!' She waddled up to him and pressed herself
against his side, pressing her cheek on his bald head. 'Ooh,
you need a shave, my lovely. Getting a bit bristly here on top.'
She planted a kiss on the priest's cowed head.

'Father Ambrosius here says that the two of you were
meditating last night,' Chaucer said, trying to keep a straight
face.

The woman let a peal of laughter screech out into the room.
'Meditating? That's a new one! We was swiving, pure and
simple. And, Master Chaucer,' she leaned forward, giving
Chaucer an unwelcome though mercifully brief glimpse of
the horrors inside her bodice, 'I have to say, that for a man
of the cloth, he's got a few surprises up his sleeve. For
example, did you know that if you—'

'Stop!' For the first and only time in their lives, Chaucer
and Ambrosius spoke as one. 'Detail of that kind is unneces-
sary, thank you, Nell,' Chaucer continued. 'Although many
men would say that your word is not worth the breath you
use to speak it, I do have a witness, one whose word I *do*
believe.'

'Can't be the miller,' the woman mused. 'He's dead. So . . .
no,' she looked up, her face wreathed in smiles. 'I can't think.
Who is it?'

'I don't think you need to know,' Chaucer said, on his
dignity. 'But you have answered my next question. I take it
that you and the miller . . .'

The woman laughed again. 'Like a couple of weasels. He
wasn't much to look at, God rest his soul, but he could . . .'
she glanced at their faces. 'Well, let's just say that yes, he did
take advantage of my good nature after Amby here had finished.
And *what* a finish!' This time she doubled up laughing and
then started coughing. Chaucer had to get up to pat her back,

because clearly Father Ambrosius didn't intend to touch her with a ten-foot pole.

'What happened when the miller had also finished?' Chaucer asked, resuming his seat.

'Well, I had a couple of groats in me placket, I didn't fancy any more of that business, so I bedded down under the new woodwork that Hardesty done. Piles of sawdust there, comfy and not as crowded as a room.'

'I think I meant, what happened to the miller?' Chaucer remarked.

'I'll *tell* you what happened to the miller,' the priest suddenly screamed, standing up suddenly and knocking the chair over, pointing with a trembling finger. 'She cut his throat for him, that's what happened to *him*!' He wiped his mouth with the back of his hand, strings of spittle flying in the warm, lifeless air. 'Take her up in chains, that's what you want to do to *her*! As it says in Thessalonians, for a prostitute is like a deep pit; a harlot is like a narrow well. Indeed, she lies in wait like a robber, and increases the unfaithful among men.'

Chaucer looked a little puzzled.

'I can see you are puzzled, Master Chaucer,' Nell said. 'Don't worry about racking your brain – let me tell you why that doesn't sound right. It's because it isn't from Thessalonians at all. It's from Proverbs. All the best bits which people trot out to try and make me and my sisters look small are.' She smiled a gappy smile at Ambrosius. 'Don't try and do the priest bit, Amby. Not till you've got a better hang of it.' She favoured Chaucer with a smile, which was unexpectedly sweet, missing teeth notwithstanding. 'Old Coggy here's no more a priest than you are.' She peered in the sun-barred gloom. 'You ain't a priest, I assume?'

'No!' Chaucer was rather outraged. 'I am, madam, the Comptroller of the King's Woollens.'

'Course you are, yes. I heard that. Only,' she wiped a grimy hand over her tangled head, 'I just wondered, with the bald bit and that. Anyway, this 'un ain't a priest either. If he quotes the Bible, he nine times out of ten gets it wrong.'

'I *knew* it,' Chaucer said. 'I *knew* the Sermon on the Mount wasn't in Luke.'

'Course it ain't,' Nell agreed. 'Matthew, every knarre knows that. Did he say Luke?' She threw an arm around Ambrosius's shoulder and gave him a malodorous squeeze. 'I don't know. He's so . . . well, to put it straight with you, Master Chaucer, he used to be plain Cog Buckley, as cunning a thief as you could wish. But then, he heard about Wat Tyler, John Ball, all these peasants . . . he could see a way of making more money, quicker than winking, than he usually took in a year.'

'So, you're saying . . .?' Chaucer didn't want to put words in her mouth.

'He's a spy, yes.' She gave the priest another squeeze. 'Don't go all sulky on me, Coggy,' she said. 'It was bound to come out in the end.'

Ambrosius found his voice. '*She's* a spy. *She* is! Not me! Her!'

He was still screaming when Hardesty and a few stout men came running at the sound of the noise and he was still screaming when they carried him off, wrapped tightly in the arms of two of Baillie's biggest lads.

In the silence which followed, Nell turned to Chaucer and shrugged a bony shoulder. 'Well,' she said, 'he would say that, wouldn't he?'

'Mary and Joseph!' Harry Baillie had been dreading this moment for days. And now, it was here. He had taken his turn on the watch because, after all, these were his rooftops and if *he* wasn't seen to be protecting them, who would? So he was the first to see the little knot of men, bristling with arms, scurrying along the alleyway beyond the Tabard. They were dragging something with them. Mother of God! Was that a bombard? Baillie had heard of such things, monstrous cannon that thundered like God's voice and smashed the walls of castles to rubble. What chance would the Tabard have against that? And here were the peasants, hauling one into position.

Tom Hardesty was at his side in an instant, scanning the roads to left and right.

'It's them, Hardesty,' Baillie half-screamed, grabbing handfuls of Hardesty's jerkin and shaking him hysterically. 'The devils. With a bombard. They're here.'

'They are,' the yeoman nodded and Baillie was both appalled and astonished that the man had not loosed a dozen arrows already. In fact, his bow was still slung across his back. He shook Baillie off and screwed up his eyes against the glare of the sun reflected off the load the little band was dragging. 'I count seven of them,' he said. 'And the odd thing is, they're coming from the north, while the peasants are across the river, to the south.'

'Well, that says it all.' Baillie refused to leave his panic behind. 'We're surrounded! We're all going to die!'

'Undoubtedly,' Hardesty said quietly, 'but not here. And not today. And that's not a bombard, by the way; it's what we here in the real world call a cart.'

Baillie blinked and took several deep breaths. Hardesty was right. But even so . . .

'Hoo the inn!' the leader of the seven souls called out, unbuckling his kettle hat and standing bareheaded in the sun. The kerfuffle on the ramparts had brought people running, Chaucer among them. Maghfield's falchion was in his hand. John Gower's heart was in his mouth.

'Ludlum?' Chaucer called down. 'Ludlum, is that you?'

'Larger than life, Master Chaucer,' the man called back.

'And Alice!' the comptroller pounded the rail, 'and Doggett! These are friends of mine, Hardesty. We must let them in.'

'Friends?' Maghfield scowled.

'Well, servants, actually, I suppose. Ludlum is the gate-keeper at the Aldgate. Doggett runs an inn, Harry, in the shadow of St Katherine Colemanchurch.'

'Joy,' Baillie growled. Just what he needed; another ale-waterer taking up space.

'Alice's blood pudding is to die for,' Chaucer told everybody. It was an unfortunate choice of words, but the damage was done.

'What's in the cart, Master Ludlum?' Hardesty wanted to know.

The gate-keeper clicked his fingers and two of his men hauled the canvas cover off the wagon. Bows lay there, long and cross, with a clutter of swords and axes. Arrows were packed in dozens in sacking bundles. Boxes and bags wedged in among the weapons held food, if the ham hock sticking out of one was anything to go by. Hardesty smiled. 'Welcome to the Tabard, sir,' he said, nudging Baillie in the ribs.

'Er . . . oh, yes,' the innkeeper said. 'My house is your house.' And Chaucer was already scrambling down the steps to the yard.

The door seemed to take an age to grind open, with the weights moving at a snail's pace, but finally, the little group were inside the walls of the Tabard and the cart was unloaded almost before the doors closed. 'What's happening at home, Ludlum?' the comptroller asked.

'Well, sir,' the man looked grim. 'That's why we're here. The Aldgate's open.'

'Open?' Chaucer felt his jaw drop. True, he'd seen the peasants massing in the fields of Whitechapel from his very own window, but he somehow never imagined they'd get any further. 'Forced by the mob?' he checked.

'Forced, my arse . . . oh, begging your pardon, sir.'

Chaucer nodded to excuse the lapse – the language was understandable, given the circumstances.

'No, Alderman Tonge let 'em in.'

'Willy Tonge?' Chaucer was astonished. 'Why, in God's name?'

'Shitting himself'd be my guess,' Ludlum said. 'Made a speech outside your very own door, sir, saying as how he could see the peasant's point of view.'

'Could he?' Chaucer said grimly. 'Could he, indeed?' The world was lost.

'At least he won't see it for long,' Ludlum beamed. 'I hit the alderman a little too hard, I think. They say he's lost an eye.'

'Shame,' Chaucer muttered. Then, realization dawned. 'Hardesty, Baillie, John, anybody else who cares to join us. The peasants are in the city. We need to talk.'

'Let me tell you, my people, how that place began.' Life on the road, after his enforced stay in Maidstone Gaol, had suited Father John Ball. His cheeks were less hollow, his eyes, still sunken, shone brightly. He was free, like all his brothers and sisters around him in Royal Street that day. 'The Marshalsea is Hell on earth, ordained by King Edward III in his dotage, to confine our people within the verge; that is, within twelve miles of his royal personage.'

'Devil take him,' Jack Chub grunted. He'd never stood this close to the powers that had become before and it had gone to his head a little.

'Devil already has,' Will Lorkin reminded him. 'Four years since.'

'Oh, yes, right.'

'Look at those walls,' Ball yelled. 'The keeper is a tormentor without pity.'

'He's got to reckon with us!' Lorkin shouted.

'Right you are, friend,' Ball smiled. 'God stands with us. And we cannot fail!'

There was a roar from the mob as gunpowder burst open the gates of the Marshalsea, its oak portal hanging loose on its hinges, burning. A handful of guards inside disappeared as the peasants swarmed in, scrabbling for keys and hauling doors off their hinges.

'Torch it!' Lorkin and Chub heard Wat Tyler shout. 'I don't want to see one stone left standing on another.'

And the slaughter went on.

Will Lorkin leaned his aching back against the Marshalsea's one remaining wall. Jack Chub was with him, sitting cross-legged on the ground.

'Somehow,' Chub said, 'I expected rather more.'

'What of, Chubby?' Lorkin asked.

'Well, a bit of gratitude, for a start, from the knarres we broke out of gaol earlier today.'

'Didn't you get that?'

'Nah. One of 'em asked if I had a handy sister hanging around, a mother at a pinch. Another nicked my knife.'

'You got off lightly,' Lorkin grunted. 'One of 'em gave me a kiss.'

'Get away!'

'That's what I said to him,' Lorkin nodded. 'I put it down to gaol fever.'

'Hoo, you fellows!'

Chub and Lorkin leapt to attention, as they had done all their lives. Wat Tyler cantered past them on somebody else's horse. 'You're not here to stand around chewing the fat and drinking my wine. Knock that wall down. That's London Bridge ahead. And it's time we crossed it.'

John Gower and Geoffrey Chaucer had been friends for years, but rarely visited each other at home. Chaucer's tiny room above the Aldgate was not built for entertaining and Gower's house, to Chaucer's mind, was too full of bustle, children and women to be conducive to chats. So Gower had never had one of Alice's signature sambocades, complete with preserved fig topping. Chaucer had grown quite used to it and sat toying with the crumbs as he usually did in the Aldgate when it appeared at his elbow as he worked, but Gower was all but bathing in it, as a bird will bathe in dust on a hot day.

'If I knew you ate like this, Geoffrey,' he said eventually, in a shower of crumbs, 'I would have visited you sooner.' He prodded the scant remains with a forefinger. 'Will she give the recipe to my Marian, do you think, when all this is over?'

Chaucer smiled, equally at the thought that Alice would part with her recipe as Gower's innocent belief that as soon as this little local difficulty was solved, everyone would be eating cheesecake. But it was good to see his friend so carefree, so he just nodded. 'I'm sure she will, John. I'm sure she will.' As he had heard Alice say more than once that her recipes would only be shared when they were prised from her cold, dead hands, he knew he was lying, but he had stopped worrying about being strictly truthful; it hardly seemed to matter, what with one thing and another.

'What other food have they brought, do you think?' Gower had now picked up every crumb with a damp forefinger and was looking longingly at Chaucer's platter, which he pushed across wordlessly.

'With Alice and Doggett, it's hard to know,' Chaucer said. 'I suppose it depends on what has been brought to the back door under cover of darkness.'

Gower was startled, but not enough to stop eating.

'I simply mean that Doggett has . . . friends, shall we call them? They bring him things which might not be considered strictly unpoached. But it's all quite fit to eat. No need to worry about that.'

Gower nodded and leaned back, as full of sambocade as a man could safely be.

Hardesty put his head around the door and Chaucer motioned him to come in. He brought a gust of the outdoors with him, a mix of dung, dust and danger.

'I just thought I'd tell you, Master Chaucer,' he said, nodding at Gower to include him. 'We've thrown Buckley the spy out through the main gates. Made a bit of a ceremony of it. He might have a few bruises he didn't have before – it's important to let men like him and the people he works for know that we don't allow that kind of behaviour. Some of the men wanted to kill him, but there'll be enough killing before this is over and I don't want blood on my hands that doesn't need to be there.'

Chaucer stayed in his seat but only because he had suddenly become weak at the knees. It was true that he hadn't given Hardesty instructions on what to do with the erstwhile priest and it was good, in a way, that the man's humanity had won through. But he had let a man out into the world who might well be – in Chaucer's mind was almost certainly – a murderer of at least two people. His mouth hung open and his eyes were wide. Hardesty became uneasy.

'Er . . . was that wrong, Master Chaucer?' he asked, knowing the answer as he did so.

'Master Hardesty . . . Tom.' Chaucer was fighting a losing battle for calm. 'Father Ambrosius, or Cog Buckley, as I suppose we should more correctly call him, was not just a spy.'

'No,' Hardesty added proudly, 'he was a thief and barrator as well. Not the kind of man we want here; and to be honest, having seen him at table, he eats for three, so we're well rid of him.' Despite this confident speech, Hardesty was still a little nervous of this plump little pen-pusher. Something told him there was a tiger within.

'He was all of that,' Chaucer agreed, 'and probably much more. A murderer, for example.'

'A . . . do you think he killed the miller?' Gower asked, agog.

'Well, yes, I do,' Chaucer said, bluntly. 'He had the opportunity, that's certain. All he needed was to step back into the shadows while Inskip and Nell . . . well, while Inskip and Nell. Then, while the miller was catching his breath, he moved silently behind him and . . .' with a graphic movement, Chaucer made the throat-slitting come alive.

'Are you saying he was *jealous*?' Hardesty could hardly contain his mirth. 'No one would be jealous where Nell is concerned. She . . . you must have noticed, Master Chaucer. Nell isn't exactly very choosy where she plies her trade. Buckley can't have imagined she was in love with him or anything. I'm not sure she knows the meaning of the word.'

'No, not jealous,' Chaucer said. 'But they have known each other for a very long while. She knew who he was, that he was a spy . . . might he be afraid that she had told the miller something?'

'If he was going to kill everyone who might have heard something from Nell,' Hardesty said, 'and I would like to say now, this is not from personal experience, but just from observation, she isn't about her business long enough to tell anyone the time of the day, let alone someone's innermost secrets. You'll have to do better than that.'

Chaucer banged his fist down on the table in frustration and made their platters jump. 'He was a thief, a barrator and a spy. What more reason does there have to be?' The comptroller just knew that Buckley was a wrong 'un, his tongue was just finding it hard to put its finger on the words.

'I assume,' Gower put in gently, trying to calm his friend down, 'that you think he killed Mistress Gillis as well.'

Chaucer looked shifty. 'That isn't quite so obvious, I will allow,' he said. 'But I can imagine that someone like Fye Gillis, who hadn't a good word for anyone, if she saw a chink in the covering armour of Buckley's habit, would have exposed him as soon as look at him. He would have had to silence her. It was you,' he nodded to Gower, 'who said the wounds were the same.'

Gower knew that was so. Hardesty grunted his agreement.

'So,' Chaucer decided to try to look on the bright side. 'Do we have any idea where Father Ambr . . . Cog Buckley might possibly be?' He smiled up at Hardesty, who wasn't fooled. The drumming fingers were too much of a giveaway.

Hardesty looked thoughtfully up at the ceiling. 'I . . . I understand he turned left, that is, to the east.'

'Very helpful, Master Hardesty,' Chaucer sighed. 'Very helpful. Well,' he looked up with defeated eyes, 'I expect you're very busy. Don't let me keep you.'

After a moment, Hardesty turned on his heel and slid out through the still-half-open door. Baillie, waiting for him outside, raised his eyebrows in silent query.

Hardesty shrugged in return then nodded slowly. 'It could have been worse,' he said. 'Much worse.' He clapped his hands and rubbed them together. 'Can't stay here, though. I have ramparts to patrol. Join me?'

# TEN

'Did you really think that Fath . . . can I still call him Ambrosius, Geoffrey? It's very confusing, all these names.'

'Whatever suits you, John.' Chaucer was almost at the point of not caring. If the murderer had gone, all to the good. If he was still in the inn, well – there were worse ways to die than a quick and merciful slash across the throat.

'I thought it was the husband, anyway,' said Gower, finding and nibbling at a piece of pie crust caught in a wrinkle in his hose.

'I know you did . . .' Chaucer paused, pensively. 'Shall we have a chat with him? See what he says when we put him in the glare of our combined brains? He would be a clever man to withstand it, I think.'

Gower sat up, intrigued. 'We can argue from both sides. That would be fun. I'll pretend to be his friend and you, because you're in a bad mood anyway, you can pretend to not like him.'

'I don't like him,' Chaucer pointed out.

'Well, in that case, it should be easy for you. As I recall from that Christmas masque at court four years or so ago, you're no actor.'

Chaucer bridled. 'I don't know how you can judge me on that. Who knows what a unicorn walks like? However, I think your idea is sound in principle. Do we know where he is?'

Gower spread his arms. 'Here, somewhere. He can't be hard to find.' Leaning back, he projected his voice to the inner door. 'Hoo! Boy! Someone!'

The door opened and Mistress Baillie's smiling face peeped round. 'Yes, Master Gower? I'm afraid I don't have any more sambocade.'

Gower smiled and rubbed his stomach. 'No more room,' he

said. 'No, what we want is a word with Master Gillis. Could he be found, do you think?'

'I'll send a lad,' she said. 'Any message?'

'No, no. Just that we would like a word.'

'You just wait there, lordings,' she said, 'and I'll get him found for you. He can't be far, can he?' And, chuckling, she went back to her kitchen.

It wasn't many minutes later that Arend Gillis walked in without knocking, leaving the door standing wide. 'You want me.' It wasn't a question.

'We would just like to have a word with you,' Gower said, 'about your wife.'

'Don't come the cooing dove with me, Gower,' Gillis said, throwing himself down on a chair and pushing it back from the table with one foot, making goblets wobble and platters jump. 'I didn't kill the miller. Like everyone else, I had a hundred reasons to, but didn't.' He stood up to go, but Chaucer, somewhat to his own amazement, was faster.

'Sit down, Master Gillis,' he said, slapping the table for emphasis. 'Not liking the bagpipes is no reason to kill a man. If you had other reasons, I would love to hear them.'

Taken completely by surprise, like a hawk attacked by a sparrow, Gillis sat back down with a thump. 'No . . . I . . . nothing specific, no. I just disliked the man. He smelt. And, yes, I hate the bagpipes. Who doesn't?'

'It seems to me,' Chaucer said, sitting down slowly in a way he hoped would appear threatening, 'that you are the only person who has a link to both dead bodies.'

Gillis looked at the poet amazed for a moment, then laughed. 'The only person? That's ridiculous!'

'Well, who else does?' Gower asked, mildly.

Gillis held up a thumb. 'To begin with,' he said, 'my children. They probably had more reason than I to kill their mother and they were here when the miller died.'

'Your *children*?' Gower for a minute forgot that he was supposed to be the nice one. 'You would accuse your *children*?'

Gillis shrugged. 'Why not? The boy is unreliable and stupid. The girl is . . . the same, I suppose I must say. I have never had much to do with them, to be brutally honest. That was my wife's duty.'

'And a fine job she made of it, too,' Chaucer said, through clenched teeth. When it came to absent parenting, he knew that he would top any list, but at least he ensured that his progeny were put into great houses where they would be given an upbringing to which he could never aspire.

Again, Gillis shrugged. 'She wasn't a nice woman,' he said. 'The miller wasn't a nice man. But I don't kill people for not being nice. No one but a madman would, surely? And if that were to be the only reason, which of us would still be alive today?'

The question stopped both his interrogators in their tracks. They took a few seconds to look back at their mildly chequered pasts and let the merchant win that one.

'So . . .' Gillis got up again. 'That's it, is it? The end of my questioning?'

It seemed wrong to say that he was right, but nothing else came to either mind, no matter how big the brains against him were. As he turned to leave, Chaucer thought of something, a question he hadn't asked.

'Where were you when the miller died?'

'I don't know when he died, so how can I answer that?'

Chaucer became more specific. 'Where were you during the hours of darkness?'

Gillis didn't sit but stood looming over Chaucer. 'I took my turn on the ramparts. Ask Hardesty when that was; he keeps a list. Then, I made sure that my children were sleeping soundly – yes, I am father enough for that. They were, and so I also went to bed, alongside my son and some others with whom I waste no chatter. These times have made for some strange bedfellows.'

'Did you go to the stables at all?' Gower asked. He was still hoping to trap the merchant by some clever questioning.

'Apart from the fact that I descended from the ramparts by the ladder near the gate, so necessarily near the stables, no. I heard muttered conversation from there, I think. I was taking no notice. Oh . . .' he held up a finger. 'I saw the priest and the drab walking that way. They made an odd couple, but these are odd times. Perhaps he was saving her immortal soul or something like that. She had her hand inside his habit; perhaps that's where he keeps his. His soul, that is.' He guffawed and they saw the man he could have been before Fye Gillis sucked the life out of him.

Chaucer nodded at Gower. This had a ring of truth, although the murderer might also know the movements of the people in question. 'You saw no one else?' Chaucer checked.

Gillis leaned down towards him, his knuckles on the table. 'I will tell you something now, Master Chaucer, and I will say it only once. If you repeat it, I will deny it. I know what you are implying and I can understand why. This inn has become a sink of iniquity. Men are roaming the place like beasts, waiting to find a likely bedfellow. The women, like-wise, have the glint of gold in their eye; there is money to be made out of every situation, Master Chaucer, and this one is no exception. I am a merchant. I know. But I am not one of those men. Believe it or not, I do have a love of my life. She is not my wife, nor ever can be, unless a miracle happens. She is married to another. But knowing that she is alive and that we can meet sometimes is what keeps me getting up each morning to meet the day. So, I do not stand in a line in the darkness to have five minutes with a woman who is not fit to let my beloved's shadow fall upon her. I do not follow kitchen maids. I did what I said I did. And now, I am going.'

His dramatic exit was rather spoiled by an unseemly colli-sion with Madame Eglantyne and her trailing nun in the doorway. Foo-Foo set up a caterwauling that the prioress soothed with crooning and a succession of treats which she kept secreted in her bosom. Eventually, she sat opposite Chaucer and next to Gower, in a billow of silk and an exhal-ation of attar of roses. Her nun stood silently just inside the door, blending into the hard shadows cast by the still-bright sun.

'Master Chaucer,' the prioress breathed, settling herself comfortably. 'As you know, I am all alone in the world now my nuns have left me and the miller is dead.'

Both men's eyes flicked to the woman by the door, but she showed nothing by word or movement.

'I know that Master Inskip was not a man to excite most people to throes of attachment, but I had got used to his little ways. You may not know, for instance, that he could play the flute quite beautifully. Oftentimes he would play for me and the sisters at our meals. Foo-Foo would be lulled quite to sleep by his playing. And now he's dead. I understand you seek his killer.'

'I have no jurisdiction, of course,' Chaucer pointed out. 'But there are similarities between Inskip's death and that of the woman found in the Thames by Hardesty, so—'

'Master Hardesty? No, he can't be the one!' The prioress buried her face in the dog's scant fur. 'He is our saviour. Oh, not our *Saviour*, of course, but he has certainly saved us from the mob.'

'No, no,' Gower placed his hand on the woman's arm for emphasis and Foo-Foo growled his warning. 'We simply mean that . . .'

'I won't have a word said against that wonderful man,' Eglantyne said, with stars in her eyes. 'You'll have to find someone else.'

Chaucer felt he must intervene. 'Like you, Madame Eglantyne,' he said, 'I can't believe it is Master Hardesty. But should it prove that we are wrong, we can't just choose someone else as the miscreant.'

The prioress raked him up and down with steely eyes and found him wanting. 'Why not?' she rapped out.

'It . . . it wouldn't be justice, madam.'

'Faugh!'

Chaucer hadn't heard anyone say that for years, not since his grandmother died.

'Justice!' she went on. 'There is no justice but God's and he would not be happy if Master Hardesty was found guilty of anything. God would be quite happy, however, if you chose some worthless knarre and . . . oh, I don't know. Cut his head off or something. Or hanged him; isn't that what happens?' She got up, tucking the lapdog under her arm. 'And don't even begin to argue with me, Master Chaucer. When it comes to knowing what God wants, I am the woman to ask.' She turned her head towards the open door. A sudden crash of falling platters made her jump. 'What's that noise?'

Harry Baillie, up on the ramparts taking water to the men watching the peasants and their steady advance, suddenly found his bowels turn to water. He wasn't sure how it had happened, but the empty roads which he had been looking at for the past days were suddenly full of men, silent, armed, all with faces upturned to the wooden walls of his inn. It was the silence which was so frightening. They didn't even seem to breathe, there was no rustle of clothing, no murmur of conversation. Just hundreds and hundreds of eyes, staring, unblinking up at them. Baillie reached out a trembling hand for Hardesty's arm – he found he needed to touch someone, just to be sure that he wasn't imagining what he was seeing. The touch of the rough cloth was reassuring, but the crowd outside remained.

'Tom.' Baillie thought that it was time enough to drop the formality. 'Tom. What do they want? Why are they so quiet?'

Hardesty had seen this just once before, at the siege of La Rochelle. Then, he had been in the silent throng and they had unnerved the castle so thoroughly that they had won the day before Nones. But now, he was on the other side and would not let anyone falter. Not on his watch. One by one, the guards on the ramparts took in the watching mob and they instinctively drew together. One, younger than the rest, shouted down to a girl crossing the yard with a pile of platters to be washed at the well, 'They're here. The peasants are here!' Although to him it was a manly shout, it came out like the squeak of a mouse. Nonetheless, the girl heard it, dropped her platters and ran for the door of the inn, shouting her news as she hurtled through the door.

Soon, everything was chaos. Hardesty had spent the days not just in building. He had been setting up watch bands, he had made sure that the more mature guests of Harry Baillie, the ones he thought would not panic or blunder about like moths in a candle flame, would be there to keep things calm and stable. So it was with some disappointment that he looked down into the yard to see Gower and Chaucer run out of the inn, eyes wild, liripipes askew.

Hardesty walked to the rail and leaned over. He lowered his voice to just above a whisper. 'Master Chaucer. Master Gower. Psst. Up here.'

The two poets swivelled their heads but didn't look up.

'Up *here*. Here! Oh, for the love of . . .' Hardesty put two fingers in his mouth and whistled. Baillie spun round as if stung and, finally, Gower focused on the yeoman, who put his finger to his lips. Gower nudged Chaucer, shushing him in his turn. They walked over to the bottom of the ladder and looked up.

'Stay down there,' Hardesty said, quietly. 'We've enough men up here for now. The peasants are outside.'

'What?' Gower's eyes were like turnips in his head. '*All* of them? I can't hear a thing.'

'Not all,' Hardesty grated. This half-whisper was hard on a man's throat. 'Some of them, though. Quite a hefty "some".'

'What are they doing?' Chaucer asked. He was looking at the wall at his level, trying to see if there was a chink through which he could peep, but Hardesty had done his job well – there wasn't room for an ant to get through.

Hardesty shrugged. 'That's it,' he said. 'They are just standing, staring. It's . . . unnerving. We'll watch and wait. That's all we can do. Wait a moment . . .' He pulled out a parchment from the breast of his jerkin. 'I have you down for a watch now, Master Gower. Look.' He pointed to a row of columns. 'In the event of a siege, Master Gower will take the sixth watch. That's now. Can you remember what you have to do?'

'Of course I can,' Gower said airily, climbing the ladder. 'But if you would like to remind me one more time, Master Hardesty, that might be best . . .'

Chaucer was not listed to be on watch until the wee small hours, but thought he could do with a reminder of exactly what he had to do, so stayed with Gower up on the ramparts. He had only intended to stay a while, but there was something about the massed crowd, about their eyes fixed on their new horizon, the top of the Tabard walls, that was mesmerizing.

The crowd was not completely silent any more. There was a low hum, not of words; something recognizable would have been a comfort, even if it was only a harbinger of doom. The hum was made of shuffling feet, rustling, rough-made clothes, the occasional sharp zing of a whetstone drawn along a blade. It seemed to get into a man's spine, running along it like St Elmo's fire, making the skin crawl and the hair crackle. It was like the calm that comes just before the lightning strikes, before the thunder splits the sky in two. Chaucer was sorely in need of something normal. A slice of Alice's home-made bread. A draught of Doggett's new ale. The smell of wool in the warehouses. Something from his old life, a life he feared he would never see again.

'Dark times, eh, Master Chaucer?' Ludlum touched the rim of his kettle hat as he arrived to relieve Gower and his crew. Chaucer had never been so glad to see anyone in his life. The comptroller's houppelande was open at the neck and his belt had gone. Ludlum was amused to see that the man whose gate he used to keep was standing with a halberd in his hand; he clearly barely knew one end from another.

'Dark indeed, Ludlum,' Chaucer murmured. 'Dark indeed. I still can't believe that William Tonge just let the peasants in.' A sudden thought struck him. 'My God! My books! The bastards have got my books!'

'One thing's for sure, sir,' Ludlum said, although it failed to cheer the poet, 'they won't have read any of 'em.'

'No, I suppose not.' Chaucer tore his mind away from imaginings of his ruined room. 'And my wine! My daily gallon from the King. They may not read my books, but they'll certainly drink my wine! What time do you think it is?'

Ludlum clicked his fingers in faked annoyance. 'Damn, I left my astrolabe behind, not that it's much good in the dark. It's time for my watch to begin, that's all I know. If you wait awhile, St Martin's le Grand's bell will tell us when the market opens. Trust in that.'

'Yes,' Chaucer sighed. 'I suppose you're right. Umm . . . have you looked . . . down, lately?'

'No,' Ludlum chuckled. 'Haven't you? I thought you were on watch.'

'Not strictly speaking. I was just keeping Gower company. It's just that . . . they're so silent. It's hard to believe they're there if you don't look.'

'My old gammer used to say to us nippers when we couldn't sleep, that if we shut our eyes, nothing could hurt us. Nothing's there if you can't see it. We'd be off to sleep like winking.'

'You believe that?' Chaucer's voice held endless hope.

'When I was *five*,' Ludlum said. 'It isn't something I would care to trust in now.' He crouched low and looked over the parapet. Down below, in the moonlight, there was a shimmer, as if from ripple in water. The crowd was thinner now, and it was harder to make out shapes. After the glaring heat and brightness of the day, the half-light was trying to the eyes. The peasants were well led – someone knew about the madness of crowds, that was certain. Chaucer joined Ludlum, but the man restrained him, a friendly hand on his arm. 'Best keep low, sir. A man on watch is a target; believe me, I know. These nightwalkers they've left behind, they will be the cream of the crop; they'll know their business. Once they stop relying on numbers, that's when we need to be on our guard.' Ludlum narrowed his eyes, attracted by some movement in the street below which meant nothing to Chaucer. 'Please keep calm, sir, but perhaps you'd care to call Master Hardesty. He'll need to—'

There was a sudden roar and a burst of flame in the street and the sound and sight of people running. Chaucer dropped the halberd as Ludlum swung down the roll into the yard, grabbing a second rope to ring the alarm bell.

'Mother of God!' Geoffrey Chaucer *had* been more worried than this, but he couldn't remember when. His knees felt at once nailed to the floorboards of the palisade and wobbling like water. For what seemed like hours, he was alone on that parapet. Then, there were people everywhere – hostelmen and pilgrims, shaking the sleep out of their eyes, hauling on their clothes, clattering up ladders onto the wall walks.

Fire. Of course they'd have fire. In that desperate madhouse, probably only Chaucer and Gower knew the story of Prometheus, who had stolen the secret of fire from the gods.

Damn his eyes! Why couldn't the Greek bastard have left well enough alone?

Hardesty was at Chaucer's side, looking down at the Comptroller of Woollens. Hardesty looked like a giant, solid on the defences that he'd built, ready to take on the world.

'Fire, Hardesty!' Chaucer gabbled. 'Fire!'

The yeoman nodded. 'And what are the two things to put out fire, Master Chaucer?'

'Er . . .'

Hardesty's hand was in the air. He was watching the peasants, even more numerous now than when they first had silently appeared, moving forward, out of the cover of the surrounding houses, chanting and shouting, their faces flickering in the light of the burning brands they carried. After their sinister silence, this chanting seemed to come from the bowels of some hell of hatred. Chaucer looked about him and couldn't believe it. Nothing was happening. Along the ramparts, to his right and left, a motley crew of defenders crouched poised, armed with anything they could find, faces grim, eyes wide, staring at the mob coming for them, its front fringed with fire.

'Now!' Hardesty's arm came down, and along the walls of the Tabard there was a rattle of chains and a thud of timbers. Barrel after barrel tilted and swung from behind shutters, revolving on the pivot that Hardesty had built over the front gate. Gallons of water crashed down on the attackers, extinguishing their brands and bowling most of them over with shouts of shock.

'Cold, isn't it?' Hardesty yelled at them. 'For flaming June, I mean.'

For several minutes, the peasants were in disarray, men falling over each other, wet through and slipping in the dust of the road, which had become suddenly a morass of sticky mud. Some were out cold; others cut and bruised from the barrels that had followed the water crashing over the palisade. While the defenders cheered, John Gower scuttled over to Chaucer. 'That'll teach them,' he said, gleefully. 'They won't do that again.'

'Oh, but they will, Master Gower,' Hardesty said. 'And we've emptied all our water barrels.'

There were still a dozen or so torches burning at street level and the mob reorganized, pulling fallen comrades out of the way, aiming for the front gate.

'We're finished,' Gower said, crossing himself.

Hardesty smiled down at him. 'Oh, ye of little faith,' he said. His hand was in the air again and Chaucer, for one, was more than a little confused. As the peasants reached the gate and the defenders heard the thud as clubs and staves hit the oak, the yeoman's arm came down again. Again, there was the scream of pivots, wood on wood and tensioned iron. More barrels were bursting out over the parapet, their hoops pinging apart into flying razors, and an avalanche of pale sand coated the front ranks at the door.

'Sand!' Chaucer yelled, back in the schoolroom as the clever boy with the right answer, 'Of course! That'll put any fire out!'

'It will,' Hardesty said, 'but it's not as simple as that. Look!'

There were screams from below. Men were falling back, covering their heads and faces, their nostrils choked, their ears full, blind and in agony. '*Hot* sand is the secret,' the yeoman said. 'Have you ever stood on a beach, Master Chaucer, at the height of summer?'

'Good Lord, no.' The comptroller was horrified. What kind of animal did Hardesty assume he was?

'If you had,' the yeoman said, 'you'd know something of the pain these knarres are feeling now.'

In the street, the peasants were pulling back, groaning and sobbing, coughing in their agony.

'Damn!' Maghfield grunted, sheathing his falchion. 'I was looking forward to tangling with those bastards.'

'You may still get your chance, sir,' Hardesty said. 'They've got a handful of torches yet and we're out of water and sand.'

The attackers had pulled back out of range of the yeoman's improvised artillery and stood in a body, shaking their weapons and yelling obscenities. Then, it fell quiet.

'Hoo, the Tabard!' a voice called.

Harry Baillie assumed the responsibility of a reply. 'What do you want?' It seemed rather an odd question after the last few minutes, but Baillie was having to make it up as he went along; in an eventful life, this was the first time he had faced down an angry mob. An angry mob of this magnitude, at least; he had had rather a torrid time with the Guild of Haberdashers once or twice, but they didn't number this many, even at a quorum.

'The Comptroller of the King's Woollens,' the voice came back. 'Give us Geoffrey Chaucer and you will all live.'

There was a stunned silence. John Gower turned to his friend. 'Mother of God, Geoff,' he whispered. 'How did they know?'

'Our friend Cog Buckley,' Chaucer told him. 'Father Ambrosius who is not Father Ambrosius. If what Nell says is true, he'll have told them all that they need to know.'

'Judging by what you've achieved so far,' Baillie shouted, 'we're all going to live anyway.'

There was a silence.

'Is that you, Baillie?' the voice came back. 'Harry Baillie, prop.? How's that nice-looking wife of yours, eh? Ready for a bit of action tonight, is she, after the birth of the sprog? And how will he look, nailed to your front door?'

Baillie's jaw twitched. He was on the parapet, sword in hand, ready to leap to the street below. Hardesty held his arm and hauled him back. 'Only one way to answer that,' he said. 'I can't see the speaker, but . . .'

There was a bow in one hand and an arrow in the other. He raised his chin, licked a finger and held it up to the slight breeze. 'Third head from the left, Master Baillie,' he said. 'Just to make a point.'

There was a hiss and a thud and the third head from the left disappeared. There was cheering from the ramparts, but Hardesty shook his head. 'He was somebody's father,' he said. 'Somebody's son.'

'Oh, no,' Ludlum growled. 'People like him don't have fathers.'

Chaucer passed the halberd he had regained to Gower. 'Here, John,' he said. 'I shan't be needing this; not where I'm going.' He clapped his old friend on the shoulder and pushed past him. He looked up and was surprised by who stood in his way.

'Oh, no, you don't, Master Chaucer.' It was Alice, a leather jerkin over her apron, a kettle hat on her head. 'If you give yourself up, who will I have to do for back at the Aldgate when all this business is over? Besides, and I hate to bring it up at a time like this, but you owe Doggett . . . well, I won't embarrass you in front of all these people.'

'Here they come again!' Maghfield drew his sword once more and everybody closed to the ramparts.

'Down!' Hardesty bellowed and the whole line ducked as a volley of arrows hissed out into the night, clattering onto the parapet and biting into the wood. The yeoman, Ludlum and his men and anybody else who dared, reached out to jerk the shafts free and add them to their quivers. Then, with a roar, the peasant line pushed forward, batting their bowmen aside and surging on the gate.

Hardesty's arm was in the air again. Chaucer and Gower looked at each other; what had the man got left?

'Now!' the yeoman shouted and more barrels spun and clanked, staves creaking and oil pouring like molten lava onto those who had reached the building. If the screams had been deafening before, as first water, then hot sand hit the attackers, it was unbelievable now.

'That's the thing about oil,' Hardesty muttered. 'It clings so, especially to sand.'

Men were floundering in the sea of chaos outside the Tabard, tumbling over each other in a mad, desperate frenzy to escape the scalding, crawling liquid. Slowly, the pandemonium died down and there was no sound but the sobbing of the maimed and dying.

Chaucer looked up to the sky. Dawn was breaking, lending an eerie light to the city over the river. But there was no great bell of St Martin's le Grand, nor any others that should have followed to mark Prime.

'My God,' somebody on the ramparts murmured, 'they're going.'

And they were. The peasants were crawling away, dragging their injured and licking their wounds. At the last, only one man stood under a tattered flag of St George, scowling at the Tabard and the battlefield in front of it. Against all the odds, one little inn had held out against thousands. Most of the defenders were on their knees, thanking God for his mercy and Tom Hardesty for his arcane knowledge.

'We'll be back,' the lone peasant said. 'All of us. And we won't just be hanging Geoffrey Chaucer. Count on it.' He turned to go, to thread his way through the still, dark tangle of Southwark streets. Then he turned back. 'In the meantime,' he said, 'look at your city; what's left of it.' And he was gone.

To a man and woman, they turned to the north. The river lay pale and dead, even the roaring below the bridge a muffled growl. Beyond, there were fires everywhere, the glow lighting up the dawn, heralding a new age that no one could quite understand. In the Tabard, they hadn't lost a man, but what of the city? The drawbridge on the bridge was open and the shops beyond it wrecked and looted. There was rubbish everywhere, scattered in the streets and floating on the water, where the eddies swirled and carried it this way and that, as Fye Gillis's body had been carried what seemed like years ago.

'That's Clerkenwell,' somebody said, pointing to one of the fires. 'The Templars' Priory of St John.'

'God, no,' somebody else chimed in. 'The Temple church; it's on fire. How can you burn a church?'

'Mother of God.' It was Geoffrey Chaucer's voice. 'That's John of Gaunt's Palace of the Savoy. It's an inferno.'

'And where is His Grace the Duke of Lancaster?' Maghfield growled. 'Where are any of the bloody nobility?'

'They'll be in the Tower,' Baillie informed him with the air of confidence of innkeepers the world over. 'Shitting themselves.'

All eyes turned to the silent stone fortress with its square towers, a bastion of civilization in a world of chaos and slaughter. And there, ranged over Tower Hill, like an Old Testament plague, were the peasants.

Waiting.

They were still erecting the tents on the Mile End Waste, on either side of the road that ran to the Aldgate. Beyond Spitalfields and Goodman's Fields, littered now with the debris of the peasants, they could see the city walls clearly and the Tower, white and solid in the June sun.

'It's a lovely day, Master Buckley.' Wat Tyler was lolling on a velvet couch he'd taken a fancy to at John of Gaunt's Palace of the Savoy, most of which now clogged the river below the Strand. 'I hope you're not going to be the bastard who spoils it.'

Cog Buckley was still wearing his sackcloth and it would be weeks before his hair would grow back. 'About the Tabard . . .' he began, but Tyler brushed it aside. His minions had closed around him, the new king in his makeshift court; one of them was actually plucking a lute.

'We'll come to that,' Tyler said. 'Tell me about the Tower.'

Buckley threw his arms wide. 'Beyond my expertise, Wat, I'm afraid.'

The peasant leader frowned. 'But you went there, didn't you, as Father Ambrosius, I mean?'

'I was with the Bishop of London for a week, yes,' Buckley nodded, 'but we were mostly in Lambeth Palace.'

Tyler put his goblet down. He could get used to Gaunt's Romonye; it tickled his palate. It tickled him to think that he'd got it for nothing. 'Well,' he said, 'from what you remember. Do the best you can.'

Buckley thought for a moment. 'The river's the best way in,' he said. 'Henry III's watergate.'

Somebody was scribbling all this down at Tyler's elbow.

'And then?'

'It's a narrow entrance. If I was a military man . . .'

Tyler snorted.

'. . . I'd make a feint from Tower Hill – you've got men there already. Use the Essex boys to hit from the north and east, down the Minories. There's a postern gate to the north. Make them think you're going for that.'

'Night attack, you reckon?'

Buckley nodded. 'That'd be best,' he said.

Tyler yawned. 'Didn't do us much good at the Tabard, though, did it?' he asked.

'Ah, well . . .'

Tyler was on his feet. 'Ah, well, there doesn't seem to be

much point in us having a man on the inside if he doesn't tell us anything.'

'I didn't know about Hardesty's contraptions,' he said, 'as I live and breathe. He kept all that close to his chest.'

'Water, sand and oil,' Tyler murmured. 'They'll have all that and more at the Tower – cannon, too. Not to mention Robert Knollys's crossbowmen. It's going to be bloody, Cog; it's going to be bloody.'

'As I live and breathe . . .' the false priest began.

'Yes, you said,' Tyler grunted. 'And that's the problem, isn't it? You do. We'll have to do something about that.' He clapped Buckley on the shoulder with his right hand and, with the other, he whipped a poignard from his belt and twirled it ostentatiously in front of the man's eyes. Buckley flinched away but the grip on his shoulder was too strong.

'No,' the man gabbled, 'no, Wat, Master Tyler, sir, please give me another chance. I'll get back in . . . I'm a master of disguise, I'll . . .'

Tyler lowered the blade a fraction and Buckley let out a sigh of relief. It was premature. The knife swung round, slitting Buckley's throat neat and clean, displaying just a glimpse of backbone as his body fell. Tyler let go and stepped back, hardly a speck of blood on him. He leaned down and wiped the blood on Buckley's sackcloth hem.

'My fault, I suppose.' Tyler looked down at him. 'I should never have sent a self-serving idiot to do a man's job.' And he drove his boot into the dead man's shoulder, kicking him into the dust of the Mile End.

# ELEVEN

This time it was Arend Gillis who saw them coming, marching from the west along the riverbank, their boots sucking in the river mud. The evening sky was aglow with fires from the still-burning Savoy and the Templar's Priory. Dozens of houses had gone up, too, crumbling into the inferno as wattle disintegrated and oak cracked in the heat. Gillis dashed across to the rope, swinging on it with all his weight to sound the alarm.

'Take post!' It was Tom Hardesty's voice, drowned out by the sound of running feet, shouted curses and the shrill scream of Madame Eglantyne.

Harry Baillie's eyes swivelled to his wife alongside him and he put an arm around her shoulders and gave her a squeeze. She was a hard woman to read, but what she needed now was a light-hearted remark and he had just the thing. 'They're coming to get you, Barbara,' he muttered and she punched him lightly on the arm.

It was what Hardesty had feared. The Tabard was surrounded now and his barrelled ammunition had been used up defending the south wall. He had made a careful count of the bows at his disposal – his own, four of Ludlum's men's and six others. Arrows? Perhaps a hundred, including those regathered from the peasants. That would stop them, all right . . . for all of ten minutes.

'Hoo, the inn!' a rough voice barked from the street.

'Who goes?' Hardesty already had the man's head in his sights.

'I am Sir Robert Knollys,' the voice called back and a banner behind him was hoisted high to show his device furling and twisting in the little breeze off the river. 'Do you have the Comptroller of Woollens lurking in there?'

John Gower was doing his best to buckle on a sword he'd found from somewhere. 'They've come for you again, Geoff,'

he muttered to his friend. 'Nice to be so popular. "Lurking"
is a bit unkind, though.'

'Sir Robert!' Chaucer called from the parapet.

'Ah, Chaucer,' the knight recognized the man's bulk at
once, half-hidden by wood and men though he was. 'Message
from the King – His Grace's compliments and would you
join him at the Aldgate in the morning? A few of us are
going out to Mile End to talk to Wat Tyler.'

'Um . . .' Chaucer, Court Poet, was lost for words. 'John,'
he turned to his old friend, 'I don't suppose you'd care to . . .'

'Er . . .' Gower, the other poet, was equally tongue-tied.

'Come with me, I mean,' Chaucer hissed. 'I feel a little like
Daniel and the lions' den.'

'Oh, Geoffrey,' Gower blustered. 'You know I would, of
course, like a shot. But . . . well, Marian and the children . . .'

Chaucer was tempted to remind him that he had a family
too, but he knew where his duty lay. 'Yes. Yes, of course,' he
said with a sigh. He looked along the ramparts. Tom Hardesty
would have been his first choice, but the man was needed
here, for when the peasants came back. Harry Baillie was
unlikely to leave the Tabard unless a team of wild horses on
bended knees was dragging him. Chaucer had already accused
Arend Gillis of murder, so he was an unlikely companion of
a mile. 'Um . . .'

There was a sigh and Gilbert Maghfield slid his falchion
away. 'If it's just company you want, Master Chaucer . . .'

'Oh.' The comptroller was a little nonplussed. 'Thank you.
Thank you, Master Maghfield.'

'Is there a problem, Chaucer?' Knollys snapped from street
level. He had been one of the knights who had fought the Battle
of the Thirty, for God's sake, hero of Nájera and the Black
Prince's right-hand man; he didn't have time for this.

'No, Sir Robert; no, indeed. Just coming.'

The king had long since gone to bed by the time Knollys,
Chaucer and Maghfield reached the Tower. The merchant
couldn't believe the astronomical sum that Knollys slipped the
waterman to ferry them across the river to the watergate. They
rowed silently, with no torches, the only sound their oar-blades

sliding into the water, slipping past the ripples as if the river was oil. Chaucer had never been so glad to see the doors of the royal palace in his life and he was soon in the kitchen, with dozens of crossbowmen gabbling away in Italian, tucking in to bread and cheese with the best of them.

It was late when Maghfield retired, leaving the comptroller in a solar with a tolerable bottle of Rhenish and an old wolf-hound, dozing before the empty, blackened hearth. Chaucer didn't hear the man come in, any more than the dog did, but he saw him clearly enough and knew the robes. It was the Archbishop of Canterbury.

'Who the hell are you?' Sudbury snapped. Chaucer struggled to his feet and bowed. Had the last few days gone differently, he might have been hobnobbing with His Grace in Canterbury itself, as the archbishop's sacristan cleared the comptroller of a considerable portion of his salary in 'fees'.

'Geoffrey Chaucer, my lord,' he said, 'Comptroller of the King's Woollens.'

'Ah, a pen-pusher.'

'We all have our place, my lord, in God's plan.'

Sudbury laughed. 'Spoken like a true crawler, Chaucer,' he said. 'You've chosen one Hell of a time to come comptrolling.'

'I'm here to accompany His Grace the King to Mile End tomorrow,' Chaucer said. 'See if we can talk some sense into the peasants.'

Sudbury guffawed. 'Good luck with that, Master Chaucer. I wish you good luck and God Speed indeed. The bastards have got all of London by now. Where are the bloody nobility when you need them?'

'I expect three of them will turn up presently, sir,' Chaucer beamed.

'Well,' Sudbury helped himself to a swig from Chaucer's bottle. 'Better to travel hopefully, I suppose.' He stopped in mid-swig. 'Look . . . er . . . Chaucer. This chance meeting may be part of God's plan too.' He ferreted in his alb and pulled out a letter, heavy with his official seal. He looked the comptroller squarely in the face. 'I'm pessimist enough to believe I may not come out of this peasant business alive. I shan't be accompanying you tomorrow; I have other plans, but . . . should it all go wrong, and should you, by a freak accident, survive, will you deliver this for me?'

Chaucer took the vellum and his jaw dropped.

'It's for the prioress of Stratford-atte-Bow . . .' Sudbury began. Then he caught the look on Chaucer's face.

'Madame Eglantyne,' the comptroller said.

Sudbury jolted upright. 'Do . . . do you know her?'

'We are . . . were to have been . . . fellow pilgrims on the road to Canterbury.'

'Canterbury?' Sudbury's eyes widened and he grabbed Chaucer's houppelande lapels. 'Is she all right? Tell me she's safe, man! Those wretched peasants haven't . . .'

'She is well, my lord,' Chaucer assured him. 'In the Tabard Inn, Southwark, as safe there as she would be in the Tower.'

Sudbury hugged Chaucer in a sudden burst of relief, surprising them both. 'Thank God,' he muttered. He crossed himself. 'Thank God. Well,' he cleared his throat and composed himself, 'in the event of my death, Chaucer,' he said, 'see that Eggy gets this, will you? It's my farewell.'

Chaucer was confused. 'Are you sending such letters to every prioress, my lord?' he asked.

'Don't be ridiculous, Chaucer,' Sudbury took to the bottle again, 'Madame Eglantyne and I . . . well, I don't suppose it'll matter much now' – his face suddenly darkened – 'but when this is over, I shall of course deny that this conversation ever took place.'

'Of course, my lord.' Chaucer was a courtier first and a comptroller second.

Sudbury closed to him, the candlelight flickering on the gold thread at his throat, his blue eyes piercing into Chaucer's soul. 'Back in the day, Madame Eglantyne and I . . . well, we were what I believe the young folk of today call "an item". I'm not afraid to admit it, despite my calling; we were – are – deeply in love.'

The image of the prioress's gold bracelet flashed in Chaucer's memory. '*Amor omnia vincit,*' it had read – Love conquers all. And it wasn't God's love the jewellery hinted at; it was the illicit love of a prioress for an archbishop.

'I said a moment ago,' Sudbury went on, 'that I'm not

ashamed to admit our love, truly, madly, deeply. But of course, there are those who would not understand. You and I are men of the world. I can trust you to keep this between us, can't I? *Vir ad virum*, so to speak?'

'Oh, absolutely, my lord.'

'Good,' Sudbury felt suddenly elated. 'Very good. Well, Chaucer,' he shook the man's hand, 'I'll bid you goodnight.' He paused in the archway. 'Oh – and good luck, tomorrow.'

There was an eerie silence over the city that morning. No bells, no shouts of the costers, no creaking of cartwheels and bellowing of oxen. A cluster of men sat in their saddles on the ground beyond the royal palace. William Walworth was there, as mayor of the city now owned by the peasants; Nicholas Brembre, in his capacity of leading light; Robert Knollys, the only man who stood a chance against the mob. And Geoffrey Chaucer, Comptroller of Woollens, wondering what the hell he was doing there.

They all, except Knollys, jumped at the blare of the King's trumpet, and Richard himself, in his white heart houppelande with a diadem glittering in the morning sun, clattered down the steps to where a groom held his grey. All the men bowed in their saddles and waited as the groom hoisted the boy onto his charger's back. He scanned their faces, then clicked his fingers at Chaucer. 'Who are you?' he asked, his voice rather higher than they had all hoped.

'Geoffrey Chaucer, sire,' the man bowed as best he could. 'Comptroller of Your Woollens and Court Poet.'

'Yes,' Richard sneered. 'I *know*. Come here.'

Chaucer urged his animal forward to stand alongside the King's. 'You may wonder,' Richard whispered, 'why I want you here.'

'It is an honour, sire,' Chaucer assured him.

'Yes, of course it is. But . . . well, the peasants have caught us all napping, haven't they, Comptroller? My uncle John is in Scotland. He'll be *livid* about the Savoy, by the way. Oxford, Salisbury, all the rest of them are taking a *hell* of a time to get here. Look about you.'

Chaucer did.

'Walworth's a fishmonger. Knollys was good in his day, but he's knocking a hundred by now. Who that other idiot is, I've no idea.'

Since the idiot in question was Nicholas Brembre, Chaucer was rather pleased by that.

'They've all got their own agenda, Chaucer,' the King went on, 'but I take you for a man of the people. You talk their language – the peasants', that is. Keep yourself close.'

'My lord,' Chaucer bowed and pulled his horse back. There was a further kerfuffle on the steps as Gilbert Maghfield hurried down then, the falchion bouncing on his hip.

'Leave that here, merchant!' Knollys ordered. 'None of us is going armed today.'

'Are you mad?' Maghfield asked.

Knollys bent low in the saddle. 'You're only here because of Chaucer. Don't build up your part.'

And the little column formed up, the knot of horsemen with the King at its head and a solid phalanx of unarmed soldiers behind him. Chaucer crossed himself. He knew that Robert Knollys had fought chevauchées without number, riding exposed through enemy territory, but the comptroller never had. Why the hell was he carrying Simon of Sudbury's farewell letter when he hadn't written one himself?

All along the King's route, the peasants stood, sullen and smug. In the space of three days, most of London had fallen to them. The Tower still stood, the rock of ages, and Knollys's mansion in Seething Lane. And there was a little inn near the Borough High Street, battered and bruised by arrows and scorched by fire, but still standing. Everything else was in the peasants' hands and they knew it. This was a royal progress like none other; no bells, no trumpets, no drums, just the hollow clatter of hoofs on the cobbles.

Chaucer looked wistfully up at the room over the Aldgate as he rode under it. There was no Ludlum there now to guard the comptroller's world. Doggett's inn had become a slum camp, people sitting over open fires in the sun, cooking the food they'd stolen from the Cheap and Billingsgate. Out beyond the city walls, in Portsoken and the Minories, the tents began in numbers, bright colours for the summer, flags fluttering, little children playing in the dirt. Everybody stopped to watch the cavalcade, but few indeed were those who bowed. One old man who knelt before his liege lord was dragged away and kicked for his subservience. This was a brave new world; the old ways had gone for ever.

Knollys rode with the King, a poignard secreted under his jupon. No weapons, he had said, so as not to inflame the rebels further, but he hadn't meant that. If it came to it, he was ready to lay down his life for his King. The Mile End was more of a waste than ever, piles of rubbish and dung heaps everywhere. The body of a priest hung down from the tower of St Mary Matfelon, the crows circling above him, waiting for their next meal. Their favourite bits, the eyes, were long gone. Around his neck someone had slung a placard which read 'traitor'. The word was written in blood, as was so much of the history unfurling in these days.

Then, the road came to an end and the King's highway was blocked by a mounted committee of welcome, the cross of St George floating wide above them. Knollys reined in his gelding and the King did likewise, standing in his stirrups to see what lay ahead. Nobody knelt. Nobody bowed. Everybody just stared – the Lord's Anointed face to face with the people's king.

Jack Chub nudged Will Lorkin; neither man could believe what he was seeing. Knollys leaned over and whispered something to the King. Still upright in the saddle, Richard called out, 'Who is your leader? With whom am I to deal?'

There was a silence; sudden, sharp, surreal. No one in those cluttered fields had ever seen the King before, still less heard his voice. And he was just a boy.

'With me,' a voice called back. 'I am Wat Tyler, man of Kent.'

There were cheers from the mob, although most of them were Essex men.

'What is it you want, Master Tyler?' the King asked.

Tyler was loving every minute of this, savouring it like the finest Romonye he'd been drinking since Rochester. 'We'll start,' he said, with no acknowledgement of the King's exalted status, 'with the end of manorial rights. Throughout the country.'

Knollys noticed that this upstart had not used the word 'kingdom'. He whispered to Richard.

'That would mean the end of the power of my nobility,' the King said.

Tyler nodded. 'That's right,' he said. He clicked his fingers. 'I have the necessary documents here. Father Ball here has drawn them up for me.'

John Ball was not sitting on his horse. He stood like an Old Testament prophet, wild-haired and bearded, a bundle of vellum in his arms.

'We have a tent for you,' Tyler told the King. 'We'll need your seal.'

Richard had no need to confer with Knollys this time. 'Will my signet suffice?' he asked, holding up his hand.

Jack Chub's eyes bulged. That gold ring would keep him in clover for life.

'It will,' Tyler said. He noted the apprehension on the faces of the riders around the King. 'There's room for you all inside, gentlemen,' he beamed. 'Except your guard. They can stand in the sun.' He frowned at them, at the strange livery stitched to their shoulders. 'Foreigners, aren't they?' he scowled. 'Let them scorch.' He turned his horse and dismounted. 'Welcome,' he said. 'We've wine aplenty, courtesy of John of Gaunt and several others. Help yourselves while young Richard wields his ring.' There were guffaws all round from Tyler's cronies and, one by one, the King's party dismounted.

'Sire,' Knollys murmured up at Richard, still sitting on his grey in silent fury. 'It's for the best. For now.'

The King's face assumed a more sullen set than usual and he bounced out of the saddle as a groom rushed to hold the animal's bridle. As they filed into the darkness of Tyler's tent where a table was laid out with a burning taper and bottles of ink, Tyler caught sight of Nicholas Brembre.

'Chaucer, isn't it?' he said. 'Pity we missed you at the Tabard. Still, there's plenty of time, isn't there?'

'Umm . . .' The man who had been London's mayor was lost for words. God damn Wat Tyler for his memory.

'Umm' was the last word in Chaucer's mind. He had Wat Tyler down for a lot of things, culminating in murderous bastard. But he'd never taken him for a mistaken idiot.

'Jack,' Tyler called to his lieutenant, 'I have places to be.'

Jack Straw nodded and took charge of the charter-sealing in the shadow of the canvas. Inside the tent smelled of trampled grass, hot hemp and unwashed bodies, and Chaucer was glad to be out again in the fresh air, not minding that it was almost as hot as Hell and almost as frightening. Tyler mounted again and clattered off towards the city, others swinging into line on the road behind him. Chaucer stood with the others, Maghfield and Knollys fuming alongside him, Brembre wishing the ground would open up and swallow him whole, Walworth just wanting his city back.

'Mother of God, no!' Simon of Sudbury couldn't believe what was happening. He'd resigned as the King's chancellor to avoid the very thing that was going on under his nose now. By handing over that wretched gold chain, he'd unburdened himself, lost his right to ride with the King to the Mile End. Now, all he had to do was slip away from the Tower. If the King had capitulated, the fortress itself was meaningless; what price a royal castle when there was no king any more?

He dashed along the walkway, past the royal palace, making for the White Tower, its walls twenty foot thick, its strength impregnable. The peasants were swarming in through the outer gates like ants, blackening the ground around the Lantern Tower and the Garden Tower. They'd let them in! Some traitor had slipped the bolts, raised the drawbridge, brought the world to an end. Below him as he ran, the rebels were laughing with the guard, pulling their beards and slapping their backs. He'd have their heads for this, nailed to their own barracks doors. What he didn't know, because he couldn't see it, was that the riff-raff had smashed their way into the King's private apartments and were rolling on his bed, laughing and joking. Next to the bed lay His Grace's wet nurse, kept on for sentiment's sake. She wasn't hurt; one of the peasants had asked her for a kiss and she'd fainted.

Sudbury reached the cool of St John's chapel. There was

nowhere else to hide now. This was his last sanctuary and he knew that the peasants would not respect it. He kissed his rosary and placed the stole around his neck. His voice echoed in the chill chamber – '*Omnes sancti orate pro nobis.*' But who was going to pray for him?

Then the door crashed back and a dozen armed men burst in.

'Here he is, the sanctimonious old bastard.'

'Hocus pocus, my Lord Archbishop,' another sneered. They tore off his stole and wrested the rosary out of his hands, kicking him out of the chapel and bundling him down the stairs.

Tower Hill was swarming with the unwashed. Their crosses of St George clothed the green in white and Sudbury found himself forced to the ground in front of a large man with a sword at his hip and an attitude the size of the Holy See of Canterbury.

'Lord Chancellor,' he said, 'I am Wat Tyler. Perhaps you've heard of me?'

Sudbury blinked in the blinding sun. 'No,' he said, coldly.

'Well,' Tyler smiled. 'No matter. I've heard of you, that's the main thing.'

'I am no longer Lord Chancellor,' Sudbury protested.

'Really?' Tyler raised an eyebrow. 'Well, that makes all the difference.'

At a nod from their leader, a dozen swords flew clear of their scabbards. Sudbury struggled on the ground but he was held too firmly. 'I am an anointed archbishop,' he screamed. 'To kill me would be a sin. Think of your souls!'

'Think of yours,' Tyler growled back and stood aside as the swords came down and blood spattered his tunic.

The royal party had not so much scattered as melted slowly away. Knollys would go with the King back to the Tower. Brembre spent the few minutes of farewell keeping at least three burly bodies between him and Geoffrey Chaucer, who kept trying to catch his eye. He had felt guilty about his earlier subterfuge, ever since the name had dropped unbidden from his mouth, but he excused himself by the thought that, at the time, he had thought there was no harm in it. Chaucer gave up trying to catch up with the man and found Maghfield, standing fingering his empty scabbard mouth on the edge of the royal group.

'Where do we go, Master Chaucer?' he asked, politely. In fact, Chaucer had been struck by the man's civility throughout this strange little adventure.

'I think they expect us at the Tower,' Chaucer muttered, 'but really – the food is so much better at the Tabard, under siege though it is. I don't know how they do it.'

Maghfield laughed. 'I thought Harry Baillie had some useful people up his sleeve,' he said, 'but that was before I met your Doggett. That man is on first-name terms with people who merchants like me can only dream of seeing in the distance. After all this, Master Chaucer, I would like an introduction, if that isn't too presumptuous.'

Chaucer looked at the man through narrowed eyes. He certainly seemed quite genuine, but with Maghfield, it was hard to be sure. 'I would be delighted, Master Maghfield,' he said. 'After all this.' Chaucer was having increasing difficulty with imagining life after all this. How could it possibly be the same? Surely, these thousands of ragamuffins would not simply go back to how things had been? Surely, the King hadn't meant a word of all the documents he had sealed? Jack as good as his master? Impossible.

'So,' Maghfield was still waiting. 'Where away?'

Chaucer chewed his lip. On the one hand, the Tower was the safest place in London. Strong walls. Strong men at arms. But it wasn't the Tabard, with the stinking huggermugger of the yard, Hardesty bestriding it all like a Colossus. And if they told them where to be tomorrow, if there was to be a tomorrow, then he and Maghfield could be there, just as well as from the Tower. 'I'll tell Knollys we're going to the inn,' he said. 'He'll have to be satisfied with that. I don't know why we need to be anywhere, truth be told.'

'*We* don't need to be anywhere,' Maghfield pointed out. '*You* do. Though I am perfectly happy to be at your shoulder tomorrow as well.' He swung into his saddle, making it look effortless, as always. 'Go and tell them and we can be away.'

The thing with Maghfield, Chaucer thought to himself as he elbowed his way towards Knollys, who was horsed and ready for the off; whoever was nominally in charge, it always ended up being Maghfield. This had been a trying day and he just wanted it to end. He grabbed Knollys's stirrup leather and the man looked down, whip raised.

'Sorry, Chaucer,' he said, when he saw who it was. 'Bit jumpy. What is it? Can we talk later at the Tower? I need to get this one home.' He might have been talking of a recalcitrant toddler out too late for bedtime.

'Just to say,' Chaucer said, shielding his eyes as he looked up, 'Maghfield and I are going back to the Tabard for the night. Don't want to intrude on your hospitality again. Difficult times for everyone, food shortages and the rest.' He was remembering the bread from breaking his fast and hardly suppressed a shudder. 'Where are we to be tomorrow? I am assuming that today was just the beginning.'

Knollys looked into the distance. Who knew? 'I'll send a galloper,' he said shortly, and urged his horse into a trot, to keep up with his wayward King.

Chaucer found Bertha standing quietly beside Maghfield and looked at her unattainably high saddle. He hadn't mounted a horse without help since he was about thirty and that was a while ago now. With a sigh, Maghfield swung his leg effortlessly over his saddle bow, jumped down, hoisted Chaucer up, and was back in the saddle before the poet had settled himself comfortably.

'How old are you, Maghfield?' Chaucer asked enviously.

'I never really think about it. Knowing how old you are makes you old, in my opinion.'

Chaucer was surprised. If asked, he would not have had Maghfield down as a philosopher. They turned their horses' heads to the Tabard and saw at once that the way would not be easy. Since they had gained entry to London, the peasants had dispersed somewhat, but this simply meant that a man could not ride a yard without going past some muttering riff-raff who stroked the leather of the horse's accoutrements, or even the rider's leg, clutching with envious fingers.

'It's going to be a rough ride, Master Chaucer,' Maghfield

said, out of the corner of his mouth. 'Try to ignore them. Don't give them reason to gather round. Can you sing, at all, something like that? Make them see you are light of heart?'

'No,' Chaucer said, louder than he had intended, because several heads snapped round in his direction. It was like riding through a flock of sheep, any one of which could be a wolf in disguise. 'No,' he dropped his voice. 'I can't sing and, even if I could, I don't exactly feel in the mood. Why don't you sing, if singing seems a good idea to you?'

Maghfield laughed, low in his throat. 'The only songs I know are the Flemish ones from my childhood. These crowds don't like Flemings, for some reason. And that is odd, because we are a peaceful people, who keep to ourselves, in the main.'

Chaucer looked at him doubtfully. As Comptroller of the King's Woollens, he had locked horns with Flemings many times and had usually been the one to back down. But it was true, they did keep to themselves, living and working in areas some would call ghettoes for all they allowed anyone else in. 'So, you and Arend Gillis, you are friends?'

Maghfield rode on for several minutes without replying and Chaucer thought he hadn't heard. The peasants in the streets were not being particularly loud, being somewhat overcome by their surroundings, but the click of the shod hoofs on the cobbles along with the hum of humanity made for quite a loud background noise. He was about to repeat himself when Maghfield answered.

'Not friends, no.'

The answer was short and very definitive. Chaucer was surprised. He had seen the men talking together in that other life, the life before the peasants had happened, when they were all on the road to Canterbury, carefree, with harness jingling and birds singing, in the warm caress of the sun. Even the sun had turned against the world, it seemed to him; its gentle fingers had become stabbing talons of heat and everything was shrivelling under its touch.

'I thought . . .' the poet ventured.

'Yes?' All Maghfield's replies were short and after a considerable pause.

'I had assumed you were friends because . . . you talk

together and you're both Flemish weavers, merchants. I . . .'
Chaucer had run out of reasons.

'Ah.' Maghfield's smile could have etched a diamond. 'I
wondered if you had assumed that because Arend Gillis is
swiving my wife, every chance he gets.'

A peasant with unusually sharp hearing looked up and
guffawed, making an obscene sign. In other circumstances,
Maghfield would have swept his whip across the man's face,
but this was not the day to make more enemies.

Chaucer swallowed hard and concentrated on his reins,
adjusting his grip and patting Bertha's mane as though she
had suddenly become a charger, trying to break into a headlong
gallop, and needed restraint.

'There is no need to feel uncomfortable, Master Chaucer.'
Maghfield stopped and turned to face the comptroller with an
unexpectedly sweet smile. 'Do you know, I feel as we are
chatting like old friends, I would like to call you Geoffrey.
There is no need to feel uncomfortable, Geoffrey. She seems
to like it, so who am I, as a loving husband, to interfere?'

'You're very understanding.' Chaucer thought momentarily
about checking Maghfield's Christian name but decided that
might be a step too far. 'Most husbands might . . . might take
matters into their own hands.'

Maghfield chuckled, an evil sound, as if the grumbling fires
of Hell were in his throat. 'Oh, I will, Geoffrey, I will. But
revenge is a dish best served cold, don't you find?'

He seemed to be waiting for an answer and Chaucer nodded.
It was something he had always lived by and it had never let
him down. But even so, he would not like to be in Arend
Gillis's shoes. A horrible thought struck him and he turned
his head towards Maghfield to whisper his disquiet. He was
startled to see that Maghfield was convulsed in silent laughter.
The merchant venturer leaned forward and whispered, 'I know
what you're thinking, Geoffrey. You're thinking, "Has this
mad-eyed Fleming with the sharp sword already wrought
his revenge? Has he killed Arend Gillis's wife, because Gillis
took his own wife from him?"' He cocked an eyebrow and
waited.

Chaucer blustered. He always found it rather disconcerting

when someone read his mind with that kind of accuracy. 'By no means! Goodness me, no! I wouldn't dream . . .'

'Of course that was what you were thinking, Geoff. I may call you Geoff? I notice that Master Gower does and I think we are now friends enough. But no, I did not kill Fye Gillis. Would you like to know why?' Maghfield cleared his throat and spat to one side, making several crowding peasants jump quickly out of the way.

'Er, yes. Please.' Chaucer wanted to edge – no, canter – away, but this man was all that stood between him and being pulled off his horse and being stripped and pulled to pieces by the crowd, he felt sure.

'Because, to kill Fye Gillis would be to do Arend Gillis and his children an enormous favour. The woman was poison, to everyone she touched. And yet, you know, Geoff, she was such a pretty little thing, back home along the Scheldt. All the young men had eyes on Fye, but she fell in love with Arend and there you are. The heart will lead in some strange directions, sometimes. Perhaps if I had married her, I would be grateful for a man to come along and take her from me.' His laugh was bitter. 'I got some comfort from the thought that perhaps poor Arend was just trying to find something beautiful in his life, made hideous by Fye. That he took my wife's love without thinking what it was doing to me because he was so unhappy. But no, Geoff, I don't believe that is true.'

Chaucer was at a loss. He and his Pippa had not spent long together, what with one thing and another. But he had never been tempted by another woman; he told himself this untruth without a blush. But as for the situation that Maghfield was in – he could only imagine what it would make him do. He had been bearing the weight of Sudbury's letter alone – could it be that Maghfield would have some wise words to help him? It was clear that his life was not as easy and simple as he had led everyone to believe. Chaucer rode on in silence by the side of the merchant venturer, becoming more aware by the second how the crowd was thickening and that the plucking hands at his hose were becoming more insistent. Listening to Maghfield's woes was a welcome diversion but now the time had come for action. He looked up at the Fleming, inches above him on his charger, and saw the same thought in his eyes.

'Yes, Geoff,' the man muttered, without preamble. 'You're right. Are you happy at a gallop?'

'A canter?' Chaucer countered, hopefully.

'A canter it is,' Maghfield agreed, touching his spurs to his horse's flanks. 'The Tabard is in sight, see. We'll be there in a flash.'

Chaucer clenched his thighs as best he could as Bertha lumbered after Maghfield. He muttered under his breath as the horse pecked her way over the cobbles, like a prayer, 'The Tabard. God be here! Oh, God be here!'

The King's leopards and lilies was hoisted high along Bankside the next morning as its bearer cantered through Southwark. It was met by jeers and spittle from the peasants, but no one had the nerve to haul the flag down. All their lives, the great unwashed had held that banner holy, as if it were Christ's shroud itself. The messenger reined in in front of the Tabard, its ramparts bristling with defenders.

'Geoffrey Chaucer!' the herald called out, his own tabard bright with the King's colours.

The comptroller jostled his way between pilgrims and inn-men. 'Norroy,' he acknowledged the messenger.

'His Grace's compliments,' the man called, 'but would you mind joining him at the abbey? The peasant leader has asked to meet him again.'

'Again?' Chaucer muttered to Gower. 'As if once wasn't enough. I was rather hoping not to have to go out again today.'

'You're *not* going, Geoff, surely?' the poet was horrified. 'Daniel and all that.'

'I *am* Court Poet, John,' Chaucer said. 'Goes with the territory really, I suppose. Master Maghfield,' he beckoned the merchant venturer. 'I wouldn't expect you to join me, not after yesterday. All those bodies . . .'

'Au contraire,' he replied in his best French. 'Tyler can kill as many Flemings as he likes, but he can't get us all. Shall we?'

Chaucer signalled to the herald that they were on their way and soon the great gates of the Tabard, made up of bedsteads, table legs and good luck, creaked open to let Geoffrey Chaucer, Comptroller of the King's Woollens and Court Poet to His Grace Richard II, King of England and Lord of Ireland, ride to his doom.

There were different guards at the bridge today. Not the militia of the Trained Bands, but slovenly peasants, lolling against the chains of the drawbridge. Chaucer's horse jinked as the comptroller looked up, 'Mother of God,' and he crossed himself.

'What's the matter?' Maghfield had not seen what Chaucer had seen. The comptroller pointed. Above the parapet, a pole projected into the sky and, on top of it, complete with his cardinal's scarlet hat, was the head of Simon of Sudbury, until yesterday Archbishop of Canterbury.

'Isn't that . . .?' Maghfield was shielding his eyes from the sun, trying to make out the distorted features. The eyes were half-closed and sunk into the head and there were several cuts, dark with congealed blood, across the throat.

'Ride on,' Chaucer hissed. 'As far as these bastards are concerned, we've never heard of the Archbishop of Canterbury.'

The King had finished his devotions at the abbey and had made his confession. The petulant little bastard was difficult to read, but he seemed calmer today, having bearded Tyler in his den at Mile End.

'Sorry to bring you here, Chaucer,' Richard said. 'The Tower has fallen and old Knollys thought it best to get here – sanctuary and all that. Pleasant day for a ride, Master Poet. Smithfield today. I'm seeing parts of London I barely knew existed.'

'Ready when you are, my lord,' Chaucer smiled. The cavalcade had formed up in the abbey precincts but none of this seemed real. Secure in the saddle of his own Bertha, he felt at home in a way, but he didn't know what to make of what Robert Knollys told him next.

'Stay close to the King, Chaucer. Whatever happens. As we near St Bartholomew's, watch the roofs.'

'Right,' the comptroller said, frowning. Why? Were the roofs closer to heaven? The place they were all – God willing – heading? And he took his place in the cavalcade. They clattered out of Westminster, along the Strand towards the Fleet. In this roasting June, the ditch was more revolting than ever, rats scurrying in the mud, dogs chasing them, gulls chasing the dogs. Then the little party was trotting up Ludgate Hill with the huge bulk of St Paul's to their left. All the way, the peasants watched them, most in rags and with bleeding feet from their march. Here and there, a stolen houppelande or liripipe stood out, clean and bright in the drab grime, and Chaucer couldn't help wondering whether their original owners were still alive.

St Bartholomew's Church and its hospital still stood, a bastion of civilization in this desolation. To the cavalcade's left, the ruined walls of the Hospitallers' priory still smouldered in the noonday sun. There would be no horse fair here today and the bells of the city were silent. Above that heavy silence, the rooks and ravens circled, watching for anything that lay on the ground that might be a meal. The comptroller was prepared to bet they'd already had a go at Sudbury's head.

The King, Chaucer and Knollys reined in sharply. Yesterday, the peasants had been a mob, sprawled all over the Mile End waste. Today, they were an army, standing to attention under their banners, bristling with pikes, halberds, all the arsenal of the Tower. All they didn't have, Knollys was relieved to note, was cannon.

William Walworth drew his horse level with Chaucer's. The comptroller couldn't help noticing that Walworth was wearing armour under his houppelande and that a poignard dangled from his belt. Knollys was armed too, his broadsword strapped to his saddle under his leg. Glancing round, Chaucer was suddenly, horribly aware that the only two in the cavalcade not armed were himself and a fourteen-year-old boy with a crown on his head.

'What's this, Sir Robert?' Walworth asked. 'The shits are drawn up for a battle.'

They were. Knollys had seen this before, countless times. Three blocks of men, archers to the front, faced the King's handful.

'Talk to him, Walworth,' he growled. 'Talk to Tyler. Tell him we want to parley.'

'Me?' Walworth said, echoing Nicholas Brembre only a few days ago, 'why me?'

'Because it's your bloody city!' Knollys snapped.

The mayor crossed himself and nudged his horse forward, making for the centre of the waiting battalions, where the cross of St George hung still and limp in the heat.

'The King would speak with you,' the cavalcade heard him say. 'Come at once.'

Wat Tyler smiled. Then he spat into the dust of Smithfield. 'It's your business to hurry, lackey,' he said, 'not mine. Tell the King I'll come when I'm good and ready.'

Walworth was beyond furious. Hadn't he made a point, all his adult life, of working with these people? He'd carried the baskets, gutted the fish, slopped ale with the lowest of the low at Billingsgate. And after all that, the people wanted to kill him. He turned his horse away and trotted back to his own side.

Chaucer patted Bertha's neck. The heat was climbing and in this, the comptroller knew, men's tempers frayed. The horses stamped and whinnied, tossing their heads and whisking their tails. The smell of burning timbers and offal from the market filled the air as the King of England sat waiting for an anonymous nobody to ride over to him to make more impossible demands.

Something caught the comptroller's eye and he remembered Knollys's enigmatic 'watch the roofs'. All along the skyline of St Bartholomew, heads bobbed up here and there, watching, waiting. Chaucer could have cried. Crossbowmen, Knollys's Italians, the archers of Genoa and Tuscany. The comptroller's heart soared. There *was* a God and he was standing, many-headed, on the roof of his own church of St Bartholomew.

There was a commotion at ground level and Wat Tyler rode out from his people with a knot of horsemen at his back. He reined in his horse alongside the King's and extended a hand. 'Brother!' he shouted. The King was as open-mouthed as the rest of them but he took the hand anyway and Tyler smiled. Knollys edged his own horse nearer. Any of these words now, any movement, might be a signal to Tyler's longbowmen to release their shafts. The old soldier thought he'd seen it all, but here was the scum of the earth laying hands on the Lord's Anointed and hailing him as an equal.

'Cheer up,' Tyler laughed at Richard's expression. 'In the next fortnight, you'll have another forty thousand of us Commons. What companions we'll make.'

Richard was not falling for the man's bonhomie. 'I granted you freedoms yesterday,' he said. 'When are you going home, back to your country?'

Tyler's smile had vanished. All England had been trodden down under the yoke of this child and his forebears for ever. Why? And he heard John Ball's words ringing in his ears, 'When Adam delved and Eve span, who was then the gentleman?'

'See these men behind me,' the peasant said. 'They've sworn fealty to me as others have to you, King. We're not leaving without our charters.'

'You'll have them,' Richard said. 'There'll be a charter for every town and village. You have my word.'

'Your word!' Tyler spat to one side of his horse. Maghfield straightened in the saddle, but Knollys touched his arm.

'Not now, merchant,' he growled. 'Best leave this to men who know what they're doing.'

'All church property,' Tyler shouted, so that the canons of St Bartholomew's couldn't fail to hear it, 'shall be distributed among the people.'

There was a stunned silence. The rabble might have burned churches and even killed priests, but this was a step too far.

'All ranks,' Tyler looked disparagingly at Knollys in his emblazoned jupon, 'shall be abolished. There will be no nobility.'

At each demand, the mob across the square cheered wildly, caps flying into the air and swords clattering on shields. The King was like a rabbit in a poacher's snare, facing the end, if not of his life then at least of his kingdom. None of this showed outwardly. He held up his hand and said calmly, 'It shall be done, Master Tyler.'

Now it was Tyler's turn to be nonplussed. Could it be this easy? Could the centuries be erased by a rag-tag army in the summer sun? He had hoped that the Boy-King would lose his temper, that Knollys or one of the plump cronies around him would crack and give the new King of England the excuse to signal to his archers. He turned in the saddle. 'Ale,' he shouted. 'Now.'

A minion dashed out between the lines, carrying a flagon which Tyler downed in one, letting some dribble from his mouth. He looked at the horsemen waiting behind the King.

'You!' he focused on Chaucer.

'Me?' The comptroller pointed instinctively to his chest, as men will, out of their depth and facing death.

'Who are you?'

'Geoffrey Chaucer,' he told him. 'Comptroller of the King's Woollens.'

Tyler blinked. 'No, you're not,' he said. 'He is!' He pointed to Brembre, who tried to shrink to the point of disappearance in the saddle.

Chaucer was as bewildered by this as anybody, but he sat his ground. 'I believe you are mistaken, Master Tyler. As for my horse piddling on your wall in Dartford, I believe you were recompensed for that.'

'You!' Tyler turned his attention to Maghfield. 'Give me your falchion.'

'The Hell I will,' the merchant growled. He had already lost one, left behind at the Tower and doubtless in the hands of one of the riff-raff.

'Do as he says.' The King spun in his saddle and, as though it were being ripped from his bowels, Maghfield obliged. Tyler took the weapon's hilt and turned it in his hand, watching the sun dance off the twisting blade.

'Nasty things, these,' the peasant said. 'Chaucer – or whatever your name is. Dismount. Let's see if this blade is as sharp as it should be. One thing we won't need when all this is over is a Comptroller of Woollens.'

No one was ready for what happened next. Robert Knollys had one hand on his sword hilt and the other resting loosely on his saddle bow, ready to give the signal to his archers to open fire. If Wat Tyler wanted to pick a fight, he was going the right way about it. But William Walworth had had enough.

These bastards had trampled all over his city, turned his own people into traitors afraid of their own shadow and contemptuous of their King. That would stop.

'How dare you?' the mayor bellowed in a way that neither Brembre nor Chaucer would have thought possible. 'How dare you insult His Grace this way?'

'His Grace?' Tyler spat again. 'I owe that little shit nothing!' He swung the falchion against the mayor's ample stomach, but he wasn't expecting the armour and it only ripped cloth.

'Arrest him!' That was the King's voice, higher than the rest and screaming.

'You stinking arsehole!' Walworth's dagger was in his hand in an instant and up to its hilt in Tyler's chest. The impact jerked the man and his horse backwards as Knollys closed in for the coup de grâce. He rammed his sword blade into Tyler, whose horse wheeled back to the peasant lines before its rider toppled to the dust of the square. For a second, no one moved. Then, all hell broke loose from the peasants and Tyler's own entourage closed around him, trying desperately to keep him alive.

'What's going on, Will?' Jack Chub was a considerable way back in the shadows of St Bartholomew's. 'I can't see a bloody thing!'

The taller Lorkin, standing on tiptoe, had missed it too but, as ever, he had his own wise take on things. 'I saw a flash of steel,' he said. 'Looks like the King's knighting old Wat.'

Chub nudged him in the ribs. '*Sir* Wat Tyler! I like the sound of that.'

'Shit!' hissed Lorkin. 'I don't like the sound of *that*!'

Robert Knollys had given his signal; all along the roofs of St Bartholomew's and the other buildings around was the click of crossbow bolts being loaded, magnified five hundred times. And *every single one* was aimed at Lorkin and Chub.

For a moment, the lines held fast. Then, with a mighty roar, the peasants launched themselves, the archers at the front bending their bows to mow down the King and his party. What had Knollys said to Chaucer? 'Stay close to the King. Whatever happens.'

And suddenly, the little royal bastard was spurring his horse towards the peasants, the gold diadem flashing in the afternoon sun. Chaucer wheeled Bertha around and trotted after him, one poignard against ten thousand. The comptroller knew, because they still spoke of it at court, that the lad's father, the Black Prince of blessed memory, had done something similar at Poitiers. Robert Knollys knew it too and he couldn't help but smile at the sight of the boy, with the fat comptroller close behind him.

'Sirs!' Richard reined in his horse as the arrows pointed at his head. 'What is it that you want? I am your captain. I am your King. Calm yourselves.'

All his life, Geoffrey Chaucer had heard of miracles, from the churchmen who preached to him from the pulpit and the stories of pilgrims on the road to their sacred shrines. He had taken it all with a pinch of salt. Now, he actually witnessed one. Archers were unstringing their bows, wandering away. Some tugged off their caps; others knelt before their King.

Richard was smiling. At that moment, he was the peasants' King, their hero and their lord. The women in the crowd looked at him with tears in their eyes; he wasn't much bigger than their own babbies and his feet barely reached the stirrups. He wheeled his horse as someone yelled, 'Three cheers for the King!' Chaucer followed him, lost in admiration for the boy he had known since he was in his swaddling bands.

'Sire,' he said, as they rode back to Knollys, Brembre and the others. 'Will you grant them their charters, now that this seems to be over?'

The King looked at his court poet. 'Are you mad, Chaucer?' he said, the smell back under his nose. 'Peasants they are and peasants they will remain.' They reined in across the square. 'Walworth?'

'Sire?' The mayor had dismounted and waddled over to his lord.

'Kneel.'

The fishmonger did.

Richard helped himself to Robert Knollys's sword and laid the flat of the blade on the man's shoulders. 'Arise, Sir William,' he said. And the man of Billingsgate kissed the boy's hand.

'What of Tyler?' the King asked.

'Dead, my lord,' Knollys told him. 'Look to see his head on London Bridge by tomorrow.'

Chaucer looked around Smithfield, where the peasants were upping stakes and going home. The grateful canons of St Bartholomew came out of their church, shaking hands with the crossbowmen who had guarded them, thanking them just for being there. If ever there was a time for Geoffrey Chaucer, too, to give thanks, to get back on the road to Canterbury, it was now. Well, perhaps not just now. Let the dust of a revolution settle first.

# TWELVE

Chaucer was pensive as he rode away from Smithfield, Maghfield at his side. As Court Poet, he was almost certainly going to be asked to write an ode about all this, to set down for posterity the rising of the peasants and the miracle of Smithfield. But he hoped he wouldn't be asked. There was nothing poetic in this. How could there be poetry in so many dead (would history ever know how many had died?), in lives torn apart which never could be mended. He thought of the women who had lost their men, of children whose parents had gone, never to return. Crops which would rot in the fields for want of anyone to harvest them. He slumped in Bertha's saddle, desolate. His world had been turned upside down all right. And when it was set back on its rightful course in the heavens, what path would it take? Surely not the one it was set on such a short time ago?

Maghfield leaned down and spoke gently. He was not a gentle man by any means, but he had become as fond as he could be of the little poet. 'Is something troubling you, Geoff?' he asked. 'Apart from . . . death, destruction, murder, the usual.'

Chaucer summoned up a smile. 'You have your finger on it as always,' he said. 'I suppose being a merchant venturer makes a man a judge of people.'

Maghfield pondered the idea and nodded. 'I believe it does,' he said. 'It would be pointless if I lent money, for example, to a rogue who never paid me back. Or dealt with a man who would sell me rotten fleece. But I have to admit, I would never have guessed the King could turn that situation around like that. I had always thought the lad a bit of a moron, if I am honest.'

Chaucer doubted that, but let it go. 'I am a little despondent, you are correct, Master Maghfield. Not at' – he waved a hand, encompassing the destruction and the disconsolate crowds of

peasants, circling randomly in the streets like a chicken with
its head cut off – 'this, necessarily. But at everything. I know
it may sound silly to still care about two dead in the midst
of all this, but I do. I still want to know who killed Fye Gillis
and Miller Inskip. And I still have to tell Madame Eglantyne
that the love of her life is dead, his head impaled on the
bridge.'

Maghfield's eyes popped. 'Madame Eglantyne's *what?*' It
was probably tasteless to gossip at such a time, but this was
too good to let go.

'Oh,' Chaucer dismissed it with a shrug. 'The prioress and
Sudbury, they had been lovers since . . . since they were little
more than children. That's all.'

Maghfield's eyes were still standing from his head, but he
suspected he would get no more for now. Although the peasants seemed to be scattering, some groups were still armed
and looked dangerous. He kept his hand on his falchion and
his eyes on the road. After a while, he said, 'Are you going
home now, or back to the Tabard?'

To Chaucer, at that moment, that sounded like one and the
same thing. 'To the Tabard, for now at least. Until Alice and
Doggett go back to their inn, my home doesn't exist in any
meaningful sense. I am in their hands in that respect. But I
also need to give Sudbury's farewell letter to Madame
Eglantyne. I have had it here,' he patted his breast, 'since he
gave it to me yesterday, although it might be in another lifetime. I didn't want to upset her unless there was need.'

'I am seeing Madame Eglantyne in a new light,' Maghfield
admitted.

'I always wondered about her,' Chaucer murmured.

'The bracelet?'

'I might have known you would notice it,' Chaucer said,
with a half-smile.

'I can't help it,' Maghfield said. 'I am a Fleming, after all.
Money is all I have that doesn't let me down. I appraise
everything, just in case.'

Chaucer was intrigued. 'How much do you appraise me at,
Master Merchant?' he said, spreading his arms as much as he
dared when riding.

Maghfield looked him up and down. Then he reached inside his houppelande and took out his little book and a scrap of charcoal. Riding with his knees, he jotted down a few numbers and looked up at the sky, muttering. 'About . . . nothing, really. Sorry, but there it is.'

'But . . . my books!'

'Who wants books?' Maghfield tucked his away and wiped his charcoal-y fingers in his horse's mane.

'My . . . gallon of wine a day? From the King.'

'Depends,' Maghfield told him. 'A gallon a day in one barrel, almost worthless. I would imagine it is pretty rough stuff, no offence. So, still nothing.'

Chaucer, offended, rode on in silence. Then, he spotted something up ahead which made him need Maghfield's keener eye. 'Is that . . . is that the Gillises there? See them? Just turning out of Pickleherring Lane.'

Maghfield looked to where the man was pointing. 'I believe it is,' he said, coldly. 'If you are worrying whether the remaining mob will hurt them, I am afraid I must leave them to their fate.'

Chaucer shrugged. He could see the man's point. 'No, not that. I just wondered what they were doing. Where they had been. What's that they're carrying?'

It was a good question. The two were hauling a canvas bag between them, roughly made on the spot by simply folding the material and running a length of it through a hole poked in it. It seemed immensely heavy.

'It isn't another body, is it?' For a horrible moment, Chaucer thought they had Fye Gillis's corpse from the crypt of St Olave, taking it in all its horror to somewhere for burial.

'No,' Maghfield said, with a laugh. 'My appraiser's eye tells me it's gold. A *lot* of gold. Where did they get that from, do you think? Though if anyone could find gold in this madness, it would be Arend Gillis.'

Chaucer thought back and suddenly, he knew. 'It's Mistress Gillis's savings from the housekeeping,' he said. 'Audric told us about that.'

Maghfield was doubtful. 'I think if she could save that much, Geoff,' he said, 'then Arend was giving her too much in the

first place. There are thousands of nobles there, if I am right.'
He grinned. 'And I always am.'

'I got the impression he kept her on quite short commons,'
Chaucer said and several of the peasants ambling along
beside him turned outraged faces up at him. They may have
lost their leader, but there was no need for folk to get nasty.
'No offence,' Chaucer hurriedly added.

'He would,' Maghfield agreed. 'But it's gold in that bag.' He
had enough foresight to drop his voice. 'I would stake my reputation on it.' He narrowed his eyes. They were gaining perceptibly
on the Gillises, burdened as they were. 'Leave this with me.'

He touched his spurs to his horse's side and was level with
Arend Gillis's ear before the man knew a thing. Chaucer saw
him bend down to whisper, saw Gillis step back, his face a
picture of terror, and tried not to laugh as he tangled his legs
in the handmade straps, and measured his length on the
highway that was once again the King's.

When he caught up with them, Gillis had regained some of
his composure and was squaring up to Maghfield. Although
not short, he was no match for the other man and was already
going on the defensive.

'How dare you do that?' he screamed at Maghfield. 'It's
none of your business what's in this bag!'

'I didn't ask what's in the bag,' Maghfield pointed out,
reasonably. 'I simply said, "Hoo". But since you bring it up
– what's in the bag, Master Gillis? Gifts for my wife, perhaps?'

Gillis looked as if he had just swallowed his own tongue.

Audric looked puzzled. 'What does he mean, Father?' he
asked. 'Why should we give any of Mother's gold to Mistress
Maghfield?'

Gillis's shoulders sagged. What a dreadful thing to have a
stupid child.

'So, it *is* Fye's gold!' Maghfield didn't mind standing
corrected when he was standing corrected over an enormous
mountain of nobles. 'How much did you give her for the
house accounts, Arend? Because I am bound to say, it was
too much!'

'We have her accounts book here,' Audric said, holding it
out. His father made a snatch at it, but was too late. Chaucer's

hand had snaked out more quickly than anyone could have expected and it was inside his houppelande as quick as winking.

The comptroller took a step forward and lowered his voice. 'I think, gentleman, that rather than stand arguing, we share the load and get this bag into the Tabard. The peasants may be no longer revolting – in only one sense, of course – but that doesn't mean that they wouldn't have the skin off your back as soon as look at you.' He turned his head and nodded in the direction they had come.

The peasants were less cohesive as a group than they had been, but there were still a lot of them, many still armed and out for a fight. The three Flemings took his point and, leaving him to lead the horses, set off at a steady trot towards the Tabard.

'How did you get out?' he heard Maghfield ask. 'I understood that Hardesty was guarding the sally port.'

Audric's broken voice rang out. He didn't seem to have any control over the volume. Chaucer tried to remember those days, but couldn't; surely, he had never sounded like that? 'We used the other one. Nell showed it to us.'

Chaucer put that piece of information into a corner of his brain. He might never need it, but one never knew.

'We'll have to go through the gates this time,' Maghfield said. 'I assume that the salley port is too small for horses.'

'Oh, yes,' Audric volunteered. 'It's round the side in . . .' He stopped as his father kicked him on the ankle. 'Ow, Father! It doesn't matter now, surely?'

Maghfield shook his head. It was a shame to see the House of Gillis come to a grinding halt like this. This lad couldn't compute his way out of a hole in the ground. 'Here we are, anyway,' he said, and raised his voice. 'Hoo! Hoo there! Let us in!'

A dubious face appeared over the top of the parapet, looking down at them sternly. 'What is the password?' the watcher said.

Chaucer pushed his way to the front. 'The password? The *password?*' It had been a busy day thus far and he was tired of all this nonsense. 'We don't have passwords now, do we?'

'Oh, yes,' the man on the parapet said, nodding his head slowly and sagely. 'We had a meeting and decided we must have passwords from now on.'

Chaucer clenched his fists to keep his temper. 'And when, my good man, did you decide on this password?'

The man was puzzled and bent his head below the parapet, to check with someone, clearly down below in the yard. After a muffled discussion, he was back. 'About an hour since,' he said.

Chaucer's eye began to twitch, always a sign that his temper was queuing up to leave the sanctuary of his brain. 'Well,' he said, his voice frighteningly level, 'how in Hell are we supposed to know? We've been gone since just after dawn, you, you . . . *imbecile.*' There were better words, he knew, but it was all he could come up with at short notice.

They heard a muffled voice calling up from the yard.

'Dunno,' the watcher said. 'I can only see the tops of their heads.' The four men obediently looked up. 'Oh, that's better. It's Master Chaucer, Master Maghfield, Master Gillis and that annoying lad.'

The voice from the yard became sharper and, with much grinding of chains and hullabaloo, the great gates swung wide and let the travellers in.

Chaucer and Maghfield were almost covered by a mob of people as soon as they got through the gates, clamouring for news. It seemed strange to them that no one knew of such momentous events, but – how could they? There were still peasants milling around outside, wandering up the road, just as before. No one could tell, from inside the inn, that they were a body with no head. The Gillises had skulked away, dragging their canvas with them, and Chaucer watched them go gratefully. It had become clear that Fye Gillis was no prize, but some people simply deserved each other. He hoped her money would make them happy; looking at their faces, avid with greed, it had, at least for now. He whispered to Maghfield, standing on tiptoe and pulling the man's ear down to his level by leaning on his shoulder, that he must find Madame Eglantyne before anyone else did and, leaving the merchant venturer to tell his tale, slipped away, taking the pretty way under the bulwarks of timber.

Before he reached the inn door, he was stopped by an arm like an iron bar stuck out suddenly from behind a ladder.

'Master Chaucer,' the yeoman said. 'Can I have a word with you?'

Chaucer was apologetic. 'I must find Madame Eglantyne . . .'

'She's resting. I need a word with you. Now.'

Chaucer sighed. 'If you insist. Why?'

'Follow me.' The yeoman sprang for the ladder and was up it like a rat on a gangplank. He stood at the top, blocking out the sun. 'Come on. Follow me.'

Chaucer stood his ground. He had had enough of being told what to do for one day. 'I will see Madame Eglantyne first,' he said. '*Then* I will follow you.' And, turning on his heel, he made for the door.

Madame Eglantyne sat with her nun beside her on a settle just by the window, in the wall opposite the door. Their heads were bowed and their fingers were busy with their rosaries. Chaucer, while never doubting their level of devotion, had never seen them at prayer before and for a moment was disoriented. He stood quietly, waiting for one of them to look up. The nun saw him first and she gently nudged the prioress.

'Mother,' she said, softly. 'It is Master Chaucer.'

It was the first time the comptroller had heard her speak.

Eglantyne looked up and folded her rosary beads into a placket in her sleeve. The ubiquitous Foo-Foo was sleeping at her feet. She looked into Chaucer's face and read it like a book. One tear slid down her cheek and dripped unheeded from her chin. She patted the nun's hand. 'Go, my child,' she said, softly. 'Get some air. I need to talk to Master Chaucer.'

The nun looked as if she might disobey, but, scooping up the unresisting dog, went out into the sunshine of the yard, where they could see her, standing still, listening to Maghfield's recitation of the day's events, stock still, like a pillar of salt.

'You must be brave, Madame Eglantyne,' he began, but she put a soft finger to his lips.

'I know he is dead, Master Chaucer,' she said. 'I have felt it in my heart since last night. A part of me ceased to beat. Did he . . . did he give you anything for me?'

'A letter, madam, nothing more.' Chaucer suddenly had a horrible thought that she was expecting gold, but being with the Gillis family could do that to a man.

'I was *expecting* nothing more, Master Chaucer,' she said, some of the old asperity rising in her voice. 'I have a similar thing addressed to him in my baggage wherever I go.' Another tear ran down her cheek. 'I suppose I can burn that, now.'

Chaucer reached inside his houppelande and pulled out something which didn't feel like Sudbury's letter. He looked at it as if he had never seen it before, then remembered – it was the book found with Fye Gillis's gold. He would look at that later, then give it back to her husband. He foraged again and found the letter, the seal and ribbon bright as blood on the vellum. He handed it to the prioress.

She took it and held it to her heart, then looked at it with eyes made short-sighted by tears. 'Look,' she breathed, holding it out to Chaucer. 'The print of his own dear fingers in the wax.' She pressed her lips to the letter and bowed her head, consumed with sorrow.

Chaucer watched her for a moment then, as silently as he could, he crept from the room and closed the door. Without a word being said, the nun moved over and stood against it. Until she wasn't needed, she would stand guard against all comers, while her prioress grieved for the man she wasn't allowed to love.

Chaucer looked up at the parapet. Maghfield, his story done, for he was a man of few words, was there now, talking to the yeoman. It wasn't possible to hear exactly what was being said, because the noise from the street was louder now, the peasants having become a mere rabble rather than a rabble led by someone, but it seemed that the merchant and Hardesty were planning the gradual decommissioning of the fortress that the Tabard had become. Neither man felt it would be wise to do too much too soon and they were both clearly enjoying the planning. Chaucer decided to leave them to it. He was tired. He was hungry. He was thirsty. And he was still more than a little frightened.

'So, what was it all about, Will?' Jack Chub asked his friend. 'In the end?'

Lorkin looked at him. 'The end, Chubby?' He shook his

head. 'Oh, no, we haven't got to the end yet. We've got to avenge Wat Tyler.'

'Have we?' Chub asked. 'Why?'

Lorkin stopped. All day he'd been carrying a halberd and his arm felt like lead. Days of no work had already made him soft and he was getting used to the good life. 'Why?' he repeated, scowling at Chub. 'We came close to changing the world, there; I don't know if you realized that. And then some stuck-up ponce of a Lord Mayor kills the man what was going to make it happen.'

'So, what are you going to do? Kill Walworth?'

'Walworth and all his kind,' Lorkin nodded, hauling the halberd over his shoulder. 'We just need to bide our time, that's all.'

At the entrance to the bridge, everything had already changed. The peasant guard had gone and grim men in kettle hats wearing the King's livery stood there.

'You'll be leaving that behind,' one of them grunted at Lorkin.

'Do what?'

'The halberd, knarre. Unless I miss my guess, that's the property of His Grace the King of England. Lift it from the Tower, did you?'

Lorkin squared up to the man, but the keeper of the bridge was bigger than he was and better armed. And there was something in his eyes that neither Lorkin nor Chub liked the look of.

'Come on, Will,' Chub said. 'Give the nice man his toy and let's go home.'

For a moment, Lorkin hesitated. The keeper was huge. And there were another dozen more just like him, waiting for the nod from their commander. Although he knew neither word, discretion was the better part of valour and Lorkin instinctively knew it. He threw the halberd to the bridge-keeper, who caught it expertly, and the pair of them trudged past the shrine of St Thomas without a second glance.

In Southwark, the Winchester geese in their yellow hoods had rarely been so busy. The average rebelling peasant couldn't afford much, but they'd clubbed together over the last few nights for the services of the girls and it had all worked quite well. Now, though, it was different; they all seemed to be leaving.

'You're not going, sweetheart?' one of them said to Chub, pushing her naked breasts out at him.

'Got to,' Chub told her. 'Be harvest time soon. That is, if they'll still let us do it.'

'You don't want to worry about all that,' the girl cooed, linking her arm with Chub's. Some of the peasants, she knew, had suddenly come into money – somebody else's – and they were worth cultivating. 'You come with me. Old Bridie'll take your mind off things.'

'Bugger off, goose!' Lorkin snarled at her.

'Ooh,' Bridie said, pulling a face at him. '*Somebody* got out of bed the wrong side . . .' But she never finished her sentence. Lorkin's right hand snaked out and caught her around the jawline. His left slapped her hard around the face and she reeled backwards. There was a knife in her bodice but she knew better than to try to use that. This knarre was built like a chantry and he'd probably just take it off her. Bridie bounced off the nearest wall and Lorkin aimed a kick which saw the girl double up in agony and slump to the street.

'That's enough, Will!' Chub shouted and held his friend back. 'Come on, now. She meant no harm. Let's go. Let's go home and put all this behind us.' He fumbled in his belt and threw the handful of groats he had there onto the ground next to Bridie. She looked up at him with hatred in her eyes. Jack Chub had never got thanks when he had worked for his lord, scratching in the dirt for what was not even close to a living. He had got no thanks from the prisoners of the Marshalsea who he'd released from Hell. And now, he had no thanks from Bridie, even though he had just saved her life. He sighed. It was the way of the world. His world, at any rate.

Chaucer was surprised to find that Alice Doggett and Barbara Baillie got on like houses afire. By rights, they should have been like two cats in a sack, but they both settled into their shared kitchen like birds in their nest. Neither would share their recipes, but collaborations were another thing altogether, and they already had their heads together concocting a sweet-meat to celebrate the bringing low of the evil that was Wat Tyler and his men. It sounded rather gruesome – there was talk of strawberry compote to take the place of blood – but they were enjoying themselves mightily and Chaucer hardly liked to interrupt them. At the sound of his voice at the kitchen door, both women looked up frowning, but when they saw who it was they were suddenly twittering over him and leading him over to the table, where they fed him titbits as though he were a toddler and waiting to hear his tale.

Finally, fuller of sugar and spice than any man had a right to be, and divested of every detail of the day, they let him go back into the sunshine, carrying a goblet of Harry Baillie's finest. He found a quiet spot and sat down, back to the sun-warmed stones, his eyes closed. He let the sounds and smells fade away first, then began to let the thoughts drift from his mind, spiralling up into a sky so blue it hurt to look at it. He was almost asleep when he remembered Fye Gillis's book. He could feel it, heavy on his breast. The sensible part of his mind told him to ignore it, to give it unopened back to Arend Gillis, to walk away from the death of his wife, her gold, the miller, the yeoman, the merchant, the prioress; but the other part, the artist's part, told him no, there was a story here as yet unfinished, and the book resting above his heart, weighing like an anvil, held the key.

Reluctantly, he opened his eyes and smothered a small scream. A man stood in front of him, black against the sun, his hand to his hip as though to draw a sword, a falchion, probably, his panic told him. He *knew* not to trust Maghfield. The man was a wrong 'un, no doubt about that.

The man stepped aside and, for a moment, Chaucer was blinded by the sun. Then he blinked, focused and saw that it was John Gower, one hand resting on his hip, as was his habit. 'I'm sorry, Geoff,' Gower said. 'Did I startle you?'

Chaucer scooted along the bench and patted it. 'Sit down, John,' he said. 'I am easily startled today. I have seen . . . well, perhaps not now. I will tell you some other time. But you are just who I need to see. I have . . . a decision to make and am having difficulty.'

Gower slapped his old friend on the thigh. 'According to your Alice,' he said, 'you have trouble deciding what side of the bed to get out of in the morning.'

Chaucer was affronted. That kind of decision could make or mar a day. 'So, Alice has been telling stories, has she?' he asked, somewhat shortly.

Gower smiled. 'She loves you, Geoff,' he said, kindly. 'You are like a father to her. She only told them out of fun. Apparently, she said, you have a tendency to stand at the window in the morning, scratching your—'

'I expect most people do that,' Chaucer headed him off. 'But my quandary, John. Can you help me with it?'

'I'm sure I would love to,' Gower told him, 'if I knew what it was.'

'Hmm?' Chaucer was still thinking things through.

'What is it? Your quandary?'

'We've been through so much, John,' Chaucer said, at something of a tangent. 'I have seen men killed today, as near to me as you are, run through without a thought. I have . . . well, I thought I was going to die today. And it made me wonder – does that kind of thing make the deaths of Mistress Gillis and Miller Inskip matter less? Or more?'

Gower sat quietly, thinking things through. There was no right or wrong answer, so he didn't worry about that. But he did worry about how his friend was feeling. He hadn't seen him as much as he should over the past year or so, but he felt that the man had aged, had something on his mind. If he could free it of just one thing, then perhaps, just perhaps, it would help. 'I think, Geoff,' he said, slowly, 'that if solving the puzzle of the deaths of those two would help you sleep at night, then you should do it. If it is one puzzle, that is?'

'Oh, yes,' Chaucer said. 'I believe it is one puzzle. Mistress Gillis was obsessed with money. Just having money, keeping it, running her fingers through it. The miller was also obsessed, but he wanted it to spend, on wine, women and song – if we could have called those terrible pipes "song". They both knew something that could make them rich, and I think they died for it.'

Gower took it in, or tried to. 'So . . . what was it that they knew?' he asked.

'That's just the thing. I think I may have the answer here.' Chaucer patted his chest, above his heart.

Gower placed his hand over his friend's and put on the sort of expression a man wears when one of his oldest friends is showing signs of treading the primrose path to utter lunacy. 'The answer is always in a man's heart, Geoff,' he said, gently.

Chaucer gave him a cutting look. 'I don't mean in my *heart*, John,' he said, flicking the man's hand away. 'I mean I have the answer here, in this book.' He reached in and pulled it out. It sat on his palm, a tiny set of pages, hand stitched and cut from other volumes, the pages different colours, thicknesses and even materials, from vellum to the cheapest of rag paper. The cover was made of leather, possibly from an old shoe. He turned to the first page and recoiled. 'Mother of God!' he said. 'I can't read that! Can you read that?' Gower looked over his shoulder and shook his head. 'Even with my glasses, I can't read that!' Chaucer held it to the light, then away, at arm's length, and then close to, but it was no good. The writing was tiny and crabbed, as writing is bound to be when done so small. Chaucer scratched his head. 'I don't know what to do now,' he said.

'I'm not a man of science, Geoff, as you know,' Gower said, 'but I wonder if you put your glasses on and then held *my* glasses between your eyes and the page, it would make some kind of . . . I don't know . . . some kind of magnifying thing.' He looked hopefully at the comptroller.

'Don't be ludicrous, John,' Chaucer said, dismissively. 'We'll just have to find someone with better eyesight.'

'Well, the best eyes in the Tabard have to be Hardesty's,' Gower said. 'While you've been gone, he has watched for your return every minute and could tell what was happening in detail across the river when most of us couldn't even see there were people there. Let's find him.'

'Not a case of finding, John,' Chaucer said, tucking the book away again. 'I know where he is. He's on the palisade with Maghfield.'

'Ooh, I don't know.' Gower was doubtful. 'I don't know whether I trust him. He is a Fleming, after all.'

'He is.' Chaucer had to concede the simple fact. 'But he was the only man here willing to watch my back, so if he is still there, I am not going to ask him to go.' He stood up and stepped smartly up to the ladder. 'Hoo! Master Hardesty. Are you there?'

Hardesty's genial face appeared and hung over the rail. 'Come on up, Master Chaucer. And Master Gower too, if you've a mind to. Master Maghfield has solved my problem for me, but I don't doubt you should know about it anyway.'

Chaucer laboured up the ladder and Hardesty pulled him over the top rung.

'Tricky bit, that, Master Chaucer,' he said. 'No rail or anything.' His brow darkened. 'Should have thought of that.' He rubbed his chin, then smiled. 'Never mind, next time, eh?'

'What was your problem, Tom?' Chaucer asked, when he had his breath back.

'You know your spy, Master Chaucer?'

'Cog Buckley? Yes? What about him?'

'He wasn't alone.'

Chaucer was taken aback. Wasn't that the thing about spies? They worked alone, clandestinely. Behind the elbow, as the Flemings would say. 'I didn't expect that,' he admitted.

'Nor did I,' Hardesty said. 'But when the sally port was breached, I thought it was because either you or Mistress Baillie had let the cat out of the bag. Then I realized that couldn't be. So I opened up the other I had built . . .'

'Cunning,' Gower muttered. 'Clever.'

Hardesty blushed a little. 'Thank you, Master Gower. Only doing what I was taught. Anyway, when the other was also breached, I wondered . . . who could it be?'

'Nell,' Chaucer said, promptly.

Hardesty was a little crestfallen. 'So I understand,' he said. 'I suppose you and Master Maghfield here heard it from the same source?'

'Yes,' Chaucer said. 'Audric Gillis. He couldn't keep a secret if his mouth was sewn shut. Was that it?'

Hardesty smiled. 'Why . . . yes, it was. So I suppose you knew Nell's real name?'

'Her real name?' Gower had nearly handed cash over to that woman. He was sincerely glad now that Harry Baillie had stopped him.

'We got it from a drunken knarre straight from Smithfield. She was Joanna Ferrour of Rochester – Wat Tyler's right-hand woman, you might say.'

'Oh, yes,' Chaucer bluffed, 'we knew that.' And he was delighted when Hardesty changed the subject.

'You called me, though,' he said. 'Did you want something, or was it simply that you were continuing with our planned meeting?' In Hardesty's world, if a meeting was planned, a meeting happened and that was final.

'Yes,' Chaucer said, 'and no. I would like you to look at this.' He fished out Fye Gillis's tiny book and handed it to the yeoman.

'What is it?' Hardesty said, looking at the tiny book nestling in his enormous, calloused palm.

'It's a book,' Chaucer said, patiently. 'I wondered if you would be able to read it for us? Apparently, you have the eyes of an eagle.'

Hardesty laughed. 'I have,' he said. 'I can see a vole poke its nose out of its nest half a mile away.'

'So . . .' Chaucer gestured to the book.

'But I can't see anything nearer than the end of my arm, not to know what it is. Sorry, Master Chaucer. It's a curse of being an archer. Too long spent looking into the distance. It takes a toll on the eyes.'

'But . . .' Chaucer was spluttering with frustration. 'You knock nails in without hesitation. You . . . you . . . you found a body in the river! How did you do that?' He narrowed his own short-sighted eyes at the man. 'You don't want to read this book. You're afraid of what it contains.'

Hardesty looked pained. 'I knock in nails because I know where the nail is. I have been knocking nails in since I was old enough to hold a hammer. The body in the river, I saw from a distance first. And she was big enough even for my long-sighted eyes to find near-to. And, without going into too much detail, the smell of her was enough; a blind man could have found her. I can't read your book, Master Chaucer. It isn't a case of won't.' He clenched his fist and made to throw the book overarm into the street.

Maghfield stepped forward. 'Let's not be hasty, Tom,' he said. He and Hardesty had become quite friendly in the current times. They were both good at what they did and recognized it in each other, though Maghfield couldn't have knocked a nail in straight if his life depended on it, and Hardesty thought that the love of money was the root of all evil. 'Let me see. My eyes are not perfect, but I would imagine . . .' He looked at Gower and Chaucer, blinking like moles at him. 'Well, let me see.' He held out his hand and, after a moment, Hardesty opened his fist and the little volume dropped into the merchant venturer's palm.

'Right,' he said, turning to the light. 'Let me see. My goodness, that *is* small! She must have written it with a hair or something. Why would she do that? I know she was mean, but . . . ink isn't that expensive, surely?' He screwed up his eyes and held it at arm's length. 'I can make out some,' he said, finally. 'It seems to be some kind of accounting book.'

Chaucer threw up his arms. 'After all that,' he said. 'The damned woman was simply skimming off the housekeeping money.'

There were sounds of heavy footsteps coming up the ladder and all four men instinctively drew back, Maghfield's hands behind his back, like a guilty thing surprised.

Arend Gillis's lugubrious face appeared at the top and he looked up before climbing the last few rungs. 'No,' he said, flatly. 'My wife – I assume that is who you mean when you say "damned woman" – was not skimming the housekeeping money. I have never given her even a fraction of the money she had hidden in our house.' He hauled himself up until he was standing level with the rest of the men. 'Audric and I have started counting it and we can't believe it. There isn't just money there, there is jewellery. Gold chalices. It's like a treasure trove.' He looked from face to face with haunted eyes. 'Was she a thief, do you think? A common thief?'

No one on the palisade spoke. What they had learned of Fye Gillis did not make her being a thief out of the question, and yet . . . she was a woman in a certain place in the world.

And, apart from anything else, when would she have found the *time*? From what they had heard, and what Gillis himself knew only too well, she was around the house and weaving sheds from dawn till dusk and badgering people to work more after dark. So unless she had found the secret of never sleeping, when would she have gone out stealing?

'There is no need to be over-nice,' Gillis said. 'My wife was a horrible woman, a bad wife to me, a cruel mother to our children. Calling her a thief will not break my heart. But . . . I just can't think it is possible.'

'Have you forgotten her book?' Chaucer said, and Maghfield uncurled his palm.

'Oh, yes, that. We found it behind the stone in the wash-house. I couldn't read it. If I had thought my wife was a woman with any feelings, I would have called it her diary.'

'We thought it was accounts,' Chaucer said. 'Which is why I was talking about the housekeeping money when you over-heard me.'

'Well, accounts would make more sense . . .' Gillis held out his hand and Maghfield reluctantly handed it over. Gillis peered at it. 'It's no good. My eyes aren't good enough. My wife had very keen sight, though, and a steady hand.' He looked again. 'It *is* accounts. Look, here on the second page, there are columns drawn. But I can't really see what it says.' He flicked through. About halfway, the book's pages were empty. The last couple of filled pages had fewer entries than earlier, and Maghfield and Gillis, peering together, thought they could make out amounts of money, larger than the early ones, and some other words that might be addresses.

'It's no good,' Gillis said. 'None of us can read this, it's stupid to pretend we can. We need some young eyes on this.'

'Audric,' Gower suggested.

'By no means!' Gillis was adamant. 'My son has learned a lot about his mother today and he doesn't need to learn more. He is with his sister and that is where he is staying.'

Hardesty swept his arm over the yard below. 'Baillie has dozens of likely lads working here,' he said. 'Why not one of them?'

Chaucer looked at the yeoman with an old-fashioned look

on his face. It was the first time since he had met him that the man had spoken anything other than perfect sense. 'I think you will find, Master Yeoman,' he said, 'that stable lads can't read.'

Hardesty nodded and raised a finger. 'Good point, well made, Master Chaucer. No, of course they can't.'

'And a good thing too,' Gower added. 'It's people with ideas above their station that has brought us to this pretty pass.' He looked out over the parapet to check, but the peasants were still passing in a steady stream, going back to the life they had known, most of them with few regrets.

The others nodded, while they tried to think of another pair of young eyes.

'I know!' Hardesty said, keen to vindicate himself. 'The nun. She's young. She can read.' He suddenly looked doubtful. 'I assume nuns can read. I've never really met one to talk to.'

Chaucer clapped the man on the back. It was like hitting a wall. 'Stout fellow,' he said, somewhat condescendingly. As the world regained its axis, certain things would have to be reinstated, and one of those was that Hardesty was not his equal. 'Of course nuns can read. Now then, shall we bring her up here, where it's private, or shall one of us go and get her?'

'I don't consider myself an expert,' Maghfield said, 'though an aunt of mine became a nun when I was still at home. But I would have thought that a nun, especially a shy, young one like . . . what is her name? Does anyone know?' He looked around. Shaken heads and shrugged shoulders told him no one did. 'A nun like . . . our nun, she wouldn't want to come up on these ramparts and be alone with five men like us. It's not what she's used to. We don't want to make her feel awkward.'

But by now, everyone wanted to know what was written in Fye Gillis's book. Even if it didn't solve the murders, it was so tantalizing to have something they could hold in their hands but which could tell them nothing.

'What if Master Chaucer goes and asks her?' Gillis suggested. 'As far as I can tell, he has spent the most time with Madame Eglantyne, and that means spending time with the nun, even though she might not have said anything.' He looked round and this time got nods. 'I've just thought of something. I suppose she *is* English, is she? She never speaks.'

Chaucer threw his hands in the air. 'Oh, that would be just perfect. The only person in this whole fortress with eyes good enough to read this and she's foreign!'

'Don't overreact, Geoffrey,' Gower admonished his friend. 'Excuse him, everyone, he's under a lot of strain. He's had a bad day.'

But Chaucer was into his stride. 'Bad day? Bad day? No, no, John. I've had bad days before. And then, today, I had a day when I saw the head of a man I had been talking to not twelve hours before, stuck on a pole on the bridge. Then, I saw a man run through feet from me by a damned fishmonger. Gutted him like a salmon, he did, just like that. No warning. And yes, before you say, it's true, the man in question was a total bastard who had somehow, because he had no discernible personality,' the Comptroller of Woollens spun round, pointing at the men on the parapet with him, 'no personality at all, that I could see, he had somehow made thousands of peasants . . . yes, *thousands*, go out and kill people, and burn beautiful places – had any of you been inside the Savoy? It was beautiful, just beautiful. And . . . and . . . rob and steal and . . .' Chaucer leaned against the rail, his hand over his eyes. 'And now, the bloody nun is foreign!'

A gentle voice behind him said, 'No, I'm not foreign, Master Chaucer. I was born here, in London. Why did you think I was foreign? And why does it matter?'

Chaucer spun round and almost fell down the ladder. Friendly hands pulled him away from the edge and he felt himself becoming calmer.

He blinked at the nun, standing demurely by his side. 'We . . . um . . . we hoped that you could read this for us.' He gestured to Gillis who passed the book across to her.

She smiled at him and turned to the book in her palm. 'This *is* tiny,' she said. 'But we do a lot of intricate work in the priory. Carolingian Minuscule, that kind of thing. Let me see. On the first page, it says, "Fye Gillis . . ." Oh, is that the poor soul in the river?' She crossed herself.

Gillis nodded. 'Yes, my wife.'

'Ah. Oh. I think perhaps foreign might have been a help, Master Chaucer. This isn't in English.'

Chaucer clapped his hand to his head again and Gower patted his back. 'Just do your best, dear,' he said to the nun. 'What is your name, by the way? I can't keep calling you dear?'

'No.' A sharper voice behind him made him jump again, but this time he recognized it.

'Madame Eglantyne. It's getting quite crowded up here. Shall we all move along?' The head of the ladder seemed to mesmerize him and he felt sure he would fall down it before the day was over.

'You can, however, call her Sister Peter, which is the name she took on taking her vows. Do your best, dear,' she said. Without turning her head, she said, 'And yes, I can call her dear whenever I want. Just say it phonetically. I'm sure Master Gillis or Master Maghfield will be able to sort it out.'

The nun peered at the book. 'I think I can work this one out. It says, "Fye Gillis. Her book".'

Maghfield and Gillis nodded at each other. In their language, the words were much the same.

Sister Peter flicked through a couple of pages and read some more. '"De bis-chop" bishop, I suppose, "li-et het geld onder het altaar. He is een dwars, maar" . . . I can't make this out. It looks like "ri-ik".'

Gillis, his hand to his eyes, muttered, 'The bishop left the gold under the altar. He is a fool, but rich.' Suddenly, he turned and raced for the ladder, stumbling and almost falling in his haste.

'Poor man,' Sister Peter said, looking after him. 'It must be terrible for him to find out what his wife really was. A black-mailer and a liar.'

Everyone on the palisade grew quiet. The sounds of the peasant band outside beat a counterpoint to their thoughts.

'That's quite an assumption, Sister,' Chaucer said softly. The prioress made a step towards the nun but Gower held her back.

'But she was, surely.' Sister Peter brandished the book. 'Why else would she mention gold under an altar and a bishop who is a fool? Our bishops are chosen by God. They are not fools.' Her smile was as innocent as the day was long, but Chaucer could see something else, something in her eyes.

'Does it say anything else in there?' he asked. 'Something about her knowing the miller, for example?'

She turned back to the book and turned the pages carefully. 'No,' she said. 'Nothing about Master Inskip – I assume that's the miller you mean, our miller from the mill at the priory?'

Chaucer nodded.

'No, no Inskip here. There's a Brembre. What a funny name, is that how you say it?'

Another nod from the comptroller.

'A Walworth. A . . . some of these pages are just numbers. Umm . . . a Maghfield.' Her eyes were wide. 'Is that a relation of yours, Master Maghfield?' she asked. 'What is this word here? It looks like . . . "horned rager"?'

Maghfield shrugged. 'I don't know what that means,' he said. 'The woman was deranged.'

Chaucer, with his interest in words, could hazard a guess, the horned cuckold, the man deceived.

She had reached the end of the book. With Gillis gone, she handed it back to Chaucer, for safe keeping. 'No Inskip, though.'

Chaucer looked at her. He realized, to his shame, that he had never looked at her properly before. With her milky skin and her clear eyes, she was a beautiful young woman. Her slightly almond eyes, pure blue, brought back a memory to Chaucer, a memory not old but already beginning to fade. A memory of her father, in the candlelight, telling him of his love for her mother, a love that would never die. He thought of all the times he had seen her since they had first met, never far away from her prioress, standing between her and a world which was sometimes a bit too much, a bit too threatening. And everything fell into place.

Chaucer took a deep breath. 'Then why did you kill him?' he asked, quietly. 'Fye Gillis, I could understand. She was hounding your father, a man you had been taught to love and revere, even though you had met him just a handful of times. Until the peasants intervened, you would have met him this summer in Canterbury, spent some days with him and your mother. Discreetly, of course. But it would have been a magical time. He has asked you for your help, asked you to leave the gold under the altar, because he couldn't bring himself to do it. We'll be generous to Simon of Sudbury, shall we, Archbishop of Canterbury and Chancellor of England? He didn't do it because he was afraid he might be hurt. He did it because if you were discovered, you were just a nun, not long into her vows. A nun who had gone wrong, stolen from the church.'

'It wasn't *like* that!' Sister Peter's eyes were bright. 'He didn't ask me to do it. I *offered* to do it. I was *proud* to do it.'

'Of course you were,' Madame Eglantyne crooned. 'Of course you were, my brave girl.'

Maghfield began to edge away, towards the other ladder.

'Stay, Master Maghfield,' Sister Peter said, without turning her head. 'I have a knife in my sleeve, sharp and bright. Before you could make that ladder, Master Chaucer's head would be all but severed from his body. You know I can do it. You know my work.'

Maghfield moved back to his place next to Hardesty. Surely, they would think of something soon, and proximity was strength.

'I hid when I had put the gold where she had demanded, and I saw her. I followed her home. Do you know?' she sounded incredulous, 'nobody notices a nun. You would think, wouldn't you, dressed like this, we would be obvious, but no. The occasion never cropped up but, if it had, and anyone had asked, no one would have said they saw a nun following a weaver's wife. And yet, what an odd thing that must have looked, had anyone opened their eyes.'

'Why did you kill her?' Gower asked. He always had a tendency to miss the obvious when under his nose.

Sister Peter looked at him, puzzled. 'It's simple, surely? She was blackmailing my parents, the best two people in the world. It isn't their fault that they shouldn't have fallen in love. Mother has told me stories since I was small about how perfect their love was and, out of their perfection, I was born. So, why should a Flemish heifer with an adulterer for a husband think she could spoil their lives? She tried to get money from mother, too. So . . .' she whipped the knife from her sleeve and it was clear to everyone that it was indeed very, *very* sharp. 'She had to die.' She looked lovingly at the weapon. 'It isn't hard, when the blade is keen. And, perhaps someone could tell Master Gillis, she probably didn't feel much. She was going out with another letter, I saw it before she stowed it away in her placket; she was laughing and muttering to herself as she made her way along the river. Some other poor soul whose life she was going to blight. So, I did the world a favour.' She turned to Madame Eglantyne. 'Don't *worry*, Mother,' she said. 'God won't be angry. He knows I had the best intentions. And you know good intentions are never bad.'

Chaucer could hardly bear it, but he had to ask again. 'And Miller Inskip?'

Sister Peter looked at her reflection in her blade and smiled. 'Ah, yes, Miller Inskip. He wanted money, of course, but more than that, he wanted my mother. He knew about her and my father. That was why she let him charge such outrageous prices for his flour. It was his way of extorting money without it showing. But when we were locked up here, his foul habits could not be assuaged, as they were when he could come and go. So, after he had finished his vile act with Nell the whore, I heard him tell her he was going to go and have his way with Mother, whether she wanted him to or not . . .' She looked again at the prioress, who was slumped against Maghfield, weeping. 'Mother, he said such vile things and so . . . I don't deny he probably did feel at least fear. I let him see the blade, you see. But he didn't see me until the last few seconds. As I told you, no one notices a nun.'

Chaucer swallowed hard. 'Why have you got your knife in your hand now, Sister Peter?' he asked her. 'We have done your parents no harm.'

She looked at him, her eyes wide and innocent. 'Of course you haven't,' she said. 'I have it out to give it to you. For safe keeping. I don't need it any more. I know that God wouldn't want me to kill anyone else. Sometimes, I feel that I would like to feel the blade go through a throat again. But that would be wrong.' She shook her head and sighed. 'If things

had gone differently today in Smithfield, well, perhaps . . .'
She smiled around at the men standing there, speechless; at
her mother, drying her eyes and blowing her nose on the end
of Maghfield's liripipe. 'So, if Mother and I could stay just
the one more night, and then get back to the priory, that would
be wonderful. God would be *so* glad, wouldn't he, Mother?'

Madame Eglantyne, almost back to her old self, nodded.
Her love for Simon of Sudbury had been pure and innocent,
but they couldn't bring a child into the world without some
recompense being due. And so, here she was, for the rest
of her life, the caretaker of a daughter with the face of an
angel and the mind of a devil, however well-meaning that
devil might be. The prioress looked around at the assembled
men. 'Could that be so?' she asked in a whisper. 'I won't
let her out. I could wall her up as an anchoress.' She looked
at her daughter, who was standing smiling, looking up at
the small clouds gathering in the deep blue sky. 'I think she
might like that.'

Sister Peter looked at her and smiled her sweet smile. 'I
believe I might,' she said and, in a silence that rang like a bell,
she climbed down the ladder, waiting solicitously for her mother
until she was safely at the bottom.

It was a while before anyone on the parapet spoke. They
were alone with their thoughts, which, had they shared them,
would not have been so different. When one of them did speak,
it was simultaneously with the rest. The cacophony settled
down to Chaucer holding the floor.

'Sister Peter is obviously a very troubled soul,' he ventured.

'Otherwise known as having bats in her thatch,' Maghfield
said. 'I've seen people like her before. But through railings
as the townsfolk poked them with sticks. We can't let this go.
People are dead.'

'Horrible people,' Gower pointed out.

'We can't be judge and jury,' Maghfield spluttered. 'Fye
Gillis and Miller Inskip were not ideal examples of humanity,
but which of us is? I will admit that perhaps sometimes my
interest rates are a little high.' He caught Chaucer's eye and
added, 'but only for people I might not trust that much. Not
for people like *you*, Master Chaucer. And you, Master Gower,

although most people would name you as the most honest
wool merchant in London, I know for a fact that you take ten
per cent of every fleece and make another from the trimmings.
A nice little mark-up, I think you will agree, Master Comptroller
of Woollens.' He looked at Hardesty, standing against his
palisade as though carved from the living rock. 'As for you,
Master Yeoman, there must be something, though I confess I
am currently unable to call it to mind. And Master Chaucer,
of course, everyone knows that you—'

'That's enough and all very well.' Chaucer was watching the
peasants and could see the end of the column in sight, trailing
on to Watling Street from the west. 'We will be able to go out
into the world again soon, and what will we say when the
sacristan of St Olave's asks us to explain a stinking body,
when Mistress Inskip, should there be such an unfortunate,
asks what happened to her husband? How will 'we explain two
bodies, linked by this inn, with their throats cut through to
the spine? Well, will we say it was a nun? An innocent-looking
girl with eyes as blue as the sky and with a hand wielding a
knife like an assassin?'

'It does sound a bit unlikely,' Gower conceded.

'And Harry Baillie won't be any too pleased that people
will say it was a traveller at his inn. You can kiss goodbye to
your discount next year,' Maghfield offered.

Chaucer whipped round. 'You get discounts?'

Maghfield shrugged.

'We need some kind of explanation.' For some reason he
couldn't fathom, Chaucer needed to be able to tell someone that
the puzzle was solved. Part of it was his own pride. The other
part was so that two souls, horrible, greedy souls though they
were, could leave Purgatory and go to where they were bound,
be that Heaven or Hell. 'We must have someone to blame,
someone so they stop looking for anyone else.' He was
sounding for all the world like Madame Eglantyne.

Down in the street, Lorkin and Chub were bringing up the
rear of the retreating peasants. The dream was over and they
were kicking up the dust as they walked. The palisades of the
Tabard were hanging in the air over them, and Lorkin suddenly
let all the hatred in his frustrated soul out against the place,

somewhere where he knew he would never enter, should he
live to be a hundred.

'Hoo!' he shouted to the walls. 'Hoo, you entitled bastards.
God be here, my arse.'

Hardesty, who could see that Chaucer was actually making
a lot of sense, picked up his bow which had been leaning
against the fortifications and, without really looking, fitted the
nock of his goose-fletched arrow onto the string. He glanced
down into the street and took aim. 'I think you are quite right,
Master Chaucer,' he said, casually letting fly. 'The tall gorm-
less one. H   l do.'

And W  ll Lorkin found out in that brief second that he was
not going to live to be one hundred after all.